Christmas Dreams

by

Cynthia Breeding

Christmas Dreams

Cover Art by *Tina Lynn Stout*

The Wild Rose Press, Inc.
PO Box 708
Adams Basin, NY 14410-0708
Visit us at www.thewildrosepress.com

Publishing History
First Edition, 2024
Trade Paperback ISBN 978-1-5092-5609-9
Digital ISBN 978-1-5092-5610-5

Published in the United States of America

Christmas is a time for hope that dreams and wishes can come true. Three young career women, friends despite their different backgrounds, find answers to their personal dilemmas as they drift into slumber on Christmas Eve...

Prologue

Caroline Campbell brushed snowflakes off her wool coat and savored the warmth inside the midtown Manhattan coffee shop as she entered and quickly closed the door to chilly gusts of wind. The aroma of fresh coffee and hot chocolate assailed her cold nose, making it hard to decide which to order.

She spotted her friends Maggie Maguire and Elizabeth Shelton already seated at a table with three cups of brew in front of them. Elizabeth usually took off early on Fridays and more than likely had already ordered for her.

"Sorry I'm late," she said as she joined them and tossed her coat and cap on the extra chair. "With the weather forecast being a big Nor'easter for this weekend, the museum stayed open a half an hour longer today to accommodate the tourists."

"No problem," Maggie said, brushing her damp, dark hair back. "I just got here myself. With the storm coming—on Christmas weekend, of all things—I wanted to be sure my insurance adjusters would be ready to go on Monday morning."

"I can't believe this storm is going to hit right at Christmas. What a mess for travelers," Caroline replied and then tilted her head as the classic "White Christmas" began playing over the store's speakers. "Appropriate song, I guess."

"I'm tired of Christmas carols," Elizabeth said. "They've been blaring in every store since early November. I'm glad I'm leaving for the sunny Caribbean next week. Sitting on a beach sipping a mai tai sounds a whole lot better than dealing with white-out conditions."

"At least these storms will mean a good fourth quarter for People's Insurance," Maggie said as she stirred her latte. "Between rising health care premiums for my employees and raises—not to mention the Christmas bonuses—my profit margins are tight. Every penny counts these days."

Elizabeth shook her head. "I don't know why people think they automatically deserve a bonus just because it's Christmas. At Nelson and Shelton, if I don't make good investment decisions, I don't make money."

"Don't remind me," Maggie said. "If I hadn't been so stupid as to lend Johnny funds for his plan-that-couldn't-fail, I wouldn't have to worry about profit margins."

"I warned you about that man, didn't I?" Elizabeth asked. "He had absolutely no credentials."

Caroline saw Maggie flinch and wished Elizabeth hadn't been quite so blunt. But then, Elizabeth came from a wealthy family, had graduated from Brown University, and was used to a life of privilege, from club memberships and designer clothes to perfectly manicured nails and a platinum, not-a-hair-out-of-place pageboy. Maggie had worked her way through college with the help of student loans. "Johnny told Maggie he needed the money to help with international medical assistance. She trusted him, Elizabeth. We shouldn't criticize her for that."

Elizabeth gave them both a look and then relented.

"Maybe not, but Daddy always told me to choose my friends wisely…especially *men* friends." She gestured toward the bar's counter where three thirtyish-looking men were seated, absorbed in their laptops. "Those guys over there may be perfectly nice, but not one of them is wearing a stitch of designer clothes."

"That doesn't mean anything," Maggie said.

"Perhaps, but they hardly look like professionals. Plain T-shirts and jeans, worn sneakers and scruffy boots. Their hair is unfashionably long, too."

Caroline turned her attention to the men in question and her breath hitched. For a split second, the man on the right, with the black hair, reminded her of her late husband, Danny. But then the man turned to his friend and she could see the profile was different.

Her breathing slowed. Danny had been killed three years ago on Christmas Day on what was supposed to have been a safe mission in Afghanistan. Those first months after his death, she'd seen his image on men in the streets, in restaurants, on buses, on the subway. She thought she'd gotten over the phenomenon, but Christmas always brought back the memories. Caroline picked up her coat, pulled her cap over her tangle of red curls, and stood.

"I think I'll head for the apartment while the trains are still running."

Maggie gathered her things as well. "Good idea. My nieces are probably waiting for me to get home so we can make snow angels in the front yard before it gets dark."

Elizabeth gave her an incredulous look. "Do adults do that?"

"I do," Maggie answered. "My nieces like to name them after the archangels. Gabriel the messenger,

Michael the protector, Rafael the healer, Ariel—"

"I know. I have heard of them." Elizabeth stood, draped her cashmere cloak over her shoulders. "I suppose that's better than believing in Santa Claus."

As they left, Caroline wished she still did believe in Santa Claus. To go back to a time when the harsh world of reality hadn't smacked her solidly in the face—back to when she had a life beyond being a museum curator. But she was an adult. Adults didn't always have choices. Maggie forever struggled with keeping her insurance agency afloat by pinching pennies, and Elizabeth, while financially sound, never seemed to enjoy her success.

"Merry Christmas," Maggie said as they stepped outside to go their separate ways. "Maybe Santa will bring each of us what we want this weekend."

Elizabeth shook her head and Caroline smiled. Options would be nice. If only dreams came true. Caroline looked at her friends, hoping they did indeed get their wishes, whatever they were. "See you guys on Monday," she said.

Maggie: Chapter One

By the time Maggie stepped off the bus at her Brooklyn stop, the snow was falling harder, swirling around her like sparkling crystals in one of the glass globes her six- and seven-year-old nieces liked so much. Of course, "snow" was much prettier when it was contained. Maggie pulled her muffler over the lower half of her face, bent her head against the raw wind, and began the three-block trudge to the row of partitioned brownstones where her aunt and uncle rented a flat. With the temperature dropping rapidly, maybe her nieces wouldn't want to do snow angels this afternoon.

She thought she was out of luck when she turned the corner to her street. Kacie and Mia were waiting on the stoop, bundled in snowsuits, mittens and boots. They jumped up and down excitedly when they saw her coming. "We already did it!" Kacie shouted.

"We wanted you to see," Mia added and pointed to two perfectly done snow angels in the small patch of dead grass blanketed in white near the steps.

Maggie smiled at her and looked at the snowy artwork. "You did a great job. They look like they might just get up and fly away."

Kacie pointed. "We left the other side for you."

"Maybe I had better wait until tomorrow," Maggie said. "It's getting pretty dark already."

"Okay," Kacie mumbled, but looked disappointed.

"It's getting colder, too," Maggie added. "You don't want Aunt Ailis to have to worry about you getting sick."

"I guess not," Mia answered and took her younger sister's hand. "Come on."

Maggie followed them into the hall and up the stairs to the second floor. She hated to squelch their enthusiasm, but her aunt didn't need the burden of caring for sick children. Uncle Sean, whose back injuries from Vietnam were growing worse, required enough of her time when she came home from work.

As Maggie hung her coat on a peg by the door, she silently berated her irresponsible sister for having dumped the girls to run off with their equally unreliable father to climb mountains in Nepal. They said they were going for humanitarian reasons, but Maggie didn't think that justified abandoning their daughters.

Especially since her sister was financing the trip on money left from their father's overseas investments after their parents were killed in an auto crash.

But then, what had Maggie done with her share of those funds? She bit her lip, remembering the conversation with Elizabeth earlier. Her friend had been right. Maggie had been warned to look beyond a handsome face and a smooth-talking line. Had she listened? No. But the incident had made her wary of causes that required monetary donations. Would she ever trust herself to know when to believe in a just cause again?

"You've got dinner started," Maggie said to her aunt as she entered the tiny, made-over kitchen a few minutes later. "It smells great."

"It's just stew," Aunt Ailis replied. "I'm saving the ham for Christmas dinner."

"Stew is perfect for a stormy, cold night." Maggie took lettuce and tomatoes out of the fridge and began the salad. "I'm just glad we can hunker down for the whole weekend. It will be a cozy, white Christmas."

Her aunt gave her a wry look. "With Mia and Kacie cooped up, you may not feel that way by Monday."

Maggie laughed. "Since we have a captive audience, maybe you should teach them how to do an Irish jig like you taught me a few years ago. That will take the cap off their energy."

"And mine too," Aunt Ailis said. "I don't know if I even remember how."

"I'll bet it comes back to you."

Her aunt smiled. "We'll see."

Much later, having watched *Frozen* for the umpteenth time—which her nieces thought was perfect for the weather—Maggie prepared for bed. The idea of the girls learning the Irish jig made her think how nice it would be if they could actually go to Ireland and absorb the culture. Although her father had convinced her there was more money to be made in business, she'd always wanted to be a teacher and it would have been fun to take her nieces overseas. Such trips were expensive, though. Had she not been gullible and given money to the jerk who ran off with it, maybe she could have afforded the trip.

Right now, she was afraid to spend a single penny more than was necessary. The girls were getting only one gift each this year. Every dollar of profit from her insurance agency was dedicated to savings.

Ireland would have to wait.

Maggie pulled back the covers to her bed and crawled in, then reached up to turn off the bedside light.

She sighed. Dreaming of Ireland was as close as she was going to get for a long while.

Chapter Two

The fragrant smell of flowers and fresh grass, along with the gentle warmth of sunshine, invaded Maggie's senses. Slowly she opened her eyes to find herself gazing at a brilliant blue sky overhead. She turned her head slightly. She was lying in a forest glade…more specifically, in a patch of primroses. Oak trees formed an almost perfect circle around her, their leaves rustling slightly in a zephyr breeze.

Maggie blinked. She must be dreaming. With the Nor'easter blowing in, her subconscious must have decided to escape to warmer weather. But where?

"I see ye have awakened," a voice said. "'Tis worried I was gettin'."

An Irish brogue? That would make sense, considering she'd been thinking about Ireland before she went to sleep. Maggie sat up and turned toward the voice. Then her jaw dropped.

Seated not far from her was a young man, rather oddly dressed in vintage clothes. Buff-colored riding breeches and Hessian boots, and a black waistcoat with silver threads, over a flowing linen shirt—he looked like he'd stepped out of the early nineteenth century, although he wore no cravat. Instead, the white shirt had several buttons open, revealing a smooth, muscular chest. She noticed his sleeves were rolled up, as well, exposing strong, tanned forearms.

Maggie had to hand it to herself…her subconscious knew how to conjure up a well-built guy. When was the last time she'd had a dream like *this*?

Her gaze traveled to his face and her breath caught. Copper-colored hair hung to his shoulders, curling slightly against the collar of his shirt, but it was his eyes that held her nearly spellbound. They were an unusual golden color, similar to those of a panther she'd once seen at the zoo, slightly tilted at the corners and fringed with incredibly thick, dark lashes that any woman would kill for.

He smiled, his teeth perfectly straight and white. "Does my appearance please ye, Maggie Maguire?"

She started. "How do you know my name?"

He drew his dark brows together. "Why would I not?"

Maggie shook her head, mainly to clear her muddled thinking. Of course he'd know her name. She was dreaming. She'd probably given him a name too, although she couldn't recall it. She might as well ask if she were going to find out where this dream was going. "And what do I call you?"

"Ye used to call me Finn."

"Finn." Maggie paused. "What do you mean, I *used* to call you Finn?"

His expression turned to one of concern. "Did ye hit your head on something? I thought ye were just napping a wee bit when I came upon ye."

She frowned. "Never mind that. What do you mean, I used to call you Finn?"

"When ye were younger, before I went to Paris for school."

Okay, this dream was getting a little weird. "I don't

know you. What is your full name?"

"Finley O'Byrne. I'm your neighbor. Why do ye ask such a question?"

"My neighbor? I'm pretty sure I would have remembered if we'd met before."

"Ummm." He looked around the clearing and then back to her. "Did ye fall from your horse? I do not see it. Perhaps that explains—"

"I don't have a horse." Where was this dream going? Why were they talking of horses?

As if he heard her unspoken question, he pointed. "Ye are dressed for riding."

"What?" Maggie looked down in bewilderment and then a shockwave went through her. Gone were her flannel pajamas—thank goodness—but she was wearing a short, fitted riding jacket of dark blue with satin cords and brass buttons. Lace peeked from under the cuffs and she could feel a ruffle around her throat. Her long, wool skirt was divided and nearly covered the leather half-boots she wore. Why in the world was she dressed—even in a dream—for riding? She'd ridden in Central Park a few times, but she'd worn jeans and a T-shirt. Not a riding habit. Certainly not one that looked like it came from the early nineteenth century…just like the clothes Finn wore.

Maggie felt her blood chill.

She looked back at Finn. He looked so *real*.

"Where am I?" she half-whispered.

"I think I need to get ye home," Finn replied and rose, coming over to offer his hand. "Come on."

She wasn't at all sure where home was at the moment, but she put her hand in his. Lord, he *felt* real. His fingers closing over hers were warm and solid, and the ease with which he helped her stand belied strength as well.

Finn whistled and Maggie turned as she heard a nicker and then the sound of hoofbeats. A horse she hadn't noticed before came through the trees, tossing its head as it stopped in front of Finn and pawed the ground. The animal was magnificent, pure white with glacier blue eyes and pinkish ears that pricked forward as it eyed her. Maggie reached out to pat the soft muzzle. The horse felt real too.

Finn put his hands on Maggie's waist and she felt a spark like an electric current flash through her. Then she was lifted as though she weighed no more than a feather pillow, and she found herself sitting sideways across the flat pommel of the saddle. Finn leaped up behind her, bracing her with one arm while he directed the horse with his free hand. Maggie had a sneaking suspicion the animal needed no guidance.

Was she still dreaming? If she were, she certainly wasn't in control of where it was heading. But if she weren't dreaming…

"I don't understand what's happening. Where are you taking me?"

Finn looked down at her, his eyes brandy color now. Maybe they just seemed darker since his face was so much closer. All of him was so much closer. Good grief, she was sprawled across the man's legs and pressed sideways against his chest. A rock-hard, *solid* chest. She could even smell his slightly woodsy outdoors scent.

"I am taking ye to your uncle's estate."

"My uncle lives in a flat."

One of Finn's eyebrows rose. "I did not know he rented a flat in Dublin. He does not care much for the city."

"Dublin?" So she was dreaming of Ireland, which was pretty obvious if she looked around at the green hills and stone fences surrounding them. She hadn't realized she was so good at creating settings. "What makes you think Uncle Sean has an estate?"

Finn smiled. "Because I am taking ye there."

Maggie was beginning to wonder if maybe a barista had slipped something into her coffee earlier that afternoon, its delayed reaction making her hallucinate. Sights, sounds, smells...all were too real to be part of a dream. Uncle Sean didn't own land, let alone in Ireland. None of this made sense. She had to find out what she could without sounding totally crazy.

"I think I might have hit my head on something after all," she said. "I'm having trouble remembering where I really am. Can you tell me?"

Finn considered her, his gaze intensifying, then he nodded. "Your uncle, Sean Adair, lives just inside the Pale at his country estate near Powercourt."

She'd put her uncle on a country estate? "What does he do there?"

"He is a textile merchant by trade, but smuggles French cognac from the Continent, which makes him quite popular with the local gentry."

"Uncle Sean designed blueprints for houses. He never smuggled anything in his life!"

"'Tis not a problem," Finn went on as though she hadn't protested. "Since England is at war with France, your uncle is seen as something of a hero."

"War with..." Maggie took a deep breath, almost afraid to ask. "Uh...what year might this be?"

His golden gaze held hers for a moment. She felt as

though she were strangely locked into some kind of mind-meld with him. But this wasn't a futuristic *Star Trek* dream. She had to know. "What year?"

"1815."

She took a deep breath. 1815. Somehow…for some reason…she had decided to dream of events two hundred years past. Why? Maggie looked into Finn's eyes again and felt herself slipping deep into the liquid amber of his gaze.

****

"Here we are."

"Where?" Maggie mumbled groggily. She must have gone back to sleep. She started to burrow her head into her pillow and then realized her pillow was not responding. In fact, what she rubbed her head against was something hard covered in cloth. Her eyes snapped open. She was leaning her head on Finn's chest and was seated sideways across his lap, although the horse had stopped. She sat up quickly.

Finn smiled and dismounted, then lifted her down and pointed. "You're home."

Maggie turned to follow the direction of his gesture and gasped. A short walk away, amidst manicured lawns, well-tended gardens and trimmed hedges, stood a Georgian mansion. The white, wooden door centrally located in the rectangular shape of the building had a portico. Four rectangular windows, equally spaced, extended on either side of the door. On the second floor, windows of the same size perfectly aligned with those below. A ninth was directly over the door. The pitched roof had smaller alcoves that stood out from the roof, indicating that level housed bedchambers with window seats. Evidently, her subconscious remembered Uncle

Sean telling her how perfectly symmetrical Georgian architecture was.

The white eaves and pane trimmings contrasted with the red brick that gave off a fiery glow from the setting sun. As she stood there, the front door opened and her Aunt Ailis hurried down the walk. "Thank goodness ye are home! 'Tis worried we were getting about ye."

Maggie frowned. Why was her aunt speaking with a brogue? And why was she dressed so funny? Well, funny might not be the right word. Considering Maggie had created this nineteenth-century setting, the clothes might even be appropriate, except that her aunt was wearing a gown of dark rose silk with a high waist, short puffy sleeves, and lots of lace trimming on what was a lower-cut bodice than Maggie had ever seen Aunt Ailis wear. For that matter, her aunt didn't like fancy trimmings and she'd never worn what looked like a ball gown, either.

"I…I am not sure—"

"'Tis my fault, Mrs. Adair," Finn said. "I persuaded the lass to go riding with me and when we stopped to rest, her mare ran off. We spent a wee bit of time looking for the horse before I brought Maggie home."

Maggie gave him a sideways glance. What on earth was he talking about? She'd not been riding with him or anyone else. She didn't have a horse…then she remembered she was dressed in a riding habit. This dream was turning really freaky, but for now, the excuse sounded as good as any.

"Well, 'tis done. Ye'll be staying for dinner, won't ye?" Aunt Ailis asked Finn.

He bowed. "I'd be honored if ye do not mind my lack of formal dress."

"'Tis just family tonight, so 'tis fine."

Just family? Maggie looked at her aunt's gown again. Why in the world would she be wearing something so dressy if she were having dinner at home?

"We'd best go inside," Aunt Ailis said. "No doubt Mrs. Jives is standing ready to lecture me on the inappropriateness of running outside without my shawl…or running outside at all."

Maggie's curiosity over who Mrs. Jives was and why the woman would want to lecture her aunt was quickly answered when they stepped inside the foyer. A tall, stout woman, her steel-gray hair pinned firmly to her head with nary a wisp or curl astray, stood ramrod-straight in a black dress and spotless white pinafore and apron her arms crossed, at the doorway that led to a parlor. From the keys dangling on a belt, she must be the chatelaine. Beside her was a rail-thin man dressed in the formal attire of a butler. At the other side of the foyer, two liveried footmen stood at the entrance to a dining hall.

Maggie stared. For some reason, she'd conjured up a perfect Regency setting. Why? She didn't read romance novels, and she certainly didn't approve of the frivolous and extravagant spending of the aristocracy of the era.

Neither her aunt nor her uncle had ever indicated they wanted to be wealthy, either. In fact, Aunt Ailis always said family was what mattered, no matter how poor. So why had Maggie dreamed up this completely illogical concept?

She was still wondering when they went into dinner a short time later. Why?

****

Finn contemplated the woman sitting beside him at

the dinner table. He knew the exact minute Maggie Maguire arrived in his time. Her appearance in the middle of a faerie ring had created quite a fluster among the Fae. Pixies, nymphs, dryads and leprechauns had set off such a cacophony of noise that the wind-singers in the trees had flown away.

He'd have the devil's time of it reestablishing order in the Other World, but that was business that would have to wait. For now, he had to focus on Maggie.

The lass was proving much harder to mesmerize than Finn had thought. His eyes narrowed. The combination of her black hair, blue eyes and fair skin made him wonder if she had the Milesian blood of the ancient Gael invaders from northwest Spain who had driven the Sidhe—the Fae—underground. It would explain why she hadn't fallen completely under his spell when she'd gazed into his eyes earlier.

When Finn had been given this assignment, he'd considered it a lark. It had been nearly a century since he'd been in charge of helping mold a mortal's destiny. Back then, women had been more impressionable. Certainly, they hadn't been given to suspicious questioning.

He sighed. That she thought she was dreaming was at least a start.

"May I say ye look lovely in that gown?" Finn said to Maggie. He'd picked out the material—silk-spun from gossamer threads, woven by faerie hands—himself.

"Uh…" Maggie looked down, giving the dress the same wide-eyed look she'd given the dining room when she'd entered and taken in the silver candelabra, the cut crystal and fine china. "I…do not remember buying anything like this."

"It arrived this morning by post, shortly after you left to go riding," her aunt said. 'I think you ordered it the last time the seamstress came to call."

Maggie frowned. "I did?"

"Yes." Her aunt smiled. "And ye chose the perfect shade of green, I must say."

He had chosen the shade, but Finn decided it best not to argue the point. He didn't want to do anything to break the enchantment that had been cast over Ailis and Sean at this time. They were crucial in getting Maggie to accept where she was. Any major dissention amongst the group might break the glamour that hung over them.

"I…" Abruptly, Maggie closed her mouth as if deciding it might be better not to say anything more. She turned her attention to the footmen, one of whom was removing her soup bowl and another who placed the second course, glazed pheasant and apple compote, in front of her. Her eyes grew round as she saw them start to prepare the third course at the sideboard. "Why are we having so much food?"

Ailis looked puzzled. "We are just having four courses this evening."

"But…" Maggie stopped, again not finishing her sentence.

Finn could sense the bewildered state of her mind, although he could not read her thoughts the way he usually could with mortals. It made him wonder again of her bloodline.

Bringing someone through a faerie ring caused confusion, but Finn was usually able to erase the memory through mesmerism. His first attempt with Maggie had not worked. He'd have to try again. Finn turned to her and gave her his most charming smile—the one that always worked.

"Perhaps you would take a stroll with me in the gardens after dinner?"

She blinked at him. "I don't—"

"Finn loves the gardens," her aunt said. "You need to show him the new roses we planted last week."

"But—"

"Yes, please," Finn interrupted before Maggie could finish. "I studied botany and should like to see them." He slanted his gaze at Ailis, who was beaming at both of them. The spell in his smile must have gone in the wrong direction, but at least the woman was aiding his cause.

. Things would be much simpler if he could simply tell Maggie why she was here, but such a thing was strictly forbidden. Such was the law of the Fae. His assignment was to help steer Maggie Maguire on the right course in her time, but the decisions she would make were her own. However, that task would be made more difficult if she were of Milesian descent. Finn was a prince of the Sidhe, and her people would be his sworn enemies.

Chapter Three

Her aunt—at least Maggie thought the woman inside the house was her aunt—had been right about the gardens. They were lovely. The beds on the front lawn were designed with smaller plants like impatiens, marigolds, snapdragons and chrysanthemums, but when she and Finn walked behind the house, the scenery changed. Clematis clung to trellises along the side of the house. Hollyhocks and hyacinth formed a border around the back lawn. The newly planted rose bushes halfway encircled a gazebo in the middle of it all. The sweet florals mingled with the fragrant aromas of basil, mint, and rosemary from a nearby herb garden.

She had thought about refusing to take this walk. Finn O'Byrne was exceptionally good-looking and he spoke with the easy confidence of a man who knew women were attracted to him. Maggie was no exception, although having scorched more than just her fingers with handsome, hunky Johnny, she'd acquired a bit of immunity to that type of charm. She was not about to let a man take advantage—any kind of advantage—of her again. Still, Maggie half-expected Finn to flirt with her once they were outside, but he walked quietly by her side, enabling her to take in the beauty of the gardens.

She wasn't sure if she was grateful for his silence or not, but then she wasn't sure about anything anymore. Finn's silence kept her from making idle chatter, but it also allowed her time to think. Thinking was becoming harder to do, as muddled as her thoughts were now. Maggie inhaled, hoping the fresh, clean air would clear her mind.

This far north during the summer, twilight lingered long, casting lavender and pink shadows along the garden walkways and deepening the hues of purple phlox bordering the paths. Finn stopped near the gazebo and Maggie looked at the two flowering hawthorn trees standing to either side of the steps like centurion guards. Their branches reached out to each other, forming a leafy arch over the gazebo's entrance. Primroses circled the bases of the trunks, reminding Maggie of the meadow where she'd seen Finn for the first time. At least, she thought it was the first time.

She looked at him now. Strangely, the setting sun seemed to highlight the copper in Finn's hair and gave a golden glow to his eyes as well. He seemed ethereal. She shook her head. She didn't need to be adding any more surrealism to her befuddlement.

"Why do ye shake your head?" Finn asked.

Even his voice sounded musical, like the strum of harp chords. Maggie shook her head again. "I don't know. I'm feeling so confused."

Finn held her gaze, his eyes turning burgundy-colored as a last ray of sun flashed across his face. For a moment, she thought he'd reached out to touch her face, but then she realized he hadn't moved. She felt lightheaded and struggled to think.

She lived in Brooklyn. Didn't she? But why were her aunt and uncle here in Ireland? They were her relatives, weren't they? They looked like her aunt and uncle. They acted as though they had known her forever.

But why the nineteenth century? And where were Mia and Kacie? And why was it summer? It should be almost Christmas. "I—"

"Ye are pale," Finn said and took her elbow. "Perhaps ye should sit."

Why could she suddenly hear wind chimes? Maggie tried to focus on Finn, but he suddenly seemed to drift in front of her eyes. Or perhaps it was fog, beginning to rise in wispy tendrils to swirl around them now that dusk had settled. She nodded slowly, hoping the movement wouldn't make her dizzy. "I would like to sit."

Finn nodded and led her to the steps. "This way."

As they passed beneath the hawthorns into the gazebo, Maggie thought she saw a glittering arch of twinkling rainbow colors and heard the sound of softly tinkling bells in the distance. And then there was nothing but beautiful white space.

****

Finn eased Maggie onto a wooden bench, propped her up, and sat down beside her. Usually, he could sense when a mortal's resistance faded away. It seeped out of the human aura like mist to drift away. He felt no such sensation now. Closing his eyes, he concentrated on creating events that would allow her mind to accept how she had come to be here. The process was always risky, even when he had full access to a mortal's memory. He had no access to Maggie's. Fae law forbade taking control over a human and allowed only the use of illusion and suggestion. Again, he couldn't be sure his thoughts were transferring. Opening his eyes, he could only hope Maggie would accept the scenario he had created and believe the year was 1815.

"Why did ye bring her here?"

He didn't have to turn to know who had spoken behind him. Only one voice could sound so soft and yet so disapproving—Moira, the Faerie Queen, his mother.

"I needed the extra magic of the hawthorn arch," he replied. "The woman's will is strong."

"I have no doubt of that." His mother materialized in front of him in a burst of radiant colors that flashed like lightning in the small space. Her pale hair swirled around her shoulders like a cape and her silvery eyes shone like shards.

"'Tis no need for such an entrance, Mother."

She raised slender arms to still the commotion and then smoothed the silk folds of her tunic. "I have heard nothing but a string of complaints from our people all day for bringing one such as that through one of our portals."

Finn sighed. "I will speak to the Sidhe."

"Better give them time to rein in their anger or ye will find yourself scattered like chaff in the wind."

"I am their prince. Ye know they cannot destroy me."

"Perhaps not, but it might take ye centuries to put yourself back together again." Moira pointed to Maggie. "You know one like her might destroy all of us."

Finn looked at his still-entranced charge. "So it's true, then? She is Milesian?"

"I am not sure. 'Tis not enough in her blood for me to scent. 'Tis likely, since ye were unable to mesmerize her as ye did others." She frowned. "Since her ancestors drove our people to the faerie mounds, why did ye bring her?"

"I had no choice. The order came."

His mother's eyes sparked. "'Tis another power that

meddles with us."

Finn shrugged. "I do not think ye want to do battle with that power. We would lose."

Flames of brilliant red and orange flared from Moira's hair and then dimmed. "At one time, the Tuatha Dé Danann would not have lost."

"Millenniums ago, perhaps."

"I suppose ye are right." She sounded resigned as she looked at Maggie. "That mortal can do damage. Do what ye must, but take caution."

"I will," Finn answered. His mother was speaking of the Fae race, but she had no idea of how much damage Maggie might truly be capable of. Already, Finn felt himself being drawn to her like he had to no other.

And that was an entirely different kind of danger.

****

Maggie awoke the next morning feeling more energized than she had in months. It probably had something to do with being in fresh, country air. It felt wonderful to be away from the sooty air and noise of the city.

She vaguely recalled arriving from Dublin by carriage yesterday afternoon. Her aunt and uncle had issued an invitation for an extended stay which she'd gratefully accepted. The parents of the young lady to whom she had been governess were returning to London, leaving her without a position.

A soft breeze blew in the open window to her bedchamber, ruffling the white lace curtain. With a start, Maggie realized the sun was already high in the sky. She must have overslept. She threw back the coverlet and padded over to the dresser where a pitcher and bowl, along with a bar of fragrant soap and a washcloth, had been placed. She made quick work of her ablutions and donned the blue muslin dress that had been laid out for her. The gown looked new and Maggie didn't recall owning it, but then it might have been in the bundle that her aunt had said the modiste delivered. The matching satin slippers looked new too. She'd have to thank Aunt Ailis for such lovely gifts.

She found her aunt sitting in the morning room sipping tea, the remnants of breakfast still on a plate in front of her. The room was aptly named for the amount of sunshine streaming in from a large rectangular window on the eastern side of the house, but it also served a practical purpose, being close to the kitchens in the back. Unlike the large, formal dining room with its imposing oil portraits of Adair ancestors lining the walls, this room had a warm, cozy feel. The walls, painted pale yellow, made the sunshine seem that much brighter. Two prints depicting hunting scenes hung on one wall while a beautiful landscape of the Moher cliffs meeting the sea adorned another. A burnished mahogany dining table with six straight-back chairs and a sideboard took up most of the space in the small room.

"I'm so sorry to have overslept," Maggie said as she helped herself to still-warm coddled eggs and ham from the chafing dish and carried it to the table.

"I suspect ye needed your sleep," her aunt replied and picked up the china pot to pour Maggie some tea. "Travelling is tiring."

"I suppose it is. I haven't really travelled much."

"Yes, your parents did prefer to stay in the city, rest their souls," Ailis said and then patted Maggie's hand. "But ye will be just fine here for as long as ye want to stay."

Maggie felt a lump in her throat rise. Her parents had been killed in a carriage accident more than a year ago, but the loss still hurt sometimes. "Thank you. I expect to earn my keep while I am here."

Her aunt gave her a quizzical look. "By doing what?"

"I can cook and clean and—"

"But we have servants for that."

"Yes, but I'm sure they have enough to do. I can take care of my own needs, at least. Really, I am quite used to doing so."

Ailis put her teacup down. "I know your father was frugal, but did he not allow your mother at least a maid?"

"There was a cleaning woman who came in once a week, but only because Mama volunteered at the hospital. Papa said we were not paying a servant to take of us since we were perfectly healthy."

"I see." Her aunt looked uncomfortable and then cleared her throat. "Do ye have any idea of the amount of your father's estate?"

Maggie shook her head. "His solicitors said it would take months to get the paperwork in order because Papa had made some kind of business venture abroad. I thought Uncle Sean was his executor."

"He is. Actually, one of the reasons we invited you to come here is because your father's solicitors have been in touch."

"Oh?" Maggie pushed back her plate, suddenly not hungry anymore. Her father must have lost his investment and her aunt and uncle were taking her in as charity. "I don't want to be a burden to you."

"A burden?"

"Yes. I realize I'm probably penniless, but I've been

a governess. I can find employment—"

"Penniless? I am sorry. I should have been more clear. Your father's business interests were very successful. All of them." Her aunt smiled. "You are quite a wealthy young woman."

Maggie stared at her. "I am?"

"Yes, my dear. Quite, quite wealthy."

Chapter Four

Maggie was still reeling from the news two days later as she stood beside her aunt and uncle welcoming their guests to the evening ball that was being given in her honor. Her emotions had run the gamut from disbelief to euphoria to uncertainty as to what to do with such an amount of money.

Her parents had not been poor but neither were they part of the English aristocracy that inhabited the Georgian terraces of Dublin's Merrion and Fitzwilliam Squares. Uncle Sean had told her the reason her father had invested overseas was, in part, because of the Penal Laws that limited what Catholics could legally own.

She'd almost questioned how her aunt and uncle were able to have such a luxurious estate, then she remembered what Finn had said. Importing cognac from behind enemy lines obviously was lucrative.

Maggie scanned the ballroom looking for Finn. Since their evening stroll in the garden, he had not stopped by. Not that she expected him to. She couldn't quite remember how that evening had ended. She recalled walking into the gazebo, but there was no memory after that. Could she have embarrassed herself by falling asleep? She'd been tired. Or worse, had the two glasses of wine at dinner been enough to make her foxed? How humiliating if she'd actually passed out in front of Finn. If she had, she needed to see him and apologize.

For the next thirty minutes, she acknowledged her aunt and uncle's neighbors as they continued to arrive. O'Tooles, O'Dempseys, McMurroughs, Gilpatricks, and even the Fitzgeralds of the Leinster duchy. The sons of these prominent folk eagerly assigned themselves a place on her dance card.

"There ye go," her aunt said, when the last blank had been filled in. "Ye will be quite the major attraction of the ball."

"I'm not sure that is what I want to be. I've not—"

"Ye will be fine," her aunt said. "Don't ye worry. Go and have some punch before the festivities begin."

As she walked toward the other side of the room, Maggie thought her aunt may have been wrong about not worrying. The daughters of the gentry eyed her with speculation. Ciara Gilpatrick seemed the most intent, but maybe that was because her green eyes slanted upward at the corners, giving the impression of a watchful cat. Erin McMurrough and Saraid O'Dempsey cast glances at Maggie and then whispered behind their hands. Maggie caught others looking at her dark hair and giving a delicate sniff of contempt. She made an effort to be cordial to all, although her face hurt from smiling. She felt like she didn't belong amongst the girls in their pastel ball gowns and their light sandy and reddish hair curled around their faces like fat little sausages.

It wasn't just that her loose hair was straight and black and made her stand out like a weathered statue in a floral garden. Nor was it her gown, which was perfectly acceptable in cut and fabric, although the color was a rich, velvet blue. She couldn't really pinpoint why she felt she didn't fit in. Maybe because she had been a governess before, ascribed to ballroom sidelines, chaperoning instead of taking part.

The trio of musicians was tuning instruments when the butler stepped forward to announce a late guest. Maggie didn't hear the name because most of the girls in attendance gave a collective squeal and moved toward the entrance like a colorful flock of fluttering butterflies. Maggie didn't need to hear the name announced. She knew Finn had arrived.

By the saints, he looked good. Standing just inside the doorway, the light from the oil lamp sconces caught the deep copper of his hair and cast interesting angles to his face. A green waistcoat fit snug against a flat stomach and his black frockcoat looked like it had been molded to his broad shoulders. Then Maggie lost sight of him as the gaggle of girls surrounded him, practically shoving their dance cards in his face. He gave each of them a smile as he signed their cards.

Maggie turned her back, busying herself with pouring a cup of punch. She should have known he'd be popular with the local gentry. Men that good-looking always were. *And not to be trusted.* Maggie frowned, wondering where that thought had come from. She had little personal experience with men, good-looking or otherwise. In any case, her dance card was full, so she didn't need to concern herself with whom Finn danced.

Still, as the evening wore on, she had no choice but to watch him with one or the other of his partners. Several times, he'd glanced her way, only to have the movements of the quadrilles and reels move them in different directions.

Finally, when Maggie was pretty sure she'd worn holes in her slippers, her last partner delivered her back to her aunt.

"It seems the evening went well for ye," she said.

"Yes, once I caught on to the steps," Maggie replied. "I'm not sure I'll be able to walk tomorrow, though."

"I hope ye are not too tired for one more dance," a voice said.

Maggie turned to see Finn standing there, smiling at her. Most of the other men were red of face and somewhat disheveled from the vigors of dancing, but not Finn. He looked as elegant as when he'd arrived.

"I think the musicians are finished," she said.

"I think not." He inclined his head toward the trio who were picking up their instruments again. "Do ye have a spot on your dance card?"

With a sinking feeling, Maggie knew she didn't. Whoever had signed up for the last dance would be appearing any minute now. "I'm afraid it's full."

Finn smiled. "Check again."

She arched a brow. "I know—"

"Just check."

"All right." Maggie tugged at the card attached to her wrist and then caught her breath. There was one blank left. How had that happened? Her aunt had made sure… "Ah, it seems no one has requested this dance."

"Someone has now," he said and took her hand to lead her to the dance floor.

She tilted her head as the music started. "What kind of a dance is this?"

"A waltz." Finn's smile widened to a grin as he placed her hands correctly and then put an arm around her waist. "Let's enjoy it, shall we?"

****

Finn knew he was doomed the minute his hand

settled on Maggie's waist. A waist so trim that when he spanned his hand, he could feel the gentle curve of her hip. He fought the urge to bring her closer. As it was, the dancers' position with the waltz was considered scandalous. He'd have matrons swooning if he actually pulled Maggie against him, but the desire to feel her bosom crushed to his chest bordered on compulsion. What in the name of Faerie had he been thinking when he sent the message to the musicians to strike a waltz? He was playing with the fires of Beltane, doing this. He just hoped his mother would not decide to put in an appearance to correct his foolishness.

Maggie's hand in his felt small and soft, and he closed his fingers around it, pressing a bit to see if she'd respond and bit back a grin when she squeezed back. The gesture may have been instinctive since her eyes were wide and guileless. No coy fluttering of lashes from this lass. He found that refreshing after spending the evening with the flirtatious females whose chatter reminded him of squirrels. Looking into Maggie's eyes, as blue as the sea on a rare cloudless day, he realized how easily he could drown in those depths. And that he had no business doing so. His instructions had not included becoming personally attached.

But, in his defense—he had a feeling he would be doing some explaining to his mother, if not to the director of his mission—once he recognized the attraction, Finn had avoided Maggie for two days. Generally, when he dallied with a mortal, a day's separation was enough to set him on a different path. After all, Fae were known for being fickle. That Maggie's face appeared in his dreams and thoughts of her intruded on his days caught Finn by surprise.

"I seem to remember this tune, but I'm sure I haven't heard it before," Maggie said as they moved around the dance floor.

Finn bit his lip. By having the waltz played, had he put a crack in the seam of this dream illusion? He hadn't thought women of the twenty-first century paid much attention to ballroom dancing. Certainly, their version of dancing looked more maniacal than measured. He'd have to be careful. "'Tis possible ye heard it in Dublin."

Maggie frowned again and he hoped the memory he'd created of life in Dublin was one her mind accepted. He knew from his background search—the Internet of her century was truly a fabulous thing—that she was keen on Irish history.

"I suppose I might have," she said, sounding doubtful, "but I can't remember chaperoning my lady at any such ball."

"Perhaps ye are a quick learner then," Finn said as the waltz ended. Grateful that the conversation about music would end too, he regretfully dropped his hands from Maggie. He reminded himself she hadn't been put in his charge so they could dance. "Ye have met the landed gentry this eve. Would ye care to have a look at the village tomorrow? 'Tis those people who do the work for such as…us." Finn reprimanded himself silently. He'd almost said *them* instead.

Her face brightened and she smiled. "Yes, I would like that very much."

He bowed slightly. "Then I shall return for ye tomorrow."

Maggie smiled. "I'll look forward to it."

So would he, Finn thought as he took his leave, but maybe for the wrong reasons.

****

The village wasn't what Maggie expected. She'd known from history books that life in the 1700s hadn't been easy for the Irish people. King William had established a ruling class of Protestant landowners and declared the official Church of Ireland to be a branch of the English Anglican church. Catholic clergy were expelled, the Irish were not allowed to maintain schools, and they lost their right to vote. This led to loss of land ownership as well, reducing many to lives of peasantry.

She'd also read conditions had gotten better in the 1800s. For certain, the landed gentry from last night's ball proved that it had for some. But as Finn handed her down from the carriage, she felt like she'd stepped back into the Middle Ages.

A narrow, dirt road wove its crooked way around several low, wooden buildings which housed the tinkers, potters, weavers, and coopers. One building looked like a general store of sorts. Another was a two-story structure that served as a public house and coaching inn. At the far end a small, stone church stood, surrounded by weathered tombstones. Beyond that was open space for weekend markets, along with a smithy and stable. Huts of whitewashed mud and wattle, with thatched roofs and small, carefully tilled patches of vegetables, lay scattered behind the tiny town. Everywhere Maggie looked people were working industriously, including children barely beyond toddling age.

"What do ye think?" Finn asked as he offered his arm and they started to walk.

Maggie took a deep breath. "I…had no idea so much work would be going on. I don't see a single idle person anywhere. "

"Life is hardscrabble. Anything that is not needed locally goes to Dublin for market, but English export taxes hurt profits. The townsmen still have to pay tithes to the English on what little money they do receive."

"But the children…why are they not in school?"

Finn shrugged. "For a long time, education was forbidden. Now, many villagers do not see the need."

"But being literate allows people to climb out of poverty."

"It does indeed," Finn said, "which is why the English chose to repress it. Banning schools would produce generations of illiterate Catholics who would then pose no threat to English control."

Maggie stared at him. "Are you telling me that all Catholic villagers and farmers in Ireland are illiterate?"

"No. Even when education was outlawed, hedge schools were still held."

"Hedge schools?"

Finn smiled. "So called because they were held in secret, often in the country, and sometimes behind hedges so they could not be seen from the road."

"Ah." Maggie turned her attention back to the children who were helping their parents work at various positions. "But education is now allowed. Are these youngsters receiving any?"

"There is not a school available for miles," Finn answered. "Their parents can't afford to let them be gone for the half day it would take to travel back and forth."

"But that isn't right. Something needs to be done."

Finn gave her a thoughtful look. "Like what?"

"I don't…" Maggie stopped suddenly as an idea occurred to her. "I was a governess. I can read and write and do numbers. What if I were to teach them? Maybe just an hour or two a day, but it would be a start."

"Do ye think your aunt and uncle would allow ye to do that?"

Maggie frowned. "Why wouldn't they? I can't just sit around all day being useless."

Finn raised a brow. "Ye think ye are useless?"

"Well, with the servants taking care of the cooking, cleaning, and laundry, what do I have to do?"

"Most aristocratic ladies spend their days in the solar or enjoying the gardens or planning parties and balls."

"Frankly, that sounds pretty dull." Maggie said.

Finn laughed. "Most of the ladies at last night's ball would be offended."

"It's true," Maggie replied. "Besides, I'm no aristocrat."

Finn stopped so abruptly Maggie almost stumbled. His eyes turned to amber as he raised his hand and ran one finger gently along her cheek. "Maybe not, but ye are a unique person, Maggie Maguire."

That soft caress sent warm quivers down her spine. She met Finn's gaze and, for a moment, felt she had the hidden potential to achieve her dreams. She just wasn't quite sure what they were.

Still, no one had ever called her unique before.

****

Finn breathed a sigh of relief when he saw the spark of aspiration in Maggie's eyes. When she said she was no aristocrat, he'd feared his illusion of this present time wasn't holding. If she were to make changes in her future life, those changes needed to begin here. That's why Maggie had been sent to him.

But he wished she'd been sent for a different reason.

Maggie was a woman he admired both for her intellect and her logic. Having spent centuries freely enjoying hedonistic pleasures—the Fae loved indulging themselves—Finn found himself intrigued by Maggie's no-nonsense approach to life. She not only recognized the children's problem in the village, but she also planned to do something about it. How many women born to privilege would even take an interest? The start of his mission had been successful.

The second part would be much harder.

Chapter Five

To Maggie's surprise, the first day she held "classes" in the pews of the stone church at least fifteen children attended. When she had spoken to parents several days ago, most of them had looked skeptical. She had hoped at least two or three children would be allowed to come, but the fact that nearly half of the youngsters had shown up was a minor miracle. Or perhaps Finn had worked some kind of magic. He'd certainly been persuasive in getting the villagers to listen to her.

Maggie had the oddest sensations when she was around Finn, as if somehow things weren't real, like when she found herself in the bed of primroses looking up at the sky. She still couldn't truly recall how she'd gotten there, although she supposed a fall from a horse could have done it. One of her uncle's horses had been found saddled nearby that day. She thought she'd been dreaming, but how long did dreams last?

Maggie was very aware of Finn leaning casually against the wall not far away. A solid wall in a solid stone church.

And the children sitting in front of her were real. Some were squirming on the benches, while others were chattering. Two were slapping hands at each other and one had crawled to the floor. None of them was paying her much attention. She cleared her throat and then again, a little louder. Several of the older ones looked at her and then battered the ears of the younger ones. "Hush now," one of them said.

"Thank you." Maggie smiled at the children, asking who knew the alphabet or could write their names or do simple sums. Her smile gradually faded when they shook their heads and she realized how much work lay ahead.

"Well, now," Finn said, straightening up and walking toward her. "Ask them about Daniel O'Connell."

"Who?"

"Daniel O'Connell!" one of the older boys exclaimed. "'Tis the mon who will free us, he will."

Maggie knit her brows. "Free you?"

"Aye!" Several voices began to speak at once.

"He'll free Ireland, me mum says."

"And me grandda will get his lands back."

"And we won't pay taxes to the filthy English."

"And me da will get to vote."

"All right," Maggie said and held up a hand to quiet the barrage. "I see this man, Mr. O'Connell, is important to you."

"Aye! Aye! Aye!" several of them shouted.

This time Finn lifted his hand for silence. "And ye know Daniel O'Connell couldn't do this if he didn't know how to read and write."

All fifteen children looked at him wide-eyed.

"So do ye want to help with his cause or not?"

Fifteen heads nodded solemnly.

"Then ye need to listen to what Miss Maguire tells ye to do."

They all nodded again and fixed their eyes on her. It was a little disconcerting to have such rapt attention all at once, but she took advantage of it.

Maggie wrote the alphabet on a slate board and then, for the next fifteen minutes, showed each student how to print his or her name. They seemed to be equally as interested in using chalk and smearing it with their fingers as in seeing what their names looked like. Well, it was a start.

"Ye did well," Finn told her after the children had returned to their chores in the village.

"I hope they'll remember how to print their names tomorrow," Maggie replied. "They seemed to know a lot about Mr. O'Connell, though."

"'Tis not surprising. Farmers and villagers have been praying for someone like him to come."

She tilted her head at Finn. "Like a savior?"

He grinned. "Something like that. To the Irish, 'tis no matter if the savior is man or god. They only wish to be rid of the English yoke."

"It's that bad?"

Finn sobered. "Over a hundred years ago, the English declared Irish Catholics rebels and seized their lands. One-time landowners had to rent property from their English landlords. Leases were a year's length, not long enough to accumulate stores." He grimaced. "People died in famines. Many were forced to move to rocky Connacht or even to the edge of the sea."

"But has that not changed? There's Trinity College. The Dublin Society and Royal Irish Academy also encourage learning."

"To the sons of what once were English immigrants." Finn gestured toward the open door of the church. "To the people out there, Dublin is a foreign world."

Maggie looked out the door. Even though a light, gentle rain was falling, none of the villagers sought shelter. They just kept on working as though they were immune to the wet. She thought she saw rainbow colors shimmering in the mist, making it seem as though the people were fading in and out of existence, but when she blinked the colors were gone and there was only gray sky overhead.

****

At the dinner party her aunt and uncle gave the next evening, Maggie listened to the conversation around the long table and thought how different it was from the concerns of the villagers.

"Midsummer is nearly upon us," Ciara said and cast a glimpse sideways at Finn, who sat across from Maggie. "We must have a ball."

"Yes, we must. I just ordered a new gown from Dublin," Erin replied and then giggled. "I need a place to wear it."

"And I have a new gown too," Saraid added.

"We can have the ball at our estate," Mr. Gilpatrick said.

"But ye had the one last year," Mrs. O'Dempsey said. "'Tis our turn to host."

Mrs. McMurrough chimed in. "We would be remiss if we didn't offer."

"Why do you celebrate midsummer?" Maggie asked.

The girls stared at her as though she'd grown another appendage somewhere. Maggie looked from one girl to another. It must not have been a good question. Most people associated midsummer with the solstice. Why was that cause for a ball? Besides, her aunt and uncle had just had a ball. Maggie wasn't all that eager to repeat the procedure, although she had enjoyed dancing with Finn. Then again, she had *not* enjoyed watching him dance with every other female in the room.

"'Tis a quarter day," Erin said.

Her tone left no doubt Maggie should know what that was. She bit her lip. If it was an obvious holiday, why didn't she know? She caught Finn watching her.

As if sensing her discomfort, he said, "Quarter days fall on the solstices and equinoxes. They may not be celebrated too much in Dublin, but in the country they are an excuse to have a feast."

"And don't forget the rents are due on quarter days," Mr. O'Dempsey said.

"Aye." Mr. McMurrough laughed. "'Tis a fine day when I can increase my bank account by what's owed me."

Maggie looked back at Finn whose eyes had darkened to amber. She remembered what he'd told her about farmer's lands having been taken away.

"Are you speaking of the villagers?" she asked Erin's father.

"Them, too," he answered. "After all, we nobles have to pay taxes on the goods they make that we export."

Maggie frowned. She understood profit was important. Her father had been frugal while amassing his fortune, but from what she'd seen, the villagers weren't that well off. They weren't starving, but their clothing was mended and their cottages small and simply furnished. "Do you provide the villagers a feast on midsummer as well?"

Mr. McMurrough frowned. "Now what would be

the purpose of that? 'Tis not harvest time. We need to keep our food stores, not waste them."

"Of course we men do not expect ye ladies to worry your heads about business," Mr. O'Dempsey said, "But whether in goods or coin, every pence counts, ye know."

Her aunt looked her way and gave a slight shake of her head. Maggie guessed, from what Mr. O'Dempsey had just said, that ladies didn't discuss business, although she didn't understand why. Something else Saraid's father had said resonated with Maggie as well. *Every penny counts.* Where had she heard that before?

****

She was still trying to recall where she'd heard that phrase the next day when she returned to the church to hold classes. Her father might have said it, since he had managed to save money and then reinvest it overseas. Maybe she just hadn't paid attention when he talked about business. But then, when had he talked about work? Vaguely, she remembered him saying the purpose of education was to gain skills that could earn lots of money.

Maggie looked at her charges, seated on the pews in front of her. Well, not all of them were seated. Some had decided to play hide-and-seek between the rows. Luckily, Finn had accompanied her again and was rounding up the rambunctious children. It gave her a moment to think.

To teach them literacy was a first step in making their lives better, but what choices would they have? Maggie put the thought aside as the renegades were returned to her and she began a lesson in reading. It was slow going and she was gratified to find out most of the older students had a grasp of doing sums, probably learned from their parents on market days.

"What choices will they have?" she asked Finn two hours later after she'd completed the lessons for the day. They were standing in the doorway of the church watching the youngsters run back to their parents.

He looked down at her and something seemed to change subtly in his expression, but it was too fleeting to identify. She became aware that the doorway to the old, medieval church wasn't that wide. Only a few inches kept her from brushing shoulders with Finn. She inhaled his woodsy scent and suddenly felt compelled to move closer.

"What choices would ye like for them to have?"

Maggie blinked, realizing she'd started to take a step and shifted her weight back onto both feet. Good heavens, what had she been about to do? She shook her head to clear it. "Choices. If the children learn to read and write, they'll be able to make choices, won't they?"

"Maybe. Most of the boys will carry on the craft they are learning from their fathers."

"But that's the point. They won't *have* to. They could go to Dublin and become clerks and learn to do business."

"Most will not want to leave home." Finn shrugged. "'Tis what they know."

"But learning how to read will open their eyes to a whole different world."

Finn gave her a direct look. "And why is it important to ye that they do?"

"I…I'm not sure." Maggie considered. "I think it's because I didn't much like the conversation at dinner last night."

He grinned. "The part about the midsummer ball?"

She wrinkled her nose. "That too. I meant what the men said about collecting rents from the villagers and then keeping the profit on the goods they make. It seems so…so feudal."

"In some ways it is." Finn sobered. "Even though the men at the table last night are fourth-generation Ireland-born, their ancestors were English Protestants, awarded land by King William that had belonged to Catholics. The loss of land and rights is what made the villagers accept the situation that ye see."

Maggie grew thoughtful. "That's what Daniel O'Connell is trying to do, isn't he? Help the common people."

"That would be an indirect result. Daniel—and most Gaels—are opposed to Ireland being a part of Britain. To change that, Catholics must first regain the power they lost when Irish Parliament was dissolved."

"Do you think he will succeed?"

"It depends. He has a large following, but as with any cause, he needs funding."

"Funding?"

Finn nodded. "The goal is to seat Catholics in English Parliament. To do that, Daniel and others need to travel to London and pay court. He also needs to convince the local aristocracy—like the ones at dinner last night—that having those seats in Parliament will not hurt their interests. 'Tis an expensive burden." Finn lifted a brow. "Why are ye so interested?"

"I…I don't know exactly. I just think there is a big gap between how poor the villagers are, even though they work hard, and the extravagance of the privileged having two balls within a week."

Finn gave her an intense look, and then took her

hand to brush a kiss across her knuckles. "Ye dream big, Maggie Maguire."

Chapter Six

Brushing a kiss across a lass's knuckles had never affected Finn in his long, immortal life. It was simply proper etiquette in some social situations. So why then was he remembering the satin softness of Maggie's hand a full twenty-four hours later? And why was he back at the her school for the third day in a row?

Finn contemplated that question as he leaned against the wall, watching Maggie put simple sentences together on a slate for the students to read and then try to copy. The easy answer—the one he'd been telling himself—was that this was part of his mission. His responsibility was to guide her in this experience so she could make the right choices in her own time. Logically, that meant he had to spend time with her.

But when had the Fae ever been known for being logical? His race liked to act on impulsive whimsy and seek hedonistic pleasure along the way. Being a prince didn't allow him the luxury of reckless spontaneity, but he was finding it difficult to curb the turbulent desire building inside him.

Although Maggie appeared calm and steady outwardly, he sensed a burning passion inside her. A part of that manifested in her wanting to help the villagers' children. It was extremely rare for a young woman of wealth and social status to actually interact physically to better an underling's position. He'd known many who donated to charities and some who treated their servants quite well, but hardly anyone cared about *bettering* those servant's lives. Finn admired Maggie for that.

But admiration wasn't what was on his mind this afternoon. Pure unbridled lust, hot as Beltane fires, was what inflamed him. That Maggie wore a long-sleeved, high-collared dress which fit loosely enough to hide her feminine curves only intensified his longing to burn brighter. He wanted to ignite the passion inside her.

He had the power to use illusion and fantasy to do just that. Strangely enough—and he was finding many things strange about his connection with Maggie Maguire—he didn't want to use magic. Finn wanted to make love to her as a mortal man would. He wanted to take his time undressing her, touching her. Stroking every inch of her silky skin, building her pleasure slowly, allowing it to escalate until she trembled in his arms. And then he wanted to take her to the brink of ecstasy and feel her shatter beneath him.

But such a thing was forbidden.

He must have sighed, because Maggie suddenly looked at him. "Are you all right?"

No, he wasn't, but he could hardly tell her why. Instead, he nodded and straightened. "I have something to attend to." He looked at the students and then back at her. "It seems you have things under control here."

"Yes. The students are behaving nicely." Maggie seemed perplexed at his sudden move toward the door. "No need to worry about anything."

Maggie may not think there was anything to worry about, Finn thought as he left, but he needed to have a serious conversation with himself before he caused the barriers between the Faerie world and the mortal one to collapse and bring doom crashing down.

****

A few days before the midsummer ball at the O'Demseys—at least that's the family whom Maggie thought had won the debate over the location—the McMurroughs decided to have a garden party in the afternoon. At least it was a Saturday and she didn't have to cancel a class.

As soon as they arrived, Maggie scanned the area quickly for Finn. Since he'd abruptly left while she was teaching two days ago, she hadn't seen him, but he wasn't in sight here either. She sighed, wondering what he'd had to attend to that took him away.

Her uncle had joined some of the older men on the porch for a card game, and Mrs. McMurrough was chatting with her aunt, giving Maggie time to look around the grounds more closely. Although similar to her aunt's in size, the gardens couldn't have been more different. Flower beds were spread out in asymmetrical plots as though a gardener had thrown seeds every which way to see where they landed. The result was startling splashes of reds, yellows, purples and pinks that chaotically blended together. A stepping-stone walkway twisted and turned along the curves of the beds like the path of a drunken sailor. White stone benches were scattered haphazardly amongst the riot of color. Also unlike her aunt's gardens, these housed no gazebo.

"I think the young people are playing *paille-maille* on the green." Aunt Ailis gestured as she turned back to Maggie. "Why don't ye go join them?"

Maggie followed the direction of her aunt's outstretched arm. Beyond the gardens was a knoll that sloped into a flat stretch of lush grass. She could see

Saraid, Erin, and Ciara, long-handled mallets in hand, laughing with three young men who were setting iron hoops on the lawn. "They seem to be partnered off."

Her aunt squinted. "So they are. Just wait a few minutes. I'm sure more young men will arrive soon."

Maggie didn't care if more young men arrived or not. The only one she wanted to see was Finn. She wasn't quite sure why she was so drawn to him, but when he wasn't around, she felt like she was all alone in a strange place. Silly of her, since her aunt and uncle had welcomed her warmly to their home, but she just didn't feel like she fit in.

"I think I might just—"

"Ah, look. There's Finn," Mrs. McMurrough exclaimed. "I'm sure he will partner you in the game."

Maggie felt her nerve endings begin to tingle as she sensed his presence behind her. She turned slowly and her breath caught. Finn stood bathed in a glow of shimmering luminescence. She blinked and then realized the glow was only the sun's rays filtering through the leafy branches of white birch that formed an archway to the gardens. Strange how light always seemed to pick up the copper streaks in Finn's hair, creating the effect of smoldering tinder.

As he stepped out of the dappled light into the brilliant sunshine, his eyes gleamed like molten gold. Maggie blinked again and Finn's eyes were their regular shade of amber. Why in the world was her imagination doing such tricks on her today?

"I shall be happy to partner ye," he said to Maggie as though he'd been privy to the whole conversation instead of just arriving. "Have ye played with a partner before?"

Played with a partner? For a moment she wasn't sure what he was asking, concentrated as she was on the nearness and woodsy male scent of him. Then her mind refocused. Play the *game* with him. "No, I haven't."

"It's quite easy," Finn said and offered his arm as they strolled down the knoll. "The object is to get the ball through the iron arch at each end with the fewest strikes of the mallet as possible. It looks like the ladies are playing the first course and the men will play the ball back."

Maggie was aware of the not-so-kind looks she got from Erin, Ciara, and Saraid as she and Finn approached the near end of the playing area. The girls' partners—men she thought she'd danced with at her aunt's ball—gave her smiles which quickly waned as Finn frowned at them.

A manservant placed a ball on the lawn a few feet from the first arch, handed Maggie a mallet, and then moved back. She studied the distance. "It can't be moved closer?"

"Afraid not," Finn replied. "'Tis one of the challenges to get it through."

"Ummm." Maggie looked at the ball again and then stepped to the side of it.

"You've got to tap it from the back," Finn said. "Let me show ye."

He put his hands on her waist to guide her into position and then moved behind her, brought his arms around her, and placed his fingers over hers on the mallet's handle. Maggie adjusted her foot for balance and bumped against him. Her breath hitched. His chest was hard as granite and his thighs, pressed lightly along the outsides of her skirts, felt solid as oak. His scent and the feel of him took over all her senses. She could have stayed wrapped in this cocoon forever, but then she felt him shift slightly away.

Finn's voice, soft and low, tickled her ear when he spoke. "Relax and let me guide ye."

How was she supposed to relax when she was engulfed in his body heat and all too aware of her own? Her breathing turned shallow and she wasn't certain her limbs would obey her.

"Slow and easy," Finn said.

His warm breath, like a cat's paw, grazed her neck as he maneuvered their arms forward in a steady stroke, a movement that also brought his whole body into contact with Maggie's again. The tingling she'd felt earlier flared into a blazing inferno so hot she thought she might combust.

Finn stepped back. "Ye did it."

Did what? All Maggie was aware of was how cold she suddenly felt without Finn's cozy embrace. She frowned and then realized the ball had gone through the hoop.

"I think you had more to do with that than I did."

He grinned. "A wee bit, perhaps." His eyes turned subtly darker. "Would ye like help on the next stroke as well?"

Maggie smiled, feeling ridiculously happy. "I would."

****

He was definitely playing with fire, and Finn didn't need anyone—Fae or otherwise—to remind him of it. He should never have touched Maggie yesterday at the garden party, let alone brought her body against his. And not once, not twice, but as many times as it took to get that ball down the course way. He had fully expected his mother—or worse—to drop in on him while he slept, but no one came.

So was he tempting the Fates by taking Maggie horseback riding this afternoon? Finn could use the excuse that Maggie had asked to go horseback riding today. He could also add since it was his responsibility to guide her he would be expected to stay near her. He was pretty sure neither reason would hold water with the powers-that-be, no more than a sieve would. The fact was he attracted to her and he had no right to be.

"It is a beautiful day," Maggie said as she brought her docile gelding alongside his magnificent white stallion on the winding country road.

He wanted to tell her she was the beautiful one, but he was already racking up enough demerits to get him sent to the frozen depths of Antarctica on his next assignment. It was bad enough he allowed his own emotions to surface. If he dallied with Maggie's, he might be stuck in the icy tundra for centuries.

"Aye. 'Tis," he said. "A cloudless day in Ireland is rare. The gods must be smiling on us." At least, he hoped they were.

Maggie drew in a deep breath and shook out her long hair, the sunlight catching the raven stresses so they looked almost blue. "Everything smells so fresh."

Finn smiled. "'Tis because it rains nearly every day."

She inhaled again. "I can smell the fragrance of grass and the sweetness of clover, even the peat from the bog and the overturned clods of earth. It's like a bouquet of nature without flowers."

Finn gave her a covert glance. If Maggie's senses

were so enhanced that she could pick up all those scents, especially as they rode, was there more than mortal blood in her veins? Perhaps a bit of pixie blood? The more mischievous of his race were known to love changelings. Could that be the reason Finn felt so attracted to Maggie? That she was—at least partially—one of them? At first, he'd thought she descended from the Milesians, but now he was not so sure.

Either way, why would she have been sent to him if there was the danger of awakening the Tuatha Dé Danann in the twenty-first century? A cool breeze swept over him and he felt a shiver slide down his spine even though the day was warm.

Could he have been given this mission *because* the Tuatha Dé Danann were needed in that time? From what he'd observed in his short journey to the future, that world was in dire need of help.

He realized Maggie was looking at him expectantly, so he smiled. "Ye do not prefer the smell of flowers?"

"I do like flowers," Maggie said. "It's just that the country is so different from being in a city. Even riding is more fun." She frowned. "It's hard to believe I fell off this sweet animal."

That got him to laugh. "Ye didn't. That was a different horse." Of course, there hadn't been a horse. Since Finn didn't know how well Maggie rode, he'd chosen this gentle, aging gelding for today's ride.

Maggie looked skeptical. "I wish I could remember how that happened."

"Sometimes a bump on the head makes ye forget. You were unconscious when I found ye." Finn did not like having to extend the illusion he'd created for her. "What's important is that you aren't afraid to get back on a horse and ride."

"I've always liked horses." She patted the horse's neck as the road narrowed through a small forest of pines, their northern sides covered in moss. She sniffed. "It smells like Christmas in here."

Finn tilted his head. "Christmas? 'Tis nearly midsummer."

"Oh, I know, but whenever I smell pines, I think of Christmas. The scent of the Christmas tree when I come in from the icy cold. The sound of pine cones crackling in a warm fire while a blizzard rages outside…" Maggie stopped and frowned. "When was the last time Dublin had a blizzard?"

Finn thought quickly. Maggie must be recalling winter in New York, which wasn't good because it meant his enchantment was weakening. And he wasn't ready— *she* wasn't ready—to leave yet. "We had snow a few years back." He managed to smile. "And ye are right. The wind blowing off the Irish Sea is brutal, coming all the way down from the Hebrides. The scent of pines does bring that memory back."

Maggie nodded as if satisfied with the explanation and Finn breathed a sigh of relief as they left the woods, but it was short-lived.

"Oh, look." Maggie pointed toward a clearing ahead. "Isn't that where you found me the day I fell off the horse?"

Of all the places…why hadn't he remembered where this road led? The last thing he needed now was for her to get near a faerie mound. "There are a lot of meadows and glades about."

She shook her head. "I'm sure that's the one. There's the stand of oak trees. And the primroses arranged in a circle. I'm going to check and see if there's a sharp rock sticking out that I might have hit my head on."

"No, don't…"

But she had nudged the gelding into a canter. Finn spurred his stallion after her, but before he could catch up, a sudden gust of wind sent a swirl of dirt rising, semi-blinding her horse as a startled hare darted in front of its path. The gelding shied and then reared. Maggie flew backward from the saddle, her body seemingly suspended in air for one horrific moment before landing with a dull thud on the ground.

Chapter Seven

Finn slid off the stallion before it came to a complete stop and knelt beside an unconscious Maggie, lying on her side. He eased her onto her back and ran his hands lightly over her, checking for broken bones. Nothing seemed broken, but she was bleeding profusely from a cut on her forehead, which had hit the gravel. He rose to get a flask of water from his saddle and quickly returned to rinse away the grime. As more blood spurted out, he realized the gash was deeper than he'd thought. He ripped off his shirt, wadded it up, and pressed it against the wound to staunch the flow and wished he'd paid more attention to the old druid who'd taught healing. Finn sent magic pulsing through his fingers, hoping it would work.

Damn it. He should have known the Queen of Faerie would not let him get by with becoming personally involved with Maggie. His first warning had been the cool breeze he'd felt earlier. This sudden gust of wind was not natural either, and he suspected his queenly mother had an invisible hand in frightening the hare as well. Finn looked around the clearing, half-expecting to see her or one of her minions, but he sensed nothing.

He turned his attention back to Maggie. The bleeding was just a trickle now, but her eyelids fluttered and she began to moan. At least he could ease her discomfort by drawing her pain into himself. He'd observed the technique enough in ancient times when the Morrigan shade appeared to escort wounded, dying warriors off the battlefield to the Other World, although Finn had no intention of letting Maggie die.

He leaned over her, cupping her face in his hands as he closed his eyes and willed more magic to reach her. Gradually, soreness seeped into his arms and infused his body with pain. Finn inhaled deeply, sucking more of it in, not wanting her to have any recollection of being hurt. Finally, he felt her body begin to relax and he opened his eyes.

Maggie lay staring up at him. "Who are you?"

****

Maggie found herself lying on her back, a half-naked man straddling her. Even in her semi-dazed state, she could tell he was quite a well-put-together specimen…sculpted, hard biceps, a broad, chiseled chest, and a flat ridged belly that was only inches from her own. She became aware that he was holding her head with his hands. The gentle strength and warmth of his fingers sent a different kind of heat coursing through her. Instinctively, she arched her back, wanting to make body contact.

The man's golden eyes widened and he moved quickly to the side of her, although he kept her face palmed in his hands. The movement served to bring his mouth closer to hers and Maggie had an urge to kiss him. She reached up to tangle her fingers in his long coppery hair. "Come—"

He pulled back. "Maggie? Are ye all right?"

He knew her name? That was good. Maybe they had done this before. She couldn't remember. She smiled at him. "Aye. 'Tis Maggie I am."

His brows drew together. "Do ye know where ye are?"

Maggie moved her eyes from side to side. "Aye. 'Tis on the ground I am." She let her hand trail down his shoulder and across his chest. "With ye."

He groaned and grabbed her hand. "No. I mean, do ye remember how ye got here?"

"Did ye not bring me?"

His eyes flickered from amber to whisky-colored and back. He hesitated. "I did bring ye here, but—"

"Well, then." Maggie used her free hand to stroke his other arm. "We should be getting on with it, then."

"Getting on with what?"

She giggled. "What does a man usually do with a lass when they take to rolling in the grass?"

He sat up abruptly, capturing her free hand and joining it with the one he already held. "We are not rolling in the grass. Ye fell from your horse and hit your head. Do ye not remember?"

"If ye say so." Maggie squirmed. All she wanted to do was keep touching this beautiful man. She tried to pull her hands away, but he held them fast. Using that leverage, she pulled herself to a sitting position. She felt a bit dizzy, but it didn't matter. She moved closer and managed to nuzzle his neck before his hands on her shoulders moved her away. She gave a disappointed sigh. "I want ye, whoever ye are."

"I am Finn."

Finn. A nice-sounding name. She'd heard it before. Someplace. It didn't matter. Now that her hands were free she placed them on his chest again, letting her fingers drift downward to trace the hard ridges of his belly. "I want ye."

She heard a muffled curse as Finn grasped her hands again. She looked up at him as the air around them began to glow with a green iridescence. Finn's hair swirled around him like coppery flames and his eyes blazed molten gold. Maggie squinted as he wavered in front of her, seeming to fade in and out her sight as though engulfed in wraithlike shreds of fog. The eerie green light grew darker, while colored lights sparkled around her. And then Maggie felt herself drifting into oblivion.

****

Finn eased Maggie to the ground unconscious once more and sat back, observing her. In healing her, he'd used way too much magic. Not only had he beguiled her—an act that made a mortal desire to couple with the Fae—but he had also ensorcelled Maggie. Her brogue proved it. He had truly brought her to nineteenth-century Ireland.

Now the question was, could he undo the enchantment?

He got up and began to pace. He'd made a mess of things, no question. He'd let himself become attached to Maggie. He wanted to keep Maggie with him. Then he'd let that emotion spill over and mix with his Fae powers. That resulted in Maggie being truly transposed to his time, rather than hovering in a dreamlike illusion.

Maggie belonged in her time. Finn knew it. He'd always known it. If she couldn't return, had he somehow changed the course of history? Not only was that forbidden in the world of the Sidhe, it was forbidden in other realms as well.

What had he done?

Finn gave a lingering look toward Maggie, lying peacefully on the ground. Her breathing was steady and even and he hoped she'd fallen into a natural sleep rather than the spelled one he'd used. He pulled his damp shirt over his head and moved toward the faerie portal, hesitating only a moment before he stepped inside the primrose circle. Facing his mother's anger was not going to be easy. Even the druids had left the Queen of Faerie alone, but Finn had to plead his case and ask for her help. He took a deep breath and waited.

Nothing.

After a few minutes, Finn stirred uneasily. He hadn't been sure the queen would help him, but he had been certain she would appear to berate him. Misuse of Fae power always incurred her wrath. For her son to misappropriate it was unforgivable. But all was still. Now that he thought on it, the normal faerie activity that surrounded any Fae mound was not present. No sylphs fluttered in the air. No pixies played amongst the flower petals. He could see no dryads in trees nor hear the wind-singers in the leaves. It was as though the place had been abandoned by the Sidhe.

Or had the portal been shut off from him? Finn raised his hands, trying to sense the passageway through which Maggie had come. He felt nothing. The door had been closed.

Finn heard Maggie stir and quickly went back to her. Kneeling beside her, he ran an index finger across her forehead, willing her to forget what happened and return to the present—or more specifically, to the present day illusion he'd created for her.

Maggie opened her eyes slowly and gazed up at him. When she smiled, he thought she was still ensorcelled. "Are ye all right?"

"I think so."

"Do ye remember what happened?"

She frowned a little. "We were riding. Something— maybe a rabbit?—ran across the road. My horse…" Maggie touched her head where the bleeding had stopped. 'I fell off again, didn't I?"

"Aye, ye did." Finn wanted to shout his relief to the world that Maggie was back where she belonged, but he didn't want her to think he'd taken leave of his wits. He stood and lifted her with him. "I will take ye home."

"It seems you are always rescuing me," Maggie said and gave him a small smile.

It was his fault she needed rescuing, but he decided not to bring that up. "Can ye ride, or do ye want to ride with me?"

Maggie looked over to where the gelding was calmly grazing. "I think I'd better show both you and the horse that I can ride."

Finn nodded and helped her mount. He supposed he should be grateful—he *was* grateful—that she was no longer beguiled. Perhaps his mother *had* helped him by having Maggie recover.

As they began the ride home, another thought occurred to him. Maybe his mother had helped him, but was she also angry enough to have banned him from his world? Was that his punishment?

Chapter Eight

Maggie had tried to beg off attending dinner at the Gilpatrick's two evenings later, but she'd used the excuse of her fall twice yesterday and once this morning to avoid other social situations, and Aunt Ailis was beginning to worry.

So here she was, seated in the Gilpatrick's formal dining room at a long linen-covered table set for twenty with enough expensive china, crystal, and silverware to satisfy King George, except he didn't step foot in Ireland. Ciara had arranged the place cards so she sat beside Finn at the far end of the table and Maggie found herself between Mr. McMurrough and Mr. O'Demsey. Not that she minded. Both men were given to talking politics and, since women weren't expected to have opinions, that gave her a chance to contemplate.

Physically, she felt fine. Once the bleeding had stopped, the gash on her head didn't turn out to be that big and she had only a small bump. Her thoughts were confused, though. She remembered riding with Finn along the winding country road and coming to the glade, but then memories blurred. She thought she'd seen green light spinning about her in changing shades, but that turned into swirling snow. Finn had his shirt off, which was strange if it were snowing, but he didn't seem cold. Of course, he was fully clothed when she'd opened her eyes.

Even now, the thought of how he'd looked with his shirt off—at least in her imagination—made her face warm. His chest and arms had been like sculpted marble, all smooth angles and planes. She'd used every bit of her will power to ride her own horse back, but Maggie had been afraid she'd tear Finn's shirt off him if he'd held her against him in the saddle. She had no idea where that urge had come from, but it was strong. Even now her fingers still itched to touch him, but she forced herself to focus on the conversation when she heard Daniel O'Connell's name mentioned.

"The villagers think O'Connell is going to save them all," Mr. O'Demsey said.

"The peasants expect too much," Mr. McMurrough answered. "They'll never have equal status to us. After all, King William granted these lands to our forefathers."

"Right," Mr.O'Demsey said, lifting his wine glass, "but I don't think we have to worry. O'Connell needs to raise a lot more money before he'll be able to influence the English Parliament."

"Does he really think he can get the Act of Union repealed?" Mr. McMurrough shook his head. "If he keeps trying to get the peasants to vote against what we landlords want—what the king wants—O'Connell will be lucky if he isn't arrested for being a traitor."

Maggie couldn't keep still. "Why would he be thought a traitor because he wants to better living conditions in the villages?"

Both men looked at her as though she'd just asked if they'd like to invite Napoleon to tea. Conversation around them stopped. People stared.

"Well?" she asked again.

"We don't expect you to understand," Mr.

O'Demsey said.

"Why not? Because I'm female?" That comment brought startled gasps from the ladies near her. Maggie had no idea where the outburst had come from. She only knew something was wrong when women weren't supposed to express—or even have—opinions. And she couldn't seem to stop. "I have a brain. And a mind—"

"No one is questioning that," Mr.McMurrough said, although his facial expression showed quite plainly that he was indeed questioning her mental capacity, "but you've lived in the city. Things are a bit different in the country. Perhaps your aunt can explain it to you later."

"Yes," Aunt Ailis said quickly and gave Maggie a warning look. "We'll talk about this later."

Maggie bit her lip to keep from retorting to her aunt, but her temper was in high dudgeon. She caught Finn watching her curiously from his end of the table. He hadn't seemed to mind when the children in the village talked about Daniel O'Connell, nor had Finn taken offense when she'd asked questions. In fact, he'd encouraged it. He didn't seem to think there was anything wrong with her having a mind and wanting to use it.

What was wrong with these other men? There must be a name for men who thought women needed to be put in their place and stay there. She just didn't know what that name was.

****

"What was that conversation about earlier?" Finn asked as they left the Gilpatricks later and were walking toward the waiting carriages. "I was too far at the end of the table to hear it, but from the expressions, I thought maybe you'd told them to prepare for a French invasion."

Maggie smiled. "It might have been better if I had."

Finn raised a brow. "What did you say?"

"They were talking about Daniel O'Connell getting arrested if he kept trying to get the villagers—they called them peasants—to vote against the landlords. I just asked what was wrong in trying to establish better living conditions for the workers."

Finn gave her a long look. "What did they say?"

"They didn't, other than to tell me I didn't understand."

He continued his level gaze. "And do you understand?"

"Maybe not everything about the politics of it, but it's easy to see conditions could be better for the villagers. They work hard. I'm sure the crofters do too."

"Ye are right."

"I've been thinking a lot since that first day I met with the schoolchildren. I know I didn't grow up wealthy, but I had much more than these children do. My parents were educated. My father made sure I was too, so I could earn a living." Maggie paused. She knew she'd been a governess in Dublin, but something niggled at the back of her mind that had to do with providing for people who might have lost everything. Where that idea came from she didn't know. Maybe she was just confusing being an orphan with losing everything. "I didn't know my father had become wealthy through overseas investments. He never talked about it. I know he spent long hours in an office and he was tired when he came home. Much like the villagers are at the end of their working day. I think Mr. O'Connell is right to try and make things better. Do you think he can?"

"Hmmm," Finn said as they came to a stop by the

Adair carriage. "He has a long road to walk. To repeal the Act of Union and free Ireland from English rule may not happen in his lifetime. But the journey will not happen at all if no one takes the first steps. Except for Ulster, and Dublin's Pale—where most of your aunt and uncle's neighbors turned Anglican generations ago—the rest of the country remains Catholic. Daniel's first goal is to get Catholics the right to seats in the British Parliament. Once there is representation of the majority, rights will slowly begin to return to the people."

"And he needs funds to do it."

"Political endeavors take money, aye."

"I have money. I want to help." Maggie paused and then added, "He is a good man, I think."

Finn tilted his head. "O'Connell is, but are ye sure ye want to give part of your inheritance away?"

Her inheritance. Maggie knew how hard her father had worked for that money. How he had saved it. Was she doing the right thing? She thought of the villagers and their mended clothing and simple furnishings. How little coin they received for their labors because of rents and taxes. She took a deep breath. "Yes. It's for a good cause."

Finn smiled, his eyes glowing like warm mead in the light from the carriage lamps. "Ye have done well, Maggie Maquire."

****

A fine mist greeted the sunrise on Midsummer Day, creating beautiful rainbows that arched and dipped over the hills and valleys of the countryside. Maggie awoke feeling happier than she had in days. Yesterday, she'd spoken to her aunt and uncle at length about helping Mr. O'Connell's cause and Uncle Sean had agreed to take her to Dublin on the morrow to arrange for funds to be transferred.

And tonight was the Midsummer Ball. Maggie was actually looking forward to it, knowing that a feast would also be provided to the villagers…her aunt and uncle had agreed to that as well. She was already thinking what she might do for the children at Christmas.

Maggie slipped out of bed and dressed quickly. Uncle Sean had promised a whole boar would be roasted for the villagers, and she wanted to oversee the kitchens today. She knew plenty of bread, potatoes, and other vegetables would be provided, but she wanted to make sure the cooks prepared cakes and pies as well.

"There she is!" one boy shouted hours later as Maggie arrived in the village with a cart that bore the efforts of the day's cooking and baking. The children crowded around her while the adults hung back, although they had wide smiles on their faces.

"Ye are kind to think of us," one woman said, wiping her hands on her apron before picking up a heavy bowl laden with food.

A second woman picked up loaves of bread and headed for the trestles that had been set up to serve as an outdoor table.

"Won't ye join us?" another woman asked as the men took the boar off the spit and carried it to a smaller table to carve it.

Although she wanted the villagers to enjoy every morsel, Maggie felt it would be rude to decline the invitation. "I would like that," she said as she helped them finish bringing the rest of the food. She would be careful to take only small portions.

After the meal, the joy—as well as the expressions

of contented fullness on the adult faces and burps by the children—made Maggie smile. "I want to start a tradition," Maggie told their parents. "We'll have another feast at harvest and then have a huge celebration for Yule."

"Aye, aye, aye!" several of the boys yelled only to be given stern looks from their mothers before the women also burst into thanks.

"There is no need to thank me," Maggie said. "Each of you works hard. You deserve to benefit from your labor."

Several of the adults gave her curious looks and one of them spoke. "No one has ever said that before, except for Daniel O'Connell."

Maggie nodded, more sure than ever she had made the right choice.

****

Finn arrived as dusk was descending, to escort them to the ball. Or, as Aunt Ailis had put it earlier, to escort Maggie to the ball. Maggie didn't argue. If they arrived together, albeit with her aunt and uncle as chaperones, it would send a message to the other girls. She might have to share her dance card and Finn would probably have to dance with others, but he'd have several slots…and he'd be escorting her home.

Finn had told her aunt he wanted to talk to Maggie before leaving for the ball this evening and her aunt had winked and said he probably would ask to pay court. Maggie smiled at her reflection in her bedchamber mirror as she tucked a strand of hair behind her ear. She hadn't thought about anyone paying court to her before, but the idea was definitely appealing. She'd been attracted to Finn ever since she'd come to her aunt and uncle's place. Even if she couldn't exactly recall knowing him before—there were other details of her life she couldn't remember either since that first fall from the horse—she felt like she'd known Finn for a long time.

Maggie smoothed the skirt of her yellow silk gown and then hurried down the stairs to greet Finn. He stood and gave her an appreciative look as she entered the parlor.

"I hope I didn't keep you waiting too long," she said.

Finn smiled. "Women are supposed to keep men waiting, aren't they? Besides, it is still early to leave." He turned to Aunt Ailis. "With your permission, I'd like to take a walk in the gardens with Maggie."

Her aunt beamed. "Of course."

"Do ye need a shawl?" Finn asked as they left the parlor. "The evening air gets a wee bit damp."

Maggie shook her head. She always felt warm around him, although she couldn't very well tell him his body heat was enough.

He offered his arm and they strolled outside and around to the back gardens. The twilight cast long shadows, spreading streaks of pale lavender and blue across much of the landscape. Tendrils of fog crept along the stone pathways, and Maggie shivered.

"Are ye sure ye are not cold?" Finn didn't wait for an answer but removed his coat and put it around her shoulders. He turned her around to face him. "There is something I need to tell ye."

His coat enveloped her in warmth and Maggie inhaled the comforting scent of him. She laid her hands on his shoulders. "What is it?"

Finn looked into her eyes. "I haven't always been…" he started to say and then stopped. "I need to tell ye—"

"Why don't you show me?" Maggie asked and looked up at him expectantly.

A furrow appeared on his forehead. "What do ye mean?"

Maggie furrowed her brow as well. "You don't want to kiss me?"

His eyes widened and then darkened to the color of brandy as his gaze moved to her mouth. "I do more than anything, but I should not."

"Why not?"

"Because I'm not…I'm not what you think I am."

Maggie smiled. "I don't care if you're a pauper or a prince."

Finn looked startled. "Ye really should know—"

"You *don't* want to kiss me, do you?" Maggie began to step away from him, feeling mortified, only to feel his arms encircle her waist as he drew her to him and then his lips were on hers.

Her breath left her in a swoosh and she felt weightless in his arms as though she were floating above the ground. Finn's lips were warm and firm, coaxing and teasing as he gently increased the pressure until her mouth opened of its own accord to invite him in. When his tongue smoothly glided across hers, Maggie moaned and clutched his shoulders, then wrapped her arms around his neck as he began a leisurely exploration of her mouth before he deepened the kiss and she found herself responding frantically, as though she could not get enough of him. Her body felt on fire.

And then she felt like she had been drenched in cold water when Finn broke the kiss and stepped away from her. A strange array of emotions swept over his face, all too fast for Maggie to read any of them. She felt disoriented, as though she were lost in a swirling cloud, and then realized the fog had moved in, hanging like ghostly shrouds on the shrubbery. She felt unsteady and started to walk toward the gazebo. "I think I need to sit down."

Finn seemed equally dazed as he stood rooted to the spot. "I must tell ye—"

"Let's wait until we're seated," Maggie said, still feeling shaky as she started up the steps. "I want—"

"No!" Finn suddenly shouted and ran toward her. "Don't go in there!"

Maggie took the final step inside and turned toward him in bewilderment. "Why ever not?"

She didn't hear his answer as the fog swirled up and enveloped her.

Chapter Nine

Maggie turned over groggily the next morning and pulled the warm quilts up to her chin. Outside, the wind howled and rattled the windowpanes. The Nor'easter must have arrived. She snuggled deeper into her bed, not wanting to leave its warmth…or the dream she'd been having.

Dream. Maggie's eyes snapped open. She looked around her familiar room in her aunt and uncle's Brooklyn walk-up. The sweater she'd worn to work yesterday lay across an armchair. Her cell phone was on the dresser. The framed college diploma she cherished hung on one wall, while another had a series of travel posters of places she wanted to see.

Travel. Maggie sat up and swung her legs over the side of the bed. She'd traveled in the dream last night. Not only to Ireland, but back to the nineteenth century. And she'd conjured up a really hunky-looking guy, to boot. Maggie touched her mouth, half-expecting her lips to be swollen. They'd been kissing…

It had all seemed so *real*.

Maggie got up and padded over to the dresser to look in the mirror. She looked the same, but she felt as though she'd aged. Feeling a little foolish, she reached for her cell phone to check the date. December 25. Christmas Day. Of course it was. What in the world was she thinking?

She slipped into the sweater and a pair of jeans and went downstairs to help her aunt with breakfast. She must have overslept, because the kitchen was empty except for her aunt cleaning a frying pan.

"Why didn't you wake me?" she asked as she went over to the sink to dry the dishes. "I told you I'd do breakfast on Christmas."

Aunt Ailis smiled. "I peeked into your room. You looked totally out, so I thought you'd had a hard day yesterday and needed the sleep."

Maggie shook her head. "The day was okay, but boy, did I have some dream last night."

"A bad dream?"

"No. I went to Ireland. In the dream, I mean."

"Maybe because we were talking about the Irish jig last night."

"I know, but this was really weird. It was like I'd stepped back in time. To 1815, to be precise."

Her aunt laughed. "Well, you always have been detail-oriented."

"You and Uncle Sean were there too, only you lived on a country estate and were rich."

"I wish I could have shared that dream. Being rich sounds good to me."

Maggie knit her brows. "I don't know if it really is."

"Why do you say that?"

"Well, your friends—in the dream—were wealthy too…something to do with English nobility. But the villagers were poor even though they worked hard. And the children weren't educated. There wasn't a school."

Aunt Ailis set down the frying pan and turned to Maggie. "That really must have been some dream. You sound so serious."

"I know. I woke up feeling like I had really been there."

"You've always had an active imagination, dear." Her aunt winked. "Did you manage to meet a nice-looking young man, too?"

Maggie felt her face warm even as her body heated. Finn O'Byrne, with his long coppery hair, golden eyes, and sculpted, muscular body, seemed more like a Prince Charming from some faerie tale than a man.

Her aunt grinned. "From your flushed face, I assume you added a little romance to your dream."

She felt her blush deepen. She'd added a romantic element all right. Maggie could still feel the gentle touch of Finn's fingers tracing her cheek, his warm embrace when he pulled her close. His demanding kiss that left her frenzied… What would have happened if she hadn't woken up? She wished now that she'd stayed in bed. "There was this nice neighbor who was really helpful…" Maggie let her voice trail off when her aunt raised an eyebrow. How could she explain Finn? That he cared about the villagers made him even more prince-like. She'd never meet someone like him in real life. He was perfect. But then, she'd created him in her mind. "Well, you know how dreams go."

"Um," her aunt said as Kacie and Mia came barreling through the door.

"Can we open presents now?" Mia asked.

"In a little while. Uncle Sean isn't up yet."

"Maggie, it snowed again," Kacie said. "Can we make more snow angels while we wait?"

"Not until the wind stops blowing, though," Mia told her with seven-year-old wisdom. "Else their wings will disappear."

"We did Gabriel and Rafael yesterday," Kacie said as though her sister hadn't spoken. "Today we can do Michael and Ariel."

"And I'll come out and watch," Maggie said. "Then we can have hot chocolate and open presents and I'll read you a Christmas story about the archangels. How does that sound?"

"Yippee!" they said in unison.

Maggie smiled, remembering in the dream that the village children didn't have quite that kind of enthusiasm, but she'd enjoyed teaching them. She shook her head as the girls scampered off to play. She was making way too much of a dream. It hadn't been real.

The feeling didn't leave her, though, as she took a granola bar out of the cookie jar and went to the back room that served as an office for her uncle, with a desk for her aunt and a study area for the girls. Two full-size bookcases stood against one wall. She'd filled one of them with books on travel and history. The yearning for travel she shared with Elizabeth, although her much wealthier friend actually could afford to do it. The passion for history she shared with Caroline.

Maggie selected a book on Irish history and settled into a comfortable old armchair near the window. Sleet pelted the glass and Maggie could feel cold air blowing through the caulking. She took the quilt lying over the back of the chair and wrapped up in it. It had been warm in Ireland…

Maggie pulled the blanket closer and opened the book. Since the dream had felt so real, she might as well check out the facts. She flipped the pages until she came to the section on Daniel O'Connell. He had been called the Liberator and had achieved his goal of Catholics being allowed seats in the English Parliament. He'd even run for Parliament himself in 1828 and won, but the significant factor was he'd refused to take the Oath of Supremacy which acknowledged the British monarch as the head of church and state—and he'd gotten by with it. After that, other Catholics were allowed to hold office without taking the oath, as well. But it wasn't until the 1920s that Ireland finally became a free state and nearly 1950 before it became a republic.

She put the book aside and smiled. So it had been a good cause, after all.

Maggie snuggled deeper into the quilt and closed her eyes. Maybe if she napped, she'd dream of Finn O'Byrne again.

****

Finn stood staring at the empty gazebo. Maggie was gone. Transported back to her own time. He clenched his fists and swore a faerie oath that had the dryads in the hawthorn trees beside him peeking out from the branches in trepidation. The colorful sparkles in the air indicating the presence of sylphs faded as they left in a flurry and the wind-singers stilled. Finn sighed. At least he still had that part of his magic left. He lifted his hand and willed the elementals to return. It wasn't the sprites' fault Maggie was gone.

But why hadn't he seen what—who—was waiting in the gazebo? Why hadn't he sensed the presence? Why had he even taken the risk of bringing Maggie to the garden and so close to a faerie portal? He'd known her time in this period was short. She'd learned to believe in herself again. Finn's mission was done.

But he'd wanted to tell her the truth. Who—what— he was. That what had started as a job had turned into much, much more. He'd never cared for a mortal like he had her.

And then he'd kissed her.

Now she was gone.

"Are you quite through feeling sorry for yourself?" his mother asked as she materialized inside the gazebo, her white gossamer gown floating ethereally around her.

He should have known she'd show up. "I am not feeling sorry for myself."

Moira raised a delicate eyebrow. "You left your thoughts wide open."

Finn frowned and closed his mind. Although his mother had the uncanny skill to pry into even closed minds sometimes, he'd been foolish not to keep barriers in place. Just another piece of evidence as to how distraught he was. "Why didn't you come earlier? You might have helped me."

"What could I have done?"

"You could have interceded."

Both brows rose. "With the one who came for her?"

Finn knew it was foolish, but he said it anyway. "Yes. Maybe she—I—would have been allowed a little more time."

"Fate did not destine her for you, my son."

"How do ye know that?"

Moira frowned and sat on the bench, patting the place beside her. "Come."

Reluctantly, he climbed the steps, not wanting to enter the place where he could smell the one who had taken her. Worse, the scent of Maggie still lingered, cutting like a dagger to his heart. He sat down on the edge of the bench. "What do ye want to say?"

"Why do you care so much for a mortal? You have

been given many missions over the centuries. Why is this one so different?"

"I cannot explain it. I only know that when I'm with her I feel happy."

"Happiness is a human emotion," Moira said.

"I know. And I like it. I want to be with her."

"We cannot bring her back. To do so might change the course of history. You know that, son, as well as I."

"Maggie was allowed to come through the portal once."

"To learn to believe in herself. Was that not the mission?"

"Yes, but she taught me something, too," Finn said. "Maggie taught me to feel again. To laugh. To embrace life—"

"Mortal life. You are Fae. There is no place for her in our world."

Finn looked at his mother. "Then perhaps there is a place in her world for me."

Silver sparks flashed in Moria's eyes. "Do not be foolish. Your powers would quickly fade in the mortal world."

"Perhaps I no longer care about immortality. Perhaps I want to experience what real love might be."

Moira stared at him. "Are you telling me you love this…this woman?"

"I think I might. I want the chance to find out."

"You are serious?"

"What you said is true, Mother. History cannot be undone, but the future is still in the making." Finn paused and took a deep breath, knowing what he had to do. "I will go to her."

Elizabeth: Chapter One

Elizabeth paid the taxi and walked toward the steps of the Upper East Side cooperative where she lived. The doorman bobbed his head and opened the door for her so she wouldn't need to use her code.

"Looks like it might be a real blow tonight, Miss Shelton," he said.

"Quite possibly," she answered as she entered the lobby and headed for the elevator. She hoped the brunt of the storm didn't hit until morning since she had an invitation to a private holiday charity event at The Cloisters this evening that included several European dignitaries. Although attendance was by invitation only and the media would be barred, she had no doubt the event would make the society page of *The New York Times*, which should make her mother happy. Elizabeth could almost hear her mega-mogul father reminding her to take the opportunity to network. With the European economy shaky, American investments looked good to those on the other side of the pond.

Elizabeth punched the button to the tenth floor, trying to recall a time when she hadn't used an invitation to a social function to network. Never miss a chance to get ahead, her daddy always said. He'd started explaining the intricacies of Wall Street to her while she was still in high school. Her mother said proper social connections were even more important and had chosen which sorority Elizabeth should pledge based on how many generations of wealth could be accounted for with the present members.

She knew, as an only child, that it was her responsibility to carry on the family dynasty, and that would eventually mean marriage to a properly affluent man.

Which was why she had tried to warn Maggie about Johnny. Elizabeth sighed as the elevator doors opened and she stepped into the tenth floor lobby with its white and gold flocked wallpaper and narrow strips of ceiling-to-floor mirrors. It was difficult to explain to someone why it was important to be discriminate without sounding like a snob. Sometimes Elizabeth envied Maggie her ability to react emotionally and not consider the long-range consequences. Then again, emotional involvement had cost Caroline dearly when her husband had been killed. He'd been her best friend, she'd said. Now Caroline kept her nose buried in past history.

Elizabeth's Italian leather boots tapped against the waxed and burnished wood floor as she made her way to one of the three solid oak doors on this level. Before she could insert her key, Jones, her middle-aged butler/chauffeur, opened the door.

"I was thinking you might call for me to bring the car, it being Christmas Eve and all," he said as he took her cloak and gloves.

"I was able to get a cab," Elizabeth answered, "but we will need the car for tonight." She noticed an almost imperceptible rise of one brow. "What is it?"

"I just thought…the event might have been cancelled due to the storm."

"Hardly. It's a thing for some international charity.

Besides, the storm isn't here yet, Jones. We'll take the Mercedes. It shouldn't have any trouble if the streets ice over."

He looked as though he wanted to say something more, but then he nodded. "As you wish, Miss Shelton. Eight o'clock?"

"That will be fine," she said as she left him and made her way down the hallway past the kitchen to her bedroom. A light had been left on over the sink, indicating the cook had already gone home—the woman always got nervous when blizzards were forecast—but at least she'd left something that smelled delicious in a chafing dish on the stovetop.

To Elizabeth's relief, the young maid Emma was tidying up in her bedroom. "I'm glad you're still here."

"Of course, Miss Shelton. I knew you had a party to go to tonight."

Elizabeth smiled. At least the girl didn't try to berate her about not going because of the weather. But then, she had probably never worked in a Manhattan high-rise before and was more starry-eyed than most. Unlike the butler—whose real name was Johannsen, but Jones was shorter—who'd been hired by her father for his experience.

"I'll be wearing the black-and-white tonight. Would you make sure it's pressed and ready?"

"The gown?"

"No. The strapless trouser suit."

Emma's face brightened. "I love that one."

"I do too. I think I'll wear the silver-threaded silk stole with it. Make sure it's not wrinkled, please."

"Yes, Miss Shelton." Emma cast a worried look outside. "Once I do that, is it all right if I leave? It is

Christmas Eve, and my husband has the baby and he gets nervous if I'm not there—"

"Fine."

Emma hesitated. "It's just…with the snow coming… I've got to get all the way out to Yonkers—"

"I said it would be fine," Elizabeth repeated, trying not to sound curt. All the maid had to say was she wanted to beat the storm and be done. Everyone used Christmas as an excuse. Using children as an excuse was something else she didn't like, not that she had known Emma had a child. "I'm going to take a hot bath," Elizabeth said, modulating her tone. "As soon as you check the clothes, you can go. I'll see you on Monday."

Emma gave her a big smile. "Thank you, Miss Shelton. And Merry Christmas."

"Yes, well. You are welcome."

Thirty minutes later, having emerged from the scented bath, Elizabeth padded barefoot onto the thick white carpet of her bedroom. Emma was gone, but the trouser suit and stole were hung by the dressing screen and her designer stilettos sat on the floor. The girl had done what she'd been asked to do and even had laid a pale blue negligee with satin wrapper across the bed.

Elizabeth glanced at the small clock on the bedside table. It was only half past six. A short nap would have her looking refreshed and give her the energy she needed to make an impression at tonight's event. She slipped the negligee over her head and added the wrapper, belting it around her waist as she lay down on top of the bedspread.

There was nothing as relaxing as a hot bath and a nap. She'd just doze off for a few minutes…

Chapter Two

Elizabeth watched several women scurrying across the courtyard from a small wooden building to the open-arched entrances of a walkway alongside an old stone, two-storied building. Some were carrying jugs and others large bowls of food and platters of steaming meat and they were all oddly clothed in ground-length gray dresses with white bib aprons and mop caps.

She frowned and looked at her surroundings. Elizabeth hadn't visited The Cloisters since she was a child, but she did remember a courtyard and stone archways. She could see the top of the tall square keep beyond the lower structures. The Hudson River flowed below the hill. She tried to recall if the invitation had indicated some kind of theme. She was certain there had been nothing about the gala being a costume ball. Maybe the 1800s garb was an organizer's idea of showcasing American history since the event was for a national charity.

Two young women with several loaves of bread came out of the smaller building and stopped when they saw her.

"Why are ye not dressed?" one of them asked.

"And why are ye standing there gawking when there's work to be done?" the other said.

"Gawking?" They spoke with English accents, although Elizabeth supposed if they were keeping to a theme, a lot of servants in the 1800s were indentured servants from England. Still, they didn't have to be rude. They'd make a horrible impression on the foreign dignitaries who would be here this evening. "You might mind your manners."

They both snickered and the first woman poked her friend. "Ain't she the clever one?"

"Givin' herself airs and all," the other answered.

Elizabeth lifted her chin. Their behavior—whether rehearsed or not, although she couldn't understand why they'd choose this type of characterization—simply would not do. Especially tonight. "Who hired you?"

"Who hired us?" the first woman rolled her eyes and turned to the other. "Ina, did ye hear the question? Who hired us?"

Elizabeth detested eye-rolling. "The mayor is going to be here tonight. You won't last an hour if you act like that."

"Well, la-de-da," Ina said. "We don't know who the mayor is, but the duke probably won't care either."

A duke was going to be present? Elizabeth had not heard of nobility—from any country—being invited. From what she'd been able to discover, the A-listers were mainly ambassadors, not aristocracy. "Which duke?"

The women gave her incredulous looks. Elizabeth wondered why. "Which duke?" she repeated. Good heavens! Might it be Prince William, the Duke of Cambridge? And maybe Kate... Kate always dressed conservatively. Maybe Elizabeth's choice of the designer suit was all wrong. Maybe she should have worn something a bit more modest.

"Byron Halliwell, the Duke of Chadworth," the first

woman replied in a tone that implied she was addressing a rather dim-witted child.

Elizabeth frowned. She'd never heard of him, but then, her father had taught her to know who the CEOs and heads of Boards of Directors were, not branches of royal bloodlines. "Well, I'm sure the duke won't appreciate your being rude to him."

Ina shrugged. "His Grace will na be payin' attention to the likes of Sara and me."

"He might find your costumes rather interesting."

"Our costumes?"

"Yes." Elizabeth gestured toward their dresses. "The servers will certainly stand out, dressed like that."

"We will?" Sara asked, and they both started laughing.

"'Tis more like ye will be noticed," Ina said and then managed to stifle another giggle. "But be warned. His Grace prefers his mistresses to stay out of sight."

"His *mistresses*? What on earth are you talking about?" Elizabeth asked.

"Aye. My friend Ina is right. The duke will na be pleased to see ye strutting around the banquet chamber."

"Strutting…" Elizabeth nearly sputtered. "I have an *invitation*."

"Aye. An invitation to His Grace's bed." Ian snickered again.

"That's enough. I'm getting a little tired of your attitude," Elizabeth said. "Whoever hired you will hear about this."

"Well, hoity-toity," Sara said and grinned at Ina. "Doesn't she just sound like a fine lady now?"

"Aye. They all think they're grand until His Grace is through with them and they're set to scouring pans for the cook."

"If they're lucky and don't get tossed back in the streets," Sara added.

Elizabeth frowned. "Tossed into the street? What—"

"What are ye girls doing, slacking yer jaws when the duke is waiting?" A plump, older woman with graying hair came out of the small building and put her hands on her hips. "Ye best be movin'."

Ina and Sara covered their bread with cloth and scampered away without another word. Elizabeth turned to the woman who sounded like she was in charge. "I really need to report—"

"Ye need to get dressed," the woman said and turned around to go back into the wooden building.

Elizabeth bit her lip. At least now she knew why the young women were so rude. They got it from their supervisor. And why did they all care how she was dressed? Maybe her outfit was a bit revealing if English nobility was going to be present, but she did have her stole around her shoulders. Elizabeth reached to pull it up more and then realized her fingers touched bare skin.

She looked down and felt her eyes widen. She was wearing her chiffon negligee and short satin wrapper. Elizabeth closed her eyes. She must be dreaming. Having one of those nightmares where people felt they were undressed in public. She'd heard those dreams were quite common. That had to be it. She took a deep breath and slowly opened her eyes to find a young man with eyes black as ebony staring at her.

He was dressed in nineteenth-century English livery.

Elizabeth felt herself grow lightheaded as the world

around her began to tilt. The last thing she remembered as she started to fall was his strong arms catching her.

****

Damnation. He'd already nearly botched this assignment and it hadn't even begun. Broc Hadon tossed his dark hair out of his eyes and swore an oath under his breath as he carried Elizabeth away from the courtyard, toward the stables, out of sight of curious, prying eyes. He was supposed to have been waiting for her when she floated through the sleep portal into this world, but his fraternal twin brother—the high-and-mighty Duke of Chadworth—had sent him on an errand that turned out to be fruitless.

Byron didn't approve of the altruistic assignments they were given. Three hundred years ago, when their mother had been burned at the stake for witchcraft, he'd refused to accept any more. At the time, Broc didn't blame him, since their mother had been innocent. It was their father who had escaped the flames, using his warlock powers.

Over the centuries, Byron had turned cold and heartless. He began using his powers for hedonistic pleasure and quickly turned cruel to anyone who stood in his way. Luckily, Broc could keep his brother's powers contained to the manor house by using special wards. The downside was that Broc couldn't enter the manor himself without breaking those bonds.

Byron hated Broc, accusing him of acting like Sir Galahad and banishing him to a life in the stables. Yet Byron couldn't kill Broc. The ultimate Master, from whence these assignments came, wouldn't allow it. Byron had tried once, only to find himself disfigured like Richard III for over seventy mortal years. He hadn't tried again, since he valued his golden-haired Adonis-like beauty too much.

But that wouldn't stop Byron from attempting to hurt this young American woman who'd been sent to Broc to heal.

Broc kicked open a stall door and laid Elizabeth down on the clean straw, then knelt beside her. Chanting an incantation, he passed his hand over her forehead, erasing her memory of the future and substituting a different history. When she woke, Elizabeth would think she was in Victorian England. The effect would only be temporary while she was in his world, but he'd found it easier than trying to explain time travel, especially since he was forbidden to explain his mission. Mortals had to find healing on their own. As a warlock, he could only guide them.

Broc studied the young woman who would be his charge. She was lovely, her pale hair the color of moonbeams. He recalled her eyes being the deep blue of an ocean swell on a summer day. Delicate porcelain skin molded to high cheekbones and a straight, short nose. Her mouth was wide and full, a ripe shade of pink that made him think of berries waiting to be tasted. Broc reached out to trace the curve of her lips and then withdrew his hand. She had not been sent to him to take his pleasure.

As beautiful as Elizabeth was, once Byron saw her, she would be in danger.

Broc frowned as he looked at what she was wearing. The night rail came only to her mid-thighs, exposing long, slender legs that were made for wrapping around a man's waist. He hoped his brother hadn't seen her in the courtyard. If Broc could get her into suitable servant's clothing, there might be a chance his twin wouldn't notice her.

"Colton!" he called and waited for the older man was in charge of the stables to appear. A short time later his gray head popped over the upper half of the stall door. "I need a servant's dress. Can your wife fetch one?"

Colton's gaze travelled to Elizabeth and his eyes rounded, but he only nodded and then disappeared. Broc listened to the man's footsteps retreat. Neither Colton nor his wife would question Broc's motives. When Byron had arrived at Chadworth to claim the title ten years ago, one of his first targets had been Colton's daughter, a girl far too young to be subject to what Byron had in mind. Broc had managed to materialize in time to mesmerize his twin temporarily and let the child escape. After that episode, he knew he could no longer leave his twin alone—and that was when he had warded the manor to keep the evil contained.

The locals had talked for days about the sudden, violent thunderstorm that erupted from a cloudless sky that same day. No one knew the storm was a battle between two warlocks hurling lightning bolts at each other, but Colton had seen burn scars on Broc's hands shortly afterward. He had given Broc a long, scrutinizing look and then taken his daughter away to safety at a relative's home. When he'd returned, he became Broc's faithful companion and, together, they'd helped more than one bruised and battered girl to escape the duke's sadistic clutches.

Colton returned shortly, his wife in tow. "This was all I could find on such short notice," she said, shaking out a long skirt and a peasant blouse.

A serving wench's attire. The blouse would do little

to conceal Elizabeth's breasts or her slender waist. Broc had hoped Colton's wife would bring a cleaning woman's garb that had long sleeves and a high neckline, but time was of the essence. Groomsmen and drivers from the guests' carriages would start to congregate by the stables soon.

Broc held out his hand for the garments. Colton's wife folded her arms around the clothing, a signal for Broc to leave. He stood, chiding himself for not thinking about modesty. The concept was pretty much foreign to a warlock—even one with good intentions—but humans had a strange sense of what they called decency. He stepped outside the stall to join Colton.

"Where do ye want me to take her?" the man asked.

Broc wished he could say "somewhere safe," but his mission meant she had to be close to him and his instructions had been specific to this place. He hoped Colton wouldn't start to ask questions.

"The girl will be staying here."

****

The smell of roasting meat filled the small wooden building where the cooking was done. Elizabeth sniffed appreciatively, suddenly aware that her stomach was growling.

"If ye do not want to be sent cleaning out the garderobes, ye'd best stop standing there like a dim-witted fool." One of the serving women thrust a heavy tray at Elizabeth and gave her a push. "The duke is waiting in the banquet hall."

She nearly dropped the platter, but managed to balance it before the food went careening to the floor and stared after the woman hurrying out the door and across the courtyard. What did she mean the duke was waiting?

"His Grace does not like his food to be cold." The plump, gray-haired woman Elizabeth remembered seeing earlier was frowning at her. "I'll not have me position questioned by having the likes of ye in the serving hall if ye cannot be swift."

Elizabeth walked out the door, more to avoid the woman's acid tongue than because she knew where she was going. She could hear strains of music and raucous laughter coming from the building behind the open-arched walkway. There must be a Christmas celebration going on. Vaguely she recalled receiving an invitation for this evening—a costume party, maybe, given the kind of clothes everyone in the courtyard was wearing. Elizabeth looked down at the peasant gown and long skirt she wore. She'd dressed for the event as well, although she didn't remember ordering a costume.

She started across the cobblestones, not sure why she'd been given a platter of meat to take in, but perhaps it was part of the holiday theme. It seemed everyone else was carrying something too. She stepped onto the walkway, nearly colliding with a man in coattails and top hat.

"Watch where you are going, wench!" he said, brushing his sleeve carefully.

"Wench?" she asked, but he'd already gone on.

Elizabeth stepped through the massive double doors that stood propped open and stopped abruptly, gazing around in wonderment. Costume party indeed. Whoever the organizer for this event was, he or she had done a wonderful job decorating. Everything looked authentic. Three huge crystal chandeliers hung from the wooden cross-beamed ceiling, each filled with dozens of beeswax candles. Wall sconces held more candles, giving a flickering glow to the large room and bringing out the richness of the velvet and brocade tapestries lining the walls. Walk-in-size hearths were centered on either side of the long walls, decorated with pine garlands and sprigs of holly. Scores of guests sat at mahogany tables glistening with china and silver. To Elizabeth's left, a quartet of musicians played.

She frowned. Why were the ladies dressed in ball gowns and the men in formal evening attire when she was dressed in such simple clothing? The other women dressed as she was were all serving food. Had she received the wrong instructions on what to wear? Looking around more carefully, she spotted a golden-haired man seated on a dais at the far end of the hall, surrounded by several fancily dressed men. He must be the duke. Surely he could explain what was going on.

Elizabeth set her tray down on a sideboard and began to start forward. Her stomach growled again, reminding her she was hungry. She halted. The duke could wait for a moment. Taking a plate from the sideboard, she helped herself to a piece of meat. She'd barely taken a bite when the food was slapped out of her hand by a furious-looking man dressed as a footman in livery.

"What do you think you are doing?"

She held onto her temper. "I was trying to eat."

His eyes widened. "You were eating His Grace's *meat*."

"I didn't think he'd mind my having a small bite. I'm not quite sure where I am to be seated."

The man's eyes turned owlish. "Where you are to be seated?"

"Do you repeat everything someone says?"

Before he could answer, the two maids she'd seen earlier came up. Sara pointed at the floor. "Look at that! She threw the duke's meat down."

Elizabeth tried not to sound annoyed. "I didn't throw it. This lout knocked it from my hand."

Ina stared at her. "Ye tried to eat His Grace's meat?"

"Really, I don't know why everyone thinks that's so bad. It's not like there's not enough to go around."

"The duke's meat!" Sara shrieked to several other maids who'd gathered around. "Miss Hoity-Toity thinks she can eat our lord's meat."

"He never gave me no meat," a buxom brunette said sullenly.

"Me either," a curvy redhead said, giving Elizabeth a dark look. "What makes ye so special?"

"Just because ye slept in His Grace's bed—"

"I did *not* sleep in anyone's bed. I don't even know your duke. I—"

"What is the commotion?" Another man, dressed in butler black with a stiff white shirt approached.

"She was eating His Grace's meat, Mr. Giles," Ina said.

The man ignored her and looked down his nose at the footman. "Can you not keep order amongst the serving wenches, John?"

"Aye, Mr. Giles. It will not happen again. This one gave herself airs…" John pointed to Elizabeth. "…because His Grace took her to his bed—"

Elizabeth's temper rose. "Your duke did *not* take me to his bed. How many times do I have to say it?"

"Why else would ye think ye could have meat?"

"Because I was hungry. I don't even know your duke."

"You deny being his latest mistress?" John asked.

Elizabeth understood now why people rolled their eyes. "*Yes.* Yes, I deny it."

Mr. Giles raised a brow. "Perhaps His Grace could settle the matter."

"Perhaps he could." Elizabeth stalked ahead of him toward the dais. Enough was enough. She was going to settle this.

Mr. Giles hurried after her. "See here. You can't just—"

"Watch me."

By the time she arrived in front of the raised platform, Elizabeth felt flushed and a bit breathless from staying ahead of the butler person while dodging between chairs. She looked up at the high table. "Mr. Halliwell. I need a word with you, please."

The duke turned slowly from the conversation he'd been having with one of the men and looked her over appreciatively, his glacier-blue eyes lighting with interest. Elizabeth became aware of her chest heaving and that the peasant blouse didn't cover a whole lot. She put her hand to the bodice edge and tugged it up. "I would like—"

"Curtsy!" Mr. Giles hissed from behind her.

Elizabeth turned to him. "Why would I do that?"

His face paled for a moment before he turned to the duke. "I am sorry, Your Grace. I will see to it that she is punished."

The duke held up his hand, an amused expression on his face. "There is no need for that." He gave Elizabeth a smile and turned back to the butler. "Have her wait in the library for me."

Chapter Three

Elizabeth looked around the library she'd been taken to after the incident at the dais. Mr. Giles had escorted her there with strict instructions to remain seated in front of the massive oak desk. She heard foot shuffling outside the door, almost as though someone was standing guard. Why anyone would be assigned to such a task, she didn't know. She also didn't understand why she was dressed as a serving girl since she'd received an invitation for this evening. At least she thought she had. Well, the duke would straighten it out soon enough.

Elizabeth tapped her foot on the Aubusson carpet and looked around the room. It was paneled in rich teak. In the area behind the desk, two oil paintings depicting hunting scenes hung on the wall, adorned on either side by oil lamps in brackets. Opposite her, a leather sofa and matching armchairs faced the hearth where a banked fire gave off a feeble glow. The side walls, from floor to ceiling, were lined with shelves packed with leather-bound books. The room had a feeling of old elegance which she found somewhat unsettling.

She looked at the big grandfather clock, the brass pendulum swinging back and forth inside its glassed case. She'd been kept waiting at least thirty minutes. How long was she expected to wait? Elizabeth pushed her chair back and walked to one of the bookcases. She might as well get something to read.

The first set of shelves held books on ancient history, several of which dealt with the fall of the Roman Empire. Other titles highlighted invasions by the Saxons, Vikings, and Normans. One entire shelf was dedicated to the Spanish and Scottish Inquisitions and even included a slim volume on the Salem Witch Trials in America. A paper stuck out from between the pages. Elizabeth took the book and opened it to find a copy of *120 Days of Sodom* by the Marquis de Sade. She wrinkled her nose, stuck the book back on the shelf, and moved on. The next row held an assortment of medieval literature, ranging from Gildas' *The Ruin of Britain* and Geoffrey of Monmouth's *Historia regum Britanniae* to Chrétien de Troyes and Thomas Mallory's tales of King Arthur.

Not much to pick from and certainly nothing modern. She removed *Le Morte d'Arthur.* Reading about Arthur and Gwenivere would at least be entertaining, even if knights in shining armor didn't exist.

"Are you finding something interesting?"

Elizabeth whirled around, nearly dropping the book. The duke stood directly behind her, so close he could have reached out and touched her. When had he come in and why hadn't she heard him? The banked fire created a golden aura around his head while the light from the oil lamps gave his eyes a silver glint and accented his high cheekbones and squared jaw. His well-tailored frockcoat emphasized broad shoulders and his waist coat molded to a flat belly.

The duke held out his hand and Elizabeth noticed his fingers were long and slender, like those of an artist. She stared at his hand a moment, wondering what he wanted her to do.

"The book," he said as though reading her mind.

The book. She'd forgotten she was holding it. It wasn't like her to feel rattled, but for some reason she did. Elizabeth held it out, feeling the cool brush of his hand over hers as he took it.

He raised an eyebrow. "Which do you like best?"

"What?"

"Which of the knights do you like best?"

"I…I'm not sure."

"Which would you choose?"

Elizabeth knitted her brows. Why was the man so insistent on wanting an answer? She had kind of always lumped all the knights together. They did the king's bidding. "King Arthur, I suppose."

The duke laughed, his teeth flashing white in the dim light. "The king himself. Perhaps I'm not surprised."

"Why do you say that?"

He reached past her to put the book back on the shelf, his arm lingering just above her shoulder. His eyes penetrated hers for what seemed an eternity before he let his arm drop to his side.

"You were quite bold coming to the dais the way you did."

"I had a reason."

His brow rose again. "And it was?"

"These clothes." Elizabeth shook out her skirt and used the gesture to move away from him. "They are a servant's."

"Yes."

"And that butler-person kept calling me a wench."

"Yes."

"I am Elizabeth Shelton. I…I had an invitation."

His other brow rose. "I do not recall anyone named Shelton. Who is your father?"

Her father. Who was her father? She couldn't recall. A split-second of panic swept through her and she fought to control it. "I...I...um—"

"Just as I thought."

Elizabeth frowned. "What do you mean?"

The duke shrugged. "Peasant girls whose fathers are of no consequence show up at my doors all the time."

"I am not a peasant! Do I sound like one?"

He tilted his head to study her and then jerked his head upright. "No. You do not. But then, it is not unheard of for parsons to send their somewhat literate daughters here, seeking to better their positions."

Elizabeth fought to keep her emotions from spinning out of control. "I am supposed to be your guest."

"A number of young ladies would like to be my guest. I must say, your approach has been very innovative."

"My approach? I'm simply saying that I had an invitation for tonight. I don't know why—or how—I ended up wearing a servant's clothes."

The duke drew his golden brows together. "Mr. Giles told me you were hired just this morning."

"Hired? As a *servant*?"

"Yes. Do you feel you are beneath your station?"

"Beneath...yes. Yes, I feel beneath my station. I—"

"Well, let me look into it."

As if by some silent signal, the servant—or guard—who'd been standing outside opened the door to escort her out.

Elizabeth started to protest, but decided against it. She was being dismissed. Her only hope in straightening out this mess was to keep the duke's good will. She simply had to get him to help her. She forced the next words out.

"Thank you, Your Grace."

He smiled. "We will meet again."

****

Byron Halliwell sobered after Elizabeth left, and he stared thoughtfully at the door. It wasn't often a woman refused him. Aside from his wealth and title along with the power it brought, he'd made sure to cultivate the perfect body and face that females found alluring. Looking like Adonis made women more compliant in fulfilling his base desires. Yet the female who just left had seemed oblivious.

Interesting.

She'd insisted she had an invitation and was a guest…a bold move even for a daughter of landed gentry. Her natural arrogance and American accent had aroused more than just his curiosity. He enjoyed subduing women who would put up a fight.

Byron also had a warlock's power to create illusion, but when he'd sent out an invisible thread to access her mind, his head had been jolted back. Her mind was closed to him completely.

His demonic horns rose. Only his damn twin could shield her like that.

Interesting.

He picked up the book on King Arthur that the wench had chosen. So she thought herself equal to a queen? And his damn brother thought himself Sir Galahad. Byron pulled his lips back in a feral growl and retracted his horns. If Elizabeth Shelton was one of his twin's protégées, Byron would take great pleasure in dominating not only her body but her soul as well.

****

Once she was out in the hall, Elizabeth didn't know which way to go. She needed to get out of here. Mr. Giles stood in the foyer, so Elizabeth turned the other way. She looked over her shoulder to make sure the butler hadn't seen her, then hurried to the back door at the end of the hall. She looked backward one more time as she stepped outside, only to collide with a brick wall.

At least that was her first impression until strong hands steadied her. She felt a moment of panic until she looked up into the dark eyes of the man who'd caught her in the courtyard earlier.

"Come this way," he said, keeping one hand cupped under her elbow. "You look as though you need some fresh air."

Elizabeth wasn't going to argue that point, although she wondered how safe she'd be with *him*. He exuded pure masculine strength. He was also a stranger, but then everyone she'd seen was a stranger. At least, he didn't appear dangerous. In spite of being as tall and broad-shouldered as the duke, he was not intimidating. His hold on her arm was gentle and the look in his eyes was concerned, not lecherous. His whole expression seemed somber and somewhat grave. Still, it wouldn't hurt to be careful. "Who are you?"

"Broc Hadon, the head groom." He tugged lightly on her arm. "We can talk once we are away from the manor."

Elizabeth nodded and picked up her skirts to keep up with his long strides as they left through a back door and crossed the courtyard, but then she pulled back as he started to lead her past the wooden outdoor kitchen.

"Where are you taking me?"

He stopped and pointed toward another building.

"The servants' quarters." Broc smiled. "Do not worry. You will be safe there."

His smile changed his face, giving a rather boyish look to his angular features. He looked trustworthy, but looks could be deceiving. How did she know he wasn't trying to lure her to some dark room? "I don't know if that is a good idea."

Puzzlement crossed his face and then it cleared. "Forgive me. I should have explained since you are new here. All the servants live in that building. The women on the ground floor, the men on the second. There will be people about."

Even as he spoke, Elizabeth could see movement past several candlelit windows. Evidently not everyone was working in the banquet room tonight. She didn't much like the idea of being housed in servants' quarters, but until she could get things straightened out with the duke, she didn't have much choice.

"I didn't mean to offend you. It's just that I'm confused about what I'm doing here. I know I had an invitation to be a guest."

"A guest?" Broc gave her a thoughtful look. "You don't know how you came to be here?"

Elizabeth shook her head, feeling panic well up again.. "The duke asked me earlier who my father was. I couldn't remember." She looked up at Broc. "I was told I'd been hired this morning. I don't remember that either. The only thing I do remember is beginning to faint—which I've never done—and you catching me. Why was I in the courtyard?"

Broc motioned toward a bench in front of the servants' quarters. "Let's sit here for a bit and I'll tell you what I know."

"Yes, please," she said as she sank down on the bench. "Help me if you can."

****

Elizabeth had asked for his help. In the warlock world, that meant he could extend the use of his magical powers, although he knew the one who had sent her here didn't approve of using any more than was absolutely necessary. Broc grimaced. Evidently, his memory erasure had worked, but the new illusion hadn't taken effect. She shouldn't have had any recollection of his catching her, although he felt a little smug that he'd left an impression. He quickly squelched that emotion. If he'd performed his job correctly, the lady wouldn't be confused now.

Broc gazed into her eyes, holding the look until they slowly glazed. He hoped this time the mesmerism would allow her to believe present conditions. For her to learn the lessons she was intended to learn, it was vital she accept the illusion. "You showed up at the manor this morning, looking for work. Your former employer tried to take advantage of you and you ran away. Your parents died of plague. Nuns took you in and educated you. You fainted because you had not had anything to eat or drink in several days. I caught you." Broc stopped speaking, observing Elizabeth. She sat enthralled. He waited a moment longer to let the information infiltrate her mind and then swept his hand across her forehead. She blinked at him.

"How are you feeling?"

"Tired," Elizabeth answered and looked toward the manor. "Do I have to go back to work?"

"Not tonight." Broc stood and helped her up. He offered his arm to walk her toward the servants' quarters.

Even with the thick cloth of his groom's jacket, the warmth of her hand seeped through, sending a different kind of heat searing deep into his belly. The reaction surprised him. Broc prided himself on remaining detached from mortal subjects, particularly when one was placed in his charge. That he should feel such a strong connection was more than a bit unsettling.

Broc left Elizabeth at the door, turning her over to the capable hands of Colton's wife Molly, who took new servants under her wing. As he walked back to the stables, he thought about Elizabeth lying asleep on her pallet, dressed in that nearly transparent blue thing she'd worn earlier, a gown that would have caused Queen Victoria to swoon. Broc wondered if Elizabeth's skin was as silky soft as it looked…

Above his head, thunder rolled. Broc looked up at starry skies as thunder rumbled once more.

It was a warning.

Chapter Four

Elizabeth was awakened early the next morning by someone crudely shaking her shoulders. She rubbed her eyes as she sat up and put a hand to her aching back. She could hardly see in the semi-darkness. Dawn hadn't even broken yet. Why in the world...

"Do ye think to sleep all day?" Ina asked.

Sara snickered. "Well, she does think she's a lady."

The sullen brunette from last night looked over their shoulders. "Still giving herself airs when His Grace didn't even keep her in his bed last night?"

"'Tis enough blethering." Molly hustled over to the three maids and glared at them. "Me thinks ye should all be getting to work unless ye want to be finding yourselves on the doorstep looking at the road."

The girls scowled but backed away.

"Thanks." Elizabeth looked up at her benefactor...a long way up. She realized then that she had been lying on a straw pallet on the floor. No wonder her back hurt. She looked around as her eyes adjusted to the dim light from a few wall sconces. She was in a large, practically bare room. Nearly two dozen pallets like hers lay scattered on the wooden floor. At the far end of the room, a few pieces of clothing hung from pegs. A misshapen curtain was strung across the corner, probably a screen for dressing. Along the side wall, a shelf held several basins and pitchers for washing. There were no tables or chairs or other furnishings.

"Ye had best get up, child," Molly said. "The housekeeper doesn't take to maids being late for their duties."

"Being late…" Good heavens, the sun wasn't even up. Elizabeth struggled to stand. Her legs were stiff, too. She shook the wrinkles out of her skirt and frowned. "I slept in this?"

"Aye. Ye were tired when Broc brought ye in last night. I'll be seeing that ye get a muslin night rail like the rest of the maids." Molly pointed toward the basins. "Ye might want to splash some water on your face before ye go to the manor."

Elizabeth wanted to do a whole lot more than that. She wanted a hot bath to soak in and fresh clothing she hadn't slept in. She needed desperately to relieve herself as well. "Where are the bathrooms?"

Molly looked at her quizzically. "There be a wooden tub behind the curtain, but we only get water to bathe on Saturdays. Most of us take a dip in the creek in the woods. It's not far."

Bathing only once a week? And washing in a creek? Elizabeth wasn't sure she'd heard correctly, but nature was making a stronger demand.

"No. I meant…where is the toilet?" She paused and then added, "the garderobe?"

Molly shook her head. "Only the manor has those. 'Tis a chamber pot behind the curtain." She gave Elizabeth a rueful smile. "A stable boy that comes to clean it once a day, but Brina—she be the housekeeper— likes to assign the duty to maids she thinks are lazy."

Elizabeth understood the message. She hurried as fast as she could in her bare feet, hoping she wouldn't pick up a splinter. As she neared the curtain, she caught the smell of the chamber pots. At least she'd gotten a pallet on the other side of the room. She tried not to inhale too deeply as she made fast work of her necessities. Then she hurried to the shelf and emptied one basin of dirty water into another and picked up a pitcher. There was only a dribble of water left at the bottom. The other pitchers were empty. There was a coarse piece of wet cloth that Elizabeth decided she didn't want to use, and she reached for the one bar of soap, wrinkling her nose as the strong smell of lye wafted from it. Putting it down, she used her hands to splash water on her face. Since she definitely did not want to be assigned latrine duty, she'd worry about cleanliness later.

Returning to her pallet, she pulled on woolen socks and pushed her feet into shoes that felt too tight. Another problem for later. "Do I go to the kitchen for breakfast?"

Molly nodded. "Alma, the cook, puts a pot of porridge on overnight for the servants and there will be leftover bread, but ye better hurry. Once dawn breaks, Alma will be setting ye to cook the morning meal for the duke and his guests."

A meal that would undoubtedly have meat, Elizabeth thought, but didn't ask. She would have to think about her situation later. Perhaps she'd have a chance to talk to Broc. He had seemed helpful last night. Maybe she'd see the duke and ask for a position as governess or something like that. She was educated, after all. She could do more than wait on tables. For now, she just nodded and walked toward the door.

"Good luck, Lizzie," Molly said.

"I prefer Elizabeth."

The older woman's eyebrows went up. "Elizabeth is a queenly name. If ye want the other maids to accept ye, I would think again."

Elizabeth sighed. Molly was right. She didn't need to antagonize the maids further. She just had to work things out.

But no one had ever called her *Lizzie*.

****

When Elizabeth entered the wooden building that served as a kitchen, she knew she was too late for breakfast. A covered pot that had probably held the porridge had been moved to the back of one of the coal-burning stoves, replaced by a kettle for boiling eggs and several pans for warming slices of ham and venison. The only bread Elizabeth could see were the molded oatcakes on tin sheets being put into the omnivorous mouths of the ovens. At least the heat felt good, since the December air outside was nippy.

Alma looked up as she carefully removed clotted cream from the surface of milk that had cooled overnight in a broad, shallow pan. "Molly let ye lie in, did she? Don't be expecting to laze about in the morn again."

Laze about? The sun's first rays were just breaking the sky with pink and lavender streaks. Elizabeth doubted even the roosters were awake yet, but she bit her tongue. Until she could talk to the duke and figure a way out of this, she'd best keep still.

She ignored the rumble in her stomach and Ina's smirk. "What do you want me to do?"

"There's butter to be churned, pudding to be made…" Alma stopped what she was doing and scrutinized Elizabeth. "Do ye know how to do either one?"

"I…"

"I wager she doesn't," Sara said.

Alma gave the girl a sharp look. "I did not ask ye, now, did I?"

Sara sulked. "She's been givin' herself airs and all."

"If ye have a care to remain a serving wench and not a dairy maid, ye'd best keep your tongue silent." Alma turned back to Elizabeth. "There's a platter of fresh scones that need to be taken to the hall."

"I will be glad to take the scones."

"There be twenty-four on the plate," Alma said. "Mind ye, Brina the housekeeper will count them."

Elizabeth nodded, understanding the unspoken warning. She picked up the plate, covered it with a clean cloth, and started across the courtyard. Evidently, the servants weren't allowed to pilfer fresh scones any more than they were to share the duke's meat. Was porridge and stale bread the only thing the servants got to eat? Why in the world was the man so miserly? From the meal that had been served last night, it didn't look like there was any shortage of food. There had even been baked apples…she remembered the heavenly scent of cinnamon that had lingered in the banquet hall.

Elizabeth looked past the manicured lawns and trimmed hedges to the fallow fields beyond. In the spring, crops would be planted. She'd already seen the large vegetable garden plot near the kitchen building. Beyond the manor house, the land sloped down to a small group of trees, probably the apple orchard. On the other side, behind the cattle barn and the stables, was a steep, wooded hill. She remembered Molly saying a creek ran through it. Fish and game should be plentiful.

The Duke of Chatworth's country estate didn't lack

for food sources. Why then were the servants not allowed to share the bounty?

Elizabeth went through the back door that she had used last night and down the dimly lit hall. The great banquet hall was empty, save for a number of maids sweeping and cleaning up. As she watched, one of the younger maids—hardly more than a child—furtively glanced around and then grabbed something off the table and buried it in her apron. Elizabeth wondered if it was remnants of food a guest hadn't eaten.

Someone snapped fingers behind her and she turned to see Mr. Giles standing in the doorway of a room across the hall. He looked irritated and snapped his fingers at her again. "This way. What are you waiting for?"

She didn't appreciate having fingers snapped at her. "You don't have to be rude."

His eyes bulged. "*You* are telling *me* what to do?"

"I am telling you there is no need to be rude." Elizabeth swept past him into another dining room. This one was smaller but no less elegant with its single crystal chandelier in the center and candelabras on each end of a highly polished table set with eighteen places of china and an array of crystal and silverware. Right now, its only occupant was the duke seated at the far end.

"Your Grace," she said, moving toward him to put down the plate. "I'd like a word with you."

"So you said last night."

"His Grace is at breakfast, you hussy!" Mr. Giles practically hissed from behind her. "He is not to be disturbed."

Elizabeth glared at him. "Can't the duke speak for himself?"

The butler's face turned purple. "How dare you—"

"It's quite all right, Giles," the duke said and smiled. "You may go."

"But—"

"Now."

"Yes, Your Grace." Mr. Giles gave Elizabeth a withering look, then lifted his chin and sniffed before he walked away.

The duke gestured to a chair. "Would you join me?"

Now *this* was much better behavior. Elizabeth pulled out the chair to his right and sat down. "Thank you."

"You are quite welcome." He picked up a scone and slathered strawberry jam on it. "Please help yourself."

"Thank you," Elizabeth said again and smiled. *This* was civilized behavior. Her first impression has been wrong. Whatever the maids or the cook thought, Mr. Halliwell seemed quite willing to share his food. She prayed her stomach wouldn't growl and forced herself not to grab for a scone. She had just dipped a spoon into the jam when Ina and Sara entered, carrying the covered platters of warm food. They nearly collided with each other when they saw Elizabeth and barely managed to keep the food from sliding to the floor.

"How—"

"What—"

"Put the food on the sideboard," the duke commanded both maids, "and send John in to serve. Let Giles know we need more tea."

They both curtsied, but not before giving Elizabeth dark looks. She was probably not endearing herself to them, but at the moment, she didn't care.

John hurried in to serve the food, raising one eyebrow in question at Elizabeth's place, but he wisely said nothing. Giles didn't speak either, although his tightly clamped mouth when he brought in the tea spoke volumes. Elizabeth hoped he hadn't poisoned it. But then, the butler had poured the duke's tea from the same pot.

"Please enjoy," the duke said when the servants had gone and he cut into the venison on his plate. "I am an early riser and my guests were up quite late, so having a companion for breakfast is quite enjoyable."

"It is my pleasure," Elizabeth answered, tapping the shell of her egg expertly with the edge of her knife so that it broke neatly in two. She used the small two-pronged fork to remove both the shell and inner lining and pushed it aside before dividing the egg and letting the soft yolk spill over the white. Feeling the duke's eyes watching her movements, she took a much more delicate bite than she would have liked. Saints alive, she was starved. "You are really very kind."

He looked amused. "I have been told I am quite charming at times."

Elizabeth looked up quickly, hoping she hadn't made a gaffe. She hadn't meant to sound like he wasn't kind, but after practically being tarred-and-feathered for taking a bit of meat last night, along with this morning's admonitions, she'd halfway expected to confront an ogre. The duke was actually quite a pleasant man. She sliced into her ham, closing her eyes for a moment to savor the succulent flavor, then taking another bite.

"There is more," the duke said when she'd finished.

As much as she would have liked second helpings, she didn't want to appear unrefined. Elizabeth patted her lips with the linen napkin and placed it beside her plate. "This has been delicious, thank you. Now if I might discuss—"

"Your plight," the duke finished for her. "I have not had time to think on it." He gave her an enigmatic smile. "Perhaps you might join me in my solar this afternoon."

Elizabeth tried not to let her disappointment show. She really wanted to get this over with, yet she had no choice. "Yes, of course."

"I shall see you then. I suspect right now the cook will be waiting for you in the kitchens."

It was a rather abrupt dismissal, but Elizabeth stood, remembering that she had been hired as a servant. Hopefully, that would no longer be the case by this evening.

****

The duke added a second lump of sugar to his tea and stared thoughtfully at the empty door through which Elizabeth Shelton had just left. The chit had a privileged upbringing. He had watched her use the correct silverware without hesitation, and she had not made a mess of the runny egg. So deft and delicate were her actions that she hadn't even left crumbs from the scone. Her hands were soft and smooth, too, not rough and calloused as a maid's would be.

But it was her attitude that intrigued him. That she was educated was obvious from her manner of speaking—albeit with the nasal American twang—but she also didn't use a tone that befitted a subordinate addressing a lord. He had observed how difficult it was for her to get out the words "Your Grace." While Americans harbored the obnoxious trait of considering themselves equal to everyone else, in this case he thought the arrogance came naturally. She had been raised with a certain amount of wealth and power. But whose?

He'd sent his man of business to London early this morning to hire Bow Street runners to investigate the wench, but he doubted anything would surface. If she were, as he suspected, another project that had been sent to his twin, the woman probably wasn't even from this time period.

Of course, that did make it more interesting.

He had found, over the centuries, that the stronger the will of a mortal, the more he enjoyed breaking the spirit…and this wench was prideful, as well. He would take great pleasure in building her hopes, allowing her to think he was helping her, and then crushing those hopes and expectations until she had no shred of dignity left. In doing so, he would not only prove his domination over his most honorable twin, but Byron would declare victory over the one who had once been his master.

Chapter Five

"Ye are making the horses uneasy," Colton told Broc as he paced back and forth just inside the stable door.

Broc halted, glancing toward the stalls where some of the animals were stomping their hooves and neighing. He should have realized the horses would react to his agitation. Taking a deep breath, he stilled his mind and sent calming effects rippling through the air. The sounds inside the stalls changed to contented huffing. "It worries me the lady has not returned from the manor. The other maids have."

"Aye, but 'tis unlikely your damn brother is even awake what with all the caterwauling that went on late into the night."

Broc shook his head. "Byron leaves those shenanigans to his guests. He prefers his decadence to be private so the other lords cannot accuse him of subversive force. Besides, he has always been an early riser." Broc turned his attention back to the empty courtyard. "I wish Miss Shelton had not approached him last night. He might not have noticed her."

Colton raised both brows. "She is the type of woman who stands out in a crowd. His *lordship* would have noticed. Maybe not right away, but he would have noticed."

"I suppose you are right." Broc sighed. "I just wish

I'd had a little more time to warn the lady. I am responsible for her welfare."

"Why do ye say that? I can understand why ye want to protect her, but she did appear on the doorstep on her own."

Broc wished he could confide in his friend, but trying to explain how someone from the twenty-first century had arrived in the nineteenth would make him a likely candidate for Bedlam, especially if Byron got wind that rumors were going around. His brother would use any excuse to try to remove Broc. "The lady seems vulnerable. That is all I meant."

Colton's brows hitched a bit higher. "Vulnerable? From what the maids told Molly, 'tis lucky for Giles the girl was not holding a knife in her hand last night."

Broc smiled. "The lady does have spirit and courage."

"Molly thought she did too," Colton said, "but if ye are going to warn her about how things are here, ye might begin by telling her not to show that spirit too much."

Again, Colton was right. Displaying a sense of independence and willfulness would only make her a more attractive target for Byron.

"And it might be better if ye stop referring to her as a lady. If her father had a title she would have claimed it by now. The other maids already think she gives herself airs."

"I will ask her if I can address her by her given name."

"'Tis a pity ye don't hold the duchy, gentleman that ye are." Colton snorted amicably. "Molly's already explained to her that she will be called Lizzie."

Broc arched his own brow. "Somehow, I do not

think she will care for that."

Colton shrugged. "Maybe not, but it's best she not rile the other maids. Ye know the cat claws women can use all the while purring in your face."

Broc nodded. He didn't understand it, but he'd encountered such behavior many times when he'd refused the advances of females who wanted to share his bed simply because they liked his body. They acted like he'd grievously insulted them when—to his way of thinking—he'd done the honorable thing by refusing to use someone he cared nothing about. The few women he had bedded had also been friends and companions and whom he had *liked*. Unfortunately, since they had all been mortal, each of the relationships ended after several decades and left him with pain and an empty heart.

"There is Lizzie now," Colton said and pointed toward the back door of the manor.

Broc felt his pulse leap at the sight of her crossing the courtyard. Elizabeth's pale hair caught the sheen of the sun's glow, framing her face like a halo and enhancing the porcelain ivory of her skin. Even dressed in peasant clothes, her bearing was regal and her walk graceful as though she glided on ice rather than rough cobblestones.

As he left the barn to intercept her, Broc reminded himself again that one of the reasons he'd been chosen to help heal someone like Elizabeth Shelton was because he no longer allowed himself to become emotionally involved. But his resolve melted a little bit when she gave him a brilliant smile and seemed genuinely glad to see him. He felt himself smiling back like some green schoolboy. "How are you this morning?"

"I feel better than I did last night," Elizabeth replied.

"I had a chance to speak to the duke this morning."

Broc's smile faded. Had his brother been lying in wait, anticipating Elizabeth would be sent to the manor this morning? He tried to keep the edge out of his voice. "You had a conversation with him?"

She gave Broc a scrutinizing look. "Yes. I know everyone seems to be in awe of him and afraid to speak, but he was actually quite nice."

Broc's misgivings increased. Byron was plotting something. "Nice is not a word often used regarding the duke."

"I don't know why not," Elizabeth answered. "I'll admit after being chastised by that horrible butler for taking a bite of meat and then being threatened with punishment for doing it, I wasn't quite sure what to expect. When we spoke last night, all His Grace would say was he would look into the matter of my position, but this morning he invited me to have breakfast with him."

Broc felt his blood chill. There were punishments much worse than what were routinely doled out to servants errant in their duties. If his brother had invited Elizabeth to share breakfast with him, he was trying to gain her trust, much like a catamount sleeping with one eye open, waiting for its unsuspecting prey to wander closer.

Mortal men had always wooed women with gifts and sweet talk, some of which was sincere and some of which was not. Broc had no argument with that. In the way of things, it was the woman's decision whether to believe or not. This situation was different. Byron Halliwell was not a mortal nor did he possess any morality. He had always used the full force of his warlock powers to get what he wanted—including the present duchy—but what did he want with Elizabeth?

"Sometimes such a thing can be perceived as favoritism."

She looked at him. "So what if it is? We had a pleasant conversation."

This was worse than Broc had thought. His twin was luring Elizabeth deliberately into some game. "The other maids might grow envious."

Elizabeth waved a hand in dismissal. "I will not be a maid for long."

His blood nearly froze in his veins. Had his demonic twin already proposed making Elizabeth his mistress? Broc's every instinct told him Elizabeth Shelton was not the type of woman to give away her favors freely, but what if Byron had ensorcelled her? While she was in the manor, his twin would be able to do it. Broc could use his own powers to sense her thoughts and make sure the shield he'd put in place held, but he would have to touch her to do it.

He reached out a hand to brush a strand of her hair back. The mere touch jolted him like a lightning bolt. Broc wondered if Elizabeth felt it too since her eyes widened and a pale blush crossed her face. She stared into his eyes and he remembered he needed to sense her thoughts. To his relief, the shield was in place. Her will was her own. He should have dropped his hand immediately since he had the information he needed, but instead his fingers traced the curvature of her cheek. Elizabeth's breath hitched and then she stepped back, breaking his own entrancement. Broc let his hand drop to his side. "Why do you say you won't be a maid for long?"

She smiled. "His Grace asked me to come to his solar this afternoon so we might discuss my situation."

By all that was holy, Broc did not want Elizabeth spending any time alone with his twin, especially not in the solar. That room was Byron's private den of iniquity where many a maid had lost her virtue and not always willingly, if torn clothing and bruised faces were any indication. The solar—with its heavy red velvet curtains kept drawn to keep sunlight out—was the room where Byron toyed with his prey. Those who consented to join in his games of pain were then invited to his bed chamber. Those who refused were turned out with nothing.

Broc could not rescue them all, but he could keep Elizabeth from that fate, at least for now. He would apply the same cunning his brother used, only against him.

****

Elizabeth nearly wept with frustration when she arrived at the manor house in mid-afternoon to be told by a smirking Giles that a post had arrived summoning the duke to London and he had left immediately.

She'd endured serving the midday meal to the duke's houseguests. Fires had been lit in the huge hearths of the main dining room so the guests did not have to don full formal wear—most had just recently risen from their beds—and could yet stay warm. Working, it didn't take long before the room felt unbearably hot. Holding heavy metal platters high enough not to bump guests quickly tired Elizabeth's arms and the steaming food brought a sheen of sweat to her face. The guests were cantankerous, as well, suffering the effects of too much wine and ale the night before. Half of them had special requests which kept Elizabeth and the other maids running back and forth to the kitchens. The guests complained if the food was too hot or too cold, as if Elizabeth had anything to do with that. The duke had not been in attendance, not that she blamed him, given the surliness of his guests.

By the time the long, drawn-out meal was over, Elizabeth was exhausted. She limped back to the servants' quarters, wondering how the maids still had energy. They had stayed at the manor after the guests finished dining, probably to eat the scraps, but Elizabeth's appetite had waned with the smell of so many unwashed bodies in such close quarters. Her only consolation was that she'd speak to the duke this afternoon. Hopefully, the noonday meal had been the last she would have to serve.

And now he was gone. Giles had just shrugged when she asked how long until he returned.

The inside of the servants' quarters was empty and quiet, a wonderful contrast to the noisy crowd in the dining hall. Elizabeth sank down on her pallet and took off her too-tight shoes. In spite of the woolen socks, she could feel blisters on her toes, and her heels were sore. The footwear was another thing she'd wanted to talk to the duke about. Why did he have to leave for London?

Sounds from outside the building began to penetrate. Elizabeth heard people laughing and talking as they walked across the courtyard toward the stables. She'd heard some of them talk about fox hunting this afternoon, which meant Broc would have his hands full saddling all the horses. She rubbed her aching feet and thought about their conversation earlier.

Broc seemed to think it odd that she thought the duke was nice. Granted, nobility usually kept themselves apart from servants. Elizabeth had not been here long, but she hadn't seen him mistreat anyone. In fact, he'd told that nasty Giles there was no need to punish her for eating a piece of meat. Molly had warned her about not eating any scones, but that was because the housekeeper counted them. The duke had waived that rule as well, inviting Elizabeth to partake.

Still, Broc had seemed upset, his dark eyes glowing with intensity when he spoke. She supposed he might have a point about favoritism, but if she wanted out of the present situation she had to capture the duke's attention. If the other girls were jealous…well, that was their problem. She had to look after herself. But it was kind of Broc to mention it. His brow had knit with concern and he'd made that endearing gesture of brushing a strand of her hair away from her face. Elizabeth couldn't remember anyone ever doing that, not even when she was child. His touch had been so gentle. Her breath grew shallow as she remembered how heat had seared through her and her body had tingled all over. *That* had never happened to her before either.

Elizabeth yawned. Goodness, she was tired. Since London was a two-days' ride away, it meant she'd have to serve meals for several more days. She'd better take a nap while she could. Scrunching the straw together in the pallet, she tried to get comfortable. Hopefully, she wouldn't have to endure these conditions for long. Elizabeth yawned again and drifted into sleep.

****

"What do you mean, I have to clean the ovens?" Elizabeth set the platter of dirty dishes from the evening meal on a shelf in the kitchen and stared at Alma. "I just finished serving the meal."

"'Tis the housekeeper's order, Lizzie. Ye did not stay to finish this afternoon."

Behind her Ina and Sara giggled. Elizabeth frowned. "No one told me too."

"We always stay," the redheaded maid Bridget said. "The housekeeper expects us to polish the tables and sweep the floors afterward."

"No one told me that," Elizabeth repeated and heard more snickers.

Alma glared at the Ina and Sara. "If ye do not want to be doing the task of oven cleaning tomorrow, ye had best be washing those dishes."

Both maids sobered and turned around quickly, although Elizabeth sensed they were enjoying this whole thing. "But I am exhausted."

Carla, the dark-haired maid, scowled at her. "We are all tired."

Elizabeth closed her eyes, trying to find some inner strength. She was weary to her bones. Every muscle ached, her arms were bruised from the heavy platters, and her feet felt on fire. If she didn't get to sit down soon and rest, her back was going to give out as well. She had never felt so miserable.

Someone poked her. Elizabeth opened her eyes slowly to see Carla holding out a small broom and a dustpan.

"You need to rake out the ashes first," she said.

Elizabeth reluctantly took the broom handle and opened the heavy iron door on the front of the oven. Heat from the smoldering embers swept over her. "They're still hot."

Carla pointed. "That's why ye use the metal pail over there to put them in."

Elizabeth sighed. Taking the dustpan in her other hand, she began to push the ashes to one side. Smoke billowed out, covering her in soot. She sneezed, which created another cloud. Her eyes began to tear and she reached up to rub them, only to have her hand caught by Alma.

"Ye will make it worse if ye rub."

Elizabeth blinked rapidly, her eyesight blurring, and hoped the sting would go away. Dear Lord in Heaven, could things get any worse?

Apparently they could, and they did. By the time she finished cleaning the flues, wiping grease off the top of the stove with newspaper, black-leading the iron surfaces before wiping them with a soft cloth and polishing the steel parts with emery, brick, and paraffin, both her mind and her body had gone numb. It was near midnight before she stumbled back to the servants' quarters with the admonishment to be back in the kitchens before dawn to get the fires started.

The last thing she remembered before falling to her pallet fully clothed was wondering how on earth she was going to endure this.

Chapter Six

Elizabeth swiped at the smudges of soot lingering on strands of her hair the next day. She'd managed to clean her face with the lye soap and water from the basin this morning, but her hair was dirty and she felt filthy. Because of the condition of her clothes, Alma had kept her in the kitchens cooking rather than serving. It seemed the breakfast dishes had hardly come back when it was time to begin preparing the midday meal. She'd had no idea how much physical labor went into kneading bread and churning butter, to say nothing of peeling and chopping vegetables for two scores of guests and turning the spit for the boar that hung from it. The air inside the kitchen quickly grew stifling, so Elizabeth was hot and sweaty as well.

She returned to the servants' quarters late in the afternoon *after* having made sure she wasn't missing another work assignment. She didn't want to have to clean the ovens again—or worse, the latrines. Alma had taken pity on her and told the housekeeper all tasks had been completed, which meant Elizabeth had about an hour before she needed to report back to start getting the evening meal ready. She looked at her pallet longingly, but she had no time for a nap...not if she was going to get rid of the soot.

Molly had left a clean serving dress on Elizabeth's pallet. She picked it up, along with the lye soap and a coarse drying cloth from the shelf, and walked outside toward the forested hill with the brook. She didn't relish how cold the water would be, this close to Christmas, but it was only Tuesday and the servants didn't get warm bath water until Saturday. She could not wait that long.

As soon as she entered the forest, Elizabeth could hear the faint sound of water gurgling over rocks. A narrow animal trail led deeper into the woods. She thought she heard snuffling, as though an animal were rooting for food, and she stopped. The sound came again, but sounded farther away. Cautiously, Elizabeth proceeded. A slight trace of smoke filled her nostrils and she followed the scent as the path curved around a cluster of small boulders and then opened to a tiny clearing where a small fire burned inside a circle of carefully laid stones. A tin pail hung suspended from a pole above it. Elizabeth looked around, delighted to see a small pool where the creek formed a bend.

A pool that was occupied by Broc.

He was partially submerged with his back to her. His black hair was wet and slicked back on wide shoulders. Water formed rivulets that followed the hard contours of sculpted back muscles to slide along his spine to the hollow of his back. The clear water allowed Elizabeth to see the shape of tight, well-formed buttocks.

She must have made a sound for he turned suddenly, his eyes widening just slightly at the sight of her.

"I…I'm so sorry. I thought…I mean, I wanted…" Elizabeth stumbled on her words. Heaven have mercy. His broad chest was even more impressive than his back. It looked like chiseled stone. Hard ridges rippled down a flat belly and… She closed her eyes. Good grief. What if he stood up?

"You can open your eyes," he said after a minute. "I'm decent."

Slowly, she opened one eye and then the other. He had wrapped a towel that she hadn't noticed around his waist as he emerged from the pool. For a fleeting second, Elizabeth felt disappointed and then mortified. Since when had she started wanting to look at naked men? Even as she had the thought, she couldn't help but notice how heavily muscled his thighs and calves were, but then what would she expect of someone who handled horses? She felt herself blush. She shouldn't be *expecting* anything at all.

Broc gestured to her towel "You are wanting to bathe?"

"I…I…well, I…uh—" What in the world was wrong with her that she couldn't get the words out? "I can come back."

Broc shook his head as he pulled a tunic over his head. "A maid's schedule doesn't allow for much free time. I'm finished, so the pool is yours."

She stared at him. Did he think she was just going to take off her clothing with him standing there? He must have sensed her hesitation because he smiled.

"I will leave you to your privacy."

"Wait. I…I thought I heard an animal earlier, digging for something."

"Probably a boar. They scour the woods."

"Is it safe here, then?"

Broc nodded. "Boars are only dangerous when they're wounded or their territory has been invaded. A herd of them lives near the rocky outcroppings at the top of this hill where the forest ends. Just don't wander up there."

"Believe me, I won't."

Broc glanced at the lye soap in her hand and then leaned down to pick up a different bar of soap and handed it to her. "You might want to use this instead."

It smelled wonderful compared to the bitter lye. "What is it?"

"Lavender and lanolin from sheep's wool," he said and then shrugged. "I didn't think it would be missed."

Having seen him nearly naked, she suspected one of the maids had managed to smuggle it to him, but Elizabeth didn't argue. It was real soap.

He walked over to the fire to bank it and pointed to the pail. "That's hot water. Pour it into the pool just before you get in so it won't feel so icy."

Elizabeth looked at it. Broc had probably meant it to rinse himself if she hadn't shown up. "Thank you," she said.

He smiled again, one corner of his mouth turning up slightly more than the other which she found endearing. "Thank you," she said again.

Broc gave her a small bow, picked up his boots and trews, and began walking away. "I will wait for you down the path to make sure no person—or boar—intrudes."

For some reason, Elizabeth believed he would do just that. She watched him disappear around the rocks and slipped off her shift and poured the pail of water into the pool. It made the water only tepid, but as she sank down into it with Broc's purloined bar of lavender soap, it felt like heaven.

****

Once he rounded the cluster of rocks, Broc took the time to put on his trews and boots. Elizabeth probably thought him totally daft for leaving the clearing only in his tunic, but she had no idea of how tempting she was…or how he felt his resolve slipping.

Normally, he didn't decide to bathe in the middle of the day. Even though Broc didn't like admitting it to himself—and certainly not to Elizabeth—he'd deliberately gone to the creek in hopes she'd come. He'd seen the soot in her blonde hair last night and knew how difficult it would be to get out, especially with just water in a basin. That was why he'd used a bit of magic so the housekeeper wouldn't notice one of her prized perfumed soaps was missing. He'd warmed the water over the fire too because he didn't think Elizabeth was used to near-frigid water. Now all he had to do was stand guard at the forest edge while she bathed.

Broc turned to walk away and then hesitated when he heard a small splash and Elizabeth's groan of pure pleasure. By all that was holy, what he wouldn't give to see her naked in the water as she had almost seen him. He didn't need to remind himself how tempted he'd been to face her without the towel in place. From the way her blue eyes had darkened and her lips curved up—so slightly that he doubted she'd been aware of her reaction—he knew she liked what she saw. He had no doubt whatsoever that he would like whatever he could see of Elizabeth in the water, even if it was just the merest glimpse of her breasts.

But Broc didn't need any more thunder rumbling out of a clear sky to remind him what his mission was. It did not include seduction.

He took a deep breath and walked away.

****

Elizabeth paused before dunking her head and

listened to the rustle behind the rocks. Broc must be dressing. She glanced at the towel lying on the grass. She'd not be able to reach it without getting out of the water if Broc returned. But would he? He'd said he was going to wait farther away in case someone else wandered this way. Somehow, Elizabeth knew he would stick to what he said. If she were the kind of person who believed in knights-in-shining-armor, she'd think Broc fitted the mold. But knights didn't exist, unless you counted the ones Queen Victoria gave a title to. Those weren't quite the same as King Arthur's.

She was being silly for even thinking of chivalrous men. Hadn't her last employer tried to take advantage of her? Even here at Chadworth, some of the maids had implied they'd shared the duke's bed. Whether by choice or coercion, Elizabeth didn't know and wasn't particularly interested. Her interaction with the duke was going to be strictly business. She wasn't quite sure how she'd manage it, but she would. He would be gone for several days, so she had time to think.

Elizabeth found her thoughts returning to Broc as she heard him walk away. He was being true to his word. He wouldn't take advantage of her, but something niggled at the back of her mind…maybe she wanted him to.

****

"You have some information regarding Elizabeth Shelton?" Byron asked the Bow Street runner after he'd been shown into the man's sparsely furnished office in London.

"We haven't been able to find out much," he replied as he picked up a single piece of paper and studied it. "In checking both Debrett's and Burke's peerage lists, we found no Lord Shelton or, at least, not one with a daughter named Elizabeth."

"So she is not a lady, then."

"Not a titled one, although many lords have supported their mistresses' by-blows. It is possible this woman is one of those."

"Um." Byron laid his gloves on the desk and tented his fingers. "She is educated, for certain, but she sounds American."

"Did you ask her if she sailed across?"

Byron gave the man—his name was James, he thought—an annoyed look. "If I had been able to get any information from her, I would not have had to hire you."

"Of course, Your Grace. I just thought—"

"You obviously did not think at all." Byron gestured toward the paper. "What else is there?"

"We put out discreet inquiries at *ton* townhouses—below stairs, of course—to determine if any governesses or nannies had left their employ. It doesn't really help that so much of Society are at country estates for the Christmas holidays—"

"Yes, yes. I know that. I have a house party of my own going on. What did you discover?"

John shook his head. "One governess and two nannies were given pensions, but they obviously were not the age of the woman you're inquiring about. Other than that, no one has left, not even an above-stairs servant. Such positions are held in high regard—"

"Yes, I know that too." By the devil's horns, was the man going to tell him something he didn't already know? House servants did not voluntarily turn themselves out into the street and certainly not ones with some element of education.

"You feel sure she was employed in London?"

No, he wasn't sure. He wasn't even sure she was from this time period, given his damn brother's propensity for good deeds. Byron had hired the Bow Street runner—or rather Martin, his man-of-business had done so—in part to confirm that Elizabeth Shelton *didn't* exist in the 1800s, but Byron could hardly explain that without a magistrate taking him directly to Bedlam. He picked up his gloves and rose, wondering why Martin had summoned him to London on such short notice for such unimportant information.

It was a question he put to Martin that evening as they dined in a private room at the Cavendish. Byron kept only a skeletal staff at his Mayfair townhouse during the non-Season and his unexpected arrival had sent them scurrying about, opening rooms and airing linens. Unfortunately, the cook had taken ill several days ago. Byron was not about to trust his palate to the pair of young maids who offered to prepare the evening meal, although he fully intended to try their more voluptuous wares later. The *duck a l'orange* the hotel served would have to do for now.

"Travel is not exactly pleasant this time of year," he said.

"I quite agree, Your Grace," Martin replied as he sampled the pheasant soup. "This is quite good. I normally do not dine here."

Byron raised a brow. "Did you ask me to come all the way to London *in December* so you could dine here?"

Martin frowned, his spoon halfway to his mouth. "Of course not."

"The paltry information the runner had could have kept. Why did you send for me?"

Martin put down the spoon. "I did not send for you."

Byron raised both brows and pulled a letter out of his pocket. "This is your handwriting. You said it was urgent."

Taking the latter, Martin scanned it quickly, his face paling. He handed the letter back. "Someone has copied my handwriting. I did not send that."

Byron felt cold fury flood his veins. Warlocks were capable of perfect forgery. It was how he'd gotten the title to the duchy. How had he not suspected his twin of this treachery? He balled a hand into a fist beneath the table.

There would be hell to pay for this. Since Broc wasn't available, he'd take his anger out on the young maids waiting for him at the townhouse.

Chapter Seven

Elizabeth tucked her hair behind her ears, trying to ignore the noise of half-sodden houseguests, and picked up the empty platter from the huge dining hall's sideboard to walk toward the door. This was the third platter of venison that she'd served from the kitchens. Clara and Bridget had each brought in several platters of boar and lamb as well, and other maids were rushing about placing bowls of steaming vegetables on the tables. The dozens of loaves of freshly baked bread had all but disappeared and these people were only on their second course of a long meal. These same people had stuffed themselves to the gills on sandwiches and tarts when they returned from the afternoon hunt and washed that down with ratafia. Elizabeth had lost count of the number of empty wine bottles she'd removed this evening, and she was pretty sure at least two barrels of ale were also empty. It was a wonder the duke's guests didn't all resemble beached walruses.

They certainly sounded like a barking, grunting herd.

Elizabeth sidestepped Ina and Sara bringing in puddings and custards and headed for the kitchens. There was still pigeon and partridge to be served along with truffles and jellied wine sauce—not that these folks weren't jellied enough already—before desserts would be brought.

The extravagance—not to mention the expense—was such a waste. The sotted guests left half the food uneaten on their plates, yet course after course was served. Since Elizabeth had been here she'd seen many of the serving women who had families to feed sneaking scraps to wrap in newspaper and stuffing them into their big apron pockets to take home. She cringed at what their punishment would be if they were caught, but maybe the housekeeper turned a blind eye. Elizabeth hoped the woman did, although after her own episode of cleaning the ovens, she wondered if the housekeeper had a heart at all.

Elizabeth entered the kitchens and set the platter down, then licked the meat juice from her fingers. She'd watched the other maids do it. At first, she'd thought it a vulgar habit, but not having had meat in three days— like bathwater, the servants were only allowed meat once a week—she'd quickly overcome her disgust. She'd also learned to shake off slivers that would stick to the platter before the meat was offered to the guests. Those were immediately consumed on the walk back to the kitchen.

She rubbed her lower back to relieve the ache. Her feet still hurt, but Molly had found some larger shoes and given her a salve for her blisters. Elizabeth refused to complain since the maids already thought she gave herself airs. And truthfully, she hadn't heard any of them grumble or whine about the hard work. That they had energy at night to laugh and talk and even improvise dancing to the music coming from the manor amazed Elizabeth. She wasn't quite sure how they managed it. She was too exhausted each evening to do more than splash water on her face and clean her teeth with powdered chalk. She'd been kept too busy with the house-party guests to have a chance to get back to the creek to bathe and she desperately needed to. She tried to put out of her mind that Broc might be there. She knew the afternoon hunts demanded his time as well. Still, the image of him naked and rising out of the water like Neptune was emblazoned in her brain.

Elizabeth sighed and reached for one of the full platters at the same time Carla did. They both hesitated and then Elizabeth picked up the larger, heavier one. She was tired of being accused of being a lightweight.

Carla's eyes widened and then one corner of her mouth lifted so slightly in a smile that Elizabeth almost didn't notice it.

"Thanks," Carla said as she took the lighter tray and walked away.

Elizabeth stared after her. Had she actually been thanked? And smiled at? She managed to smile herself. At least one maid didn't seem to hate her anymore.

It was a start.

****

Two hours later the last dish had been removed from the large dining hall and most of the guests had staggered off to their bedchambers. Elizabeth helped Alma bank the fires in the ovens and then bit her lip to keep from cursing when a cloud of soot rose. She stepped back quickly, but some of it still settled on her face and hands. Luckily, she'd tucked her hair back and worn the mop cap Molly had given her. Elizabeth had thought the thing hideous, but now she understood why the maids wore them. At least her hair remained clean.

Still, she felt filthy. The creek water would be cold, but at this time of night no one else would be there…and she didn't think boars hunted at night. A quick dip with that bar of lavender soap she kept hidden sounded wonderful. Elizabeth took a drying cloth from the stack kept in the kitchen so she wouldn't draw attention to herself by leaving with one from the servants' quarters and retrieved her soap from under a low shelf where the big kettles stood. She'd kept the bar in her apron for a whole day pondering a place to hide it. The servants' quarters were too open and putting it under her pallet wasn't wise since they were picked up to be pounded every other day. She'd finally decided the kitchen with its busy activity was the last place someone would notice her. She smiled when her hand closed over it and quickly tucked the bar into her pocket.

Several maids were finishing stacking platters. None of them paid her any mind when she slipped out the door and walked around the side of the servants' quarters to head for the woods. She was still in the dark recessed shadow of the wall when she heard a stifled scream from behind the building. Elizabeth quickened her pace, rounding the corner in time to see the red-haired maid Bridget trying to fend off a drunken guest. He had her backed against the wall, one hand muffling her mouth while the other pawed at the bodice of her dress. Elizabeth heard the material tear just as Bridget whacked a fist at the man's ear.

"You bitch!" he snarled and slapped her across her face. Her head snapped back, resounding on the wood. He wrapped one huge paw around Bridget's throat.

"Stop it!" Elizabeth shouted, dropping her towel and rushing toward him. She began hitting the man's back with her own fists. "Stop it, stop it."

The man snarled again, swinging his free arm around. Before his fingers could close on her, Elizabeth suddenly felt herself being lifted, swung around, and set a safe distance away. She looked up in time to see Broc grab the man's arm, pulling it up and behind his back, causing the sotted fool to grunt and let Bridget go. She sidled along the wall, rubbing her throat and then took off running.

"I'll have you flogged for this!" the man bellowed.

Broc raised the captured arm higher, turning the man's bellow to a whimper of pain. "I think not."

"Let me go, you damned fool."

"Not until you give me your word you'll not molest another maid."

"I am a guest here! Unhand me at once."

Broc inched the man's arm up. "Not until I have your word."

"I do not— *Ow*," he screeched as his arm rose more. "You are breaking my arm!"

"If that is what you prefer."

"I…*no. Ow, ow, ow.* All right. Fine. My word I will not touch another maid."

Broc released his arm. "A wise choice on your part."

The man turned to glower at him, rubbed his arm, and then turned his angry gaze on Elizabeth. "You have both assaulted an *earl*. His Grace will hear about this when he returns."

Broc shrugged. "You might think twice on that. His Grace favors Bridget, and she will have bruises on her throat. Not to mention there were two eyewitnesses to *your* assault of her."

Elizabeth could see the man's face pale even in the near-darkness. "His Grace will not believe you," he said as he backed away.

Broc took a step toward him. The earl stumbled,

cursed, and stalked off.

Elizabeth watched him go. "That man needs to be arrested."

"Nobles rarely get arrested."

"That's not right. He nearly killed Bridget. We can't just let him walk away."

"There is not much we can do," Broc said. "The wealthy have the power to do what they want."

Elizabeth frowned. "But he attacked a defenseless maid."

"He tried to attack you too," Broc replied and reached over to brush a strand of her hair back. "Did he hurt you?"

"No." Elizabeth caught Broc's hand and pressed it to her cheek. His touch was so light, yet comforting. "You came along just in time. I owe you a lot of thanks."

An unreadable expression flitted across his face. "You do not owe me anything. I was coming back from the barn and heard the struggle."

"Still." Elizabeth gazed up at him. Light flickered in the depths of his dark eyes. It was probably just the result of a cloud passing over the moon, but it made her want to step closer. She let his hand drop and put hers on his shoulder. "I want—"

"You should get back inside," Broc said, stepping back. "Let me walk you."

Elizabeth felt her face heat and was grateful that it was dark so he wouldn't see how mortified she was. Goodness, she had been about to kiss him. She'd never acted so forward with a man in her life. Worse, she still wanted to kiss him, even though he had turned away. "Of course. It is late. We all need sleep."

Broc nodded and they walked in silence the short

distance to the front of the building. Elizabeth turned to him as he left her at the door. "Thank you for helping."

The light she'd seen in his eyes earlier flickered again and she wondered if it was due to the oil lamp hanging nearby. But the spark was so fleeting that when she blinked it was gone. Broc's eyes were simply dark, like midnight blue velvet, and his gaze focused on her mouth. He dipped his head toward her. Instinctively, Elizabeth parted her lips, her breath becoming shallow as unfamiliar tingles flashed through her.

He straightened abruptly and opened the door to the women's quarters. "You'll be safe here. Good night."

****

Broc turned and stomped back to the barn after she'd gone inside. By all that was holy, he'd nearly kissed Elizabeth. Had *wanted* to kiss her. *Still* wanted to kiss her.

He didn't even remember how long it had been since he'd desired a mortal woman as much as he did Elizabeth.

When he'd heard the sounds of a struggle, he'd figured one of the clouts from the house party was trying to take advantage of an unwilling maid. It was damnable enough that his hedonistic brother seduced some of them, often mesmerizing the poor women into willingness. Broc was not about to let slothful houseguests abuse them as well.

He just hadn't expected to see Elizabeth when he rounded the corner. The last he'd seen of her was as she finished up tasks in the kitchen. What in the world had she been doing along the side of the servants' quarters anyway? Had she heard the struggle as well? Unlikely, given the noise from the manor across the courtyard.

The sight of Elizabeth pounding her small fists on the idiot's back had brought back visions of earlier warrior queens like Boudicca and Gwenhwyfar. Women capable of defending themselves and their people. When Broc saw the man's arm swing back to knock Elizabeth away, the memory vanished instantly. Elizabeth Shelton was no trained warrior woman, even though she'd shown remarkable courage.

Once inside the stables, Broc did a quick inspection of the horses. Most were lying down in their stalls, a few stood dozing, a front or back hoof propped against the other leg. His favorite mount, a gray stallion named Warrior, poked his head over the half-open stall door and nickered. Broc stroked his muzzle and then turned at a sound behind him.

"Is something wrong with one of the horses?" Colton asked as he came out of the tack room.

"No. There was an altercation behind the servants' quarters. I wanted to make sure the horses hadn't gotten spooked by the commotion."

"I didn't hear anything, but then, the noise coming from the main hall would be enough to drown out Gabriel's trumpet." Colton shook his head. "Not that any angel would likely be visiting that crowd, even if it is close to Christmas."

Broc grimaced. "I could have used St. Michael's sword a short time ago."

"That bad? What happened?" When Broc told him, the corners of Colton's mouth drew down. "'Tis getting worse. 'Tis bad enough the duke is depraved."

If Colton knew how base Broc's twin really was, he'd probably run for the faraway hills of Scotland. Unfortunately, Byron had always been clever enough to keep his darkest deeds well hidden—like orchestrating two assassination attempts on Queen Victoria which had failed due to what Broc was pretty sure was divine intervention of the archangels themselves. Even if Broc had proof of such treason, he didn't think a duke had ever been hanged.

"I doubt the earl will bother any more women while he's here."

Colton snorted. "If I were the man, I would be gone come dawn."

"The aristocracy doesn't work that way," Broc answered. "The earl will want to get to the duke first with his version of what happened before Bridget does."

"How can he defend bruises around her throat?"

Broc clenched his jaw. "We have seen bruises on Bridget before. The duke likes to inflict pain, so that won't shock him."

"But isn't the girl one of his favorites?"

"Only to the point she acquiesces to him. He cares for none of them."

"'Tis a crime, truly. No man should be above the law, even if he is a duke."

"I agree, but commoners bringing charges against nobility often lands the wrong person in the gaol." Broc wanted to tell Colton that he was working toward seeing justice done with his abominable brother, but the possibility of implicating his friend posed too much danger. "For now, all we can do is be vigilant."

Colton hesitated. "What about the new girl, Lizzie? My wife says the duke already invited her to his solar. 'Tis not a good omen."

Broc would have smiled at the understatement except the situation was far too serious. He'd bought

Elizabeth some time with the false summons to London, but by now Byron would have figured out who had sent it. Broc didn't fear his twin's wrath—he couldn't kill him, after all—but if Byron suspected Elizabeth was under Broc's direct care, she would be the one to suffer the consequences.

He couldn't let that happen, whatever the cost.

Chapter Eight

Elizabeth slipped inside the women's quarters and hoped she wouldn't be seen. She wasn't a crier. She'd never seen much sense in letting tears flow to engage someone's sympathy. She didn't want anyone's sympathy or worse, pity, but she felt tears stinging the back of her eyes. Broc had not only stepped away from her when she'd touched him, but he'd practically shoved her inside the door just now. She'd never felt so rejected in her whole life.

She took a steadying breath, thankful the oil lamps had already been turned down and the room was in near-darkness. Maybe she was overreacting. She wasn't used to running into someone being accosted by a man. Her nerves felt as jittery as though a cannon had gone off beside her. Good heavens, what if she hadn't rounded the corner when she did? Would Bridget be dead?

Elizabeth looked around the room for the other girl, but with so many women already asleep, she couldn't make out who anyone was. If she started walking around, she'd no doubt wake half of them up and no one would be happy. She tiptoed to her own pallet and lay down. She knew Bridget had survived. She'd just have to wait until morning to find out the extent of her injuries.

Far too restless to sleep, Elizabeth replayed the events of the evening in her head. The inequality between servants and nobility was nothing new, but what bothered her was how little servants' lives meant to those who were privileged to be born to titles. That servants were allowed real meat and hot bath water only once a week was bad enough, especially when it seemed food was plentiful and it was the servants who heated the water for bathing, but would any action have been taken if Bridget were seriously hurt? Or killed? Would the earl even have been reprimanded? Or would the incident have been brushed under the carpet? Elizabeth had the uneasy feeling that she knew the answer.

Slavery was illegal in England, but being treated like a slave apparently was not. Elizabeth had never worked so physically hard in her entire life, nor had she ever been this exhausted. She had hoped she wouldn't have a serving maid's position long. After all, she was educated. At the least, a governess position should be secured. However, having witnessed the debauchery of the last two evenings, Elizabeth was beginning to wonder how willing the duke would be to help her...or worse, what he would expect in return if he did. She hoped she could persuade the Duke of Chadworth it was the right thing to do.

Wasn't everyone human, after all?

****

Elizabeth awoke with a start. Sunlight streamed in the small windows. She bolted upright, grabbing her shoes and rushing for the door without bothering to wash her face or take care of any other needs. Lord have mercy. She'd been warned if she didn't get to the kitchens before dawn broke, she'd be penalized. Cleaning the ovens had been bad enough. She didn't think she could face cleaning the latrines. Why had she overslept?

She shook her head as she stopped outside the door to slip into a shoe and then hopped while she put on the other, trying to move forward at the same time. She'd spent half the night fuming over the unfairness of her plight and the other half thinking about Broc, drat him. He'd even filled her dreams—with wonderfully amorous desire—when she'd managed to doze shortly before dawn. Now, dreaming of lying wrapped in Broc's warm embrace while he showered tender kisses on her was going to cost Elizabeth dearly.

She raced through the kitchen door, nearly barreling into Alma. Elizabeth looked around for Bridget but didn't see her. Seeing Carla, Ina and Sara removing dirty dishes from platters, Elizabeth froze in her tracks. She had really slept late if the morning meal was already over. Not only would she be cleaning latrines, probably for several days, but she'd have to face the wrath of the other maids for sloughing her duties. Strangely, though, none of them were glaring at her.

"I am so sorry for oversleeping," she said to Alma and then turned to Sara. "Give me the platter. I'll wash it…and all the rest too."

Sara continued cleaning it as though she hadn't heard. Ina gave her a sideways glance and then went back to work as well.

"It is all right," Carla said.

"What is all right?" Elizabeth asked, picking up pewter mugs to plunge into a basin of soapy water.

"Your sleeping in. You earned it."

Elizabeth wasn't sure she heard correctly. "I overslept. I didn't help with serving the morning meal. The housekeeper is going to—"

"Do nothing," Alma interjected.

Elizabeth sent her a startled glance. "I am being let go?"

"No."

"But I—"

"Bridget told us what happened last night," Carla replied.

"Ye helped her escape," Ina said.

"And ye weren't afraid to attack the earl," Sara added, a slight trace of admiration in her voice.

"Any of you would have done the same," Elizabeth countered. "Besides, Broc was the one who really ended the attack."

"But ye got there first," Carla said. "That was brave."

Elizabeth shrugged, still not sure she was believing what she was hearing. The maids weren't angry with her. "It was the right thing to do."

"Aye." Alma patted her shoulder. "It was. There will be no punishment because ye slept late."

Elizabeth saw the other maids exchange glances and she could practically hear their thoughts. No punishment from the housekeeper because she came to the aid of a maid. How the duke would feel about a servant attacking an earl might be an entirely different matter.

****

For once, the evening banquet seemed subdued. Instead of the boisterous, ribald remarks and laughter, the conversation at the long tables held to a steady hum. Elizabeth felt the covert looks of the female guests while the men watched her openly, some with curious expressions, others with contemplative looks, as if they were deciding what her fate should be for daring to strike an aristocrat. The earl glared at her. The butler assigned

Elizabeth to serve at the far end of the hall. She wondered if the man thought she might spill an entire platter of food on the earl. Elizabeth hid a grin as she took empty plates back to the kitchen. She had thought about doing just that.

"'Tis as quiet as I have heard that bunch," Ina said as she took the empty plates from Elizabeth.

"They're like vultures waiting for the prey to die before they descend," Carla said.

Elizabeth had the feeling that Carla was right. With the duke still gone, gossip had probably run rampant all afternoon. What steps would he take? What punishment would he mete out? Would he even listen to any version of what happened other than what the earl told him? Elizabeth doubted it.

"I say ye put the fear of God in them, ye did," Sara said.

"I don't think any of them fear God…or the devil," Carla replied.

"Maybe not," Sara answered and pointed at Bridget, who was at the far counter placing more food on a platter. "But they have seen the bruises around her neck. 'Tis no denying that. His Grace won't be pleased."

Ina snickered. "Aye. Those uppity snoots may not fear Heaven or Hell, but falling out of the duke's favor is another matter."

Sara batted her eyelashes and pretended her towel was a fan as she bobbed a curtsy. "Just imagine if they stopped receiving invitations to all the balls and parties."

Elizabeth glanced over to Bridget. The earl had squeezed her throat so hard last night that her voice was barely a whisper and Alma had told her not to talk. The cook had even tried to get Bridget to stay in the kitchen today and away from the crowds, but Bridget's eyes had flashed fire and she'd tugged the neckline of her bodice a bit lower so every bruise would show when she served the midday meal. The butler had managed to keep her away from the earl's table, but that didn't stop Bridget from glowering at the man the entire time.

It didn't take long after that for the tongues to start wagging…and Elizabeth had heard her name mentioned as well. Since she'd refused to acknowledge any of the remarks with even a glance, the gossip had accelerated by the evening meal.

"Society can be fickle," Elizabeth said, "maybe they deserve to be shunned."

"Shunned?" Carla asked. "You mean passed over like they didn't matter?"

"Yes," Elizabeth replied. "Kind of the way they treat you…us…servants."

The maids all glanced at her and Ina shook her head. "When ye first got here the other day, ye acted just like them. All hoity-toity, as though ye were better than us. I thought ye were giving yourself airs."

"We all did," Sara added, "but saving Bridget last night changed our minds."

Elizabeth felt her cheeks warm. "Well, Broc actually did the saving. We were lucky he happened by."

Ina and Sara exchanged glances and then Ina spoke. "I don't think luck had to do with it. Broc followed ye."

"Followed me? Why?"

Sara giggled. "'Tis plain the man is interested in ye."

"Interested?" If they knew what had happened—or didn't happen, to be more precise—last night, they wouldn't think so. He'd all but slammed the door behind her.

"Aye. He watches ye when he doesn't think ye are looking."

She was the one who spent time watching Broc. Elizabeth felt her face heat again. Had *she* been that obvious? Maybe the maids were making fun of her. She looked at them for signs of derisiveness, but only saw sincerity. Still, better to change the subject. "Whatever made him come around the corner last night, he saved Bridget. I'm grateful to him for that because I don't know how long I would have been able to hang on."

There was a grunt from the counter. Bridget walked over and pointed to Elizabeth. "Ye were first," she whispered and then thrust a rolled newspaper into Elizabeth's hands. "Ye take."

Elizabeth looked down. Inside the paper was a good portion of mutton. She gave Bridget a startled look. "I better not take this."

Bridget folded her arms across her chest. "Take."

Elizabeth looked at the other maids. Their eyes all widened as they gathered around her. She felt herself smiling too and held the paper out. "Let's all be bad, then," she said as Alma grinned and closed the door to the kitchen.

****

Elizabeth watched from the kitchen door as the ducal carriage rolled into the courtyard late the next afternoon. From the way the duke stomped into the manor house, his face grim, she assumed whatever had taken him to London had not gone well. She doubted his mood would improve once he heard news about the incident.

To Elizabeth's surprise, she saw Bridget cross the courtyard from the servants' quarters and enter the manor house from the postern door. She didn't blame the girl for wanting to get to the duke first before the earl had a chance to slant the story in his favor, but Elizabeth wished she'd been able to warn Bridget that the duke appeared to be in a foul mood.

Then again, if Bridget had actually gone to his bed before, she probably would be able to ascertain that herself. Elizabeth just prayed the duke would believe Bridget.

The evening meal was served without its usual fanfare. The duke had not put in an appearance since his return, but he had summoned the earl to his solar. The guests, perhaps sensing one of their own was actually being questioned, kept their comments and speculations to a low murmur. No one had seen Bridget. Elizabeth couldn't decide if that was cause for hope or concern.

As she was helping the other maids clean the kitchen before retiring to their quarters, a note came from the housekeeper.

The duke had requested Elizabeth's presence in his solar at once.

Chapter Nine

Broc stood in the doorway of the stables watching the back entry to the manor. The hour was getting late. Elizabeth should have finished serving by now. In fact, she should be in the kitchens cleaning the dishes and getting ready for the next day. When he had checked nearly a half hour ago, she wasn't there nor was Bridget. Neither woman was in the servants' quarters either.

Broc resisted the urge to pace even though every muscle in his body screamed for action instead of this innate stillness. There was no use in making the horses restless. As it was, Warrior was already stamping his hooves. Colton was in the tack room polishing harnesses. Broc didn't need him coming out to ask questions Broc couldn't answer.

The biggest question for which he had no answer was when had he come to care for Elizabeth Shelton. Not that he didn't *care* about any of the other charges who had been his responsibility, but Elizabeth was special. Even though he'd try to deny it, in his heart—that organ that he'd thought had grown immune to emotion—he knew this time with this woman was different.

That thought made Broc even more uneasy. Byron reveled in making the lives of servants generally miserable, hence the once-a-week-only rituals of bathing and eating meat. He delighted in putting obstacles in the way of the mortals sent to Broc, partly to make Broc's assignment more difficult, but also because Byron believed evil would overcome good eventually. Any person's spirit could be broken. If Broc's twin even had an inkling that this mission had become personal to him, the results would be disastrous.

Broc turned his attention back to the manor house. He supposed it was possible that Elizabeth and Bridget had decided to have a chat in an empty room, but he doubted it. He'd seen Bridget race across the courtyard after the duke returned. It was highly likely that his damnable brother had made Bridget pleasure him before he would even listen to her story. That would explain the maid's absence, but it didn't explain Elizabeth's. Had the earl cornered her somewhere? Broc didn't think the man would be foolish enough to assault another woman during his stay, but he might have insisted to the duke that she be locked in the cellar with the rodents for the night. If only Broc could gain entrance to the house without breaking the wards that kept Byron's magic contained.

His thoughts were interrupted when he saw Bridget step out the back door and walk toward the servants' quarters. He tried to appear unhurried as he strode toward her.

"Have you somewhat recovered from your ordeal?"

"I am better," Bridget replied. "I am grateful you happened by when you did."

"It is Elizabeth you should thank," Broc answered. "If she hadn't pounded on the earl to distract him, I might have been too late."

Bridget nodded. "I know. I've thanked her, but I'd like to do more. None of us were very nice to her when she first came."

"I'm sure Elizabeth will value your friendship," Broc said and then hoped he sounded casual, "Do you know where she might be?"

"I think she's with His Grace."

Broc's heart nearly leapt out of his throat. "With the duke?"

"Aye. He summoned her."

"Why?"

Bridget gave him a look that left no doubt she thought him a dimwit, then she shrugged. "He dismissed me when Lizzie got there."

Broc had troubled keeping his voice pitched at a reasonable level. "How long ago was this?"

She shrugged again. "Ten…maybe fifteen minutes ago. I finished wiping the tables before I came out."

His heart sank with a thud to the bottom of his stomach. In that amount of time, who knew what his brother would do? Elizabeth wasn't safe with his brother, but she didn't know it. "Thanks," Broc said and then spun on his heel to sprint to the manor.

To hell with his wards. He was going in.

****

Elizabeth met Bridget in the hall outside the duke's solar as the maid was leaving. "Did you have a chance to tell His Grace your side of the story?"

"Aye, but I don't know if he believes me."

"Why wouldn't he? He saw the bruises, didn't he?"

"He did just now. I tried to see His Grace earlier when he returned, but he kept me waiting all afternoon. I saw the earl go to his solar."

"So the duke got the earl's side of the story first?" Elizabeth asked. Then, when Bridget nodded, she patted the other girl's hand. "Well, don't worry. I'll tell him what happened too. It's probably why he wants to see me."

Bridget gave her a long look. "Maybe. Be careful."

Elizabeth didn't have time to contemplate what she meant when the door to the solar swung open. The duke stood there. "I do not like to be kept waiting."

Bridget bobbed a curtsy and scurried off. Elizabeth scrutinized him and lifted her chin. "You wanted to see me, Your Grace?"

He raised an eyebrow. He probably thought she should curtsy too, but Elizabeth didn't really see any reason to. She'd been attending to aristocratic demands for several days now. All that had done was convince her not only were the nobility *not* any better people than the servants, but many of wealthy were also petty, rude, and quite vain. She held the duke's gaze. "I believe you asked me to come to your solar?"

His facial expression changed. The haughtiness vanished from his eyes to be replaced with a sharper, more intent look. Then that, too, disappeared and he smiled jovially. "Indeed, I did. Please come in."

Elizabeth walked past him into the room and then stopped, taking it in. Solars were normally light and airy, with a number of bare-framed windows to let the sun shine in during the day. Heavy, red velvet curtains covered the windows in this room. The other three walls were a dull gold with every conceivable type of vine and foliage painted over them and across the ceiling, giving the impression of being in a jungle. A large, black lacquered wardrobe stood against one wall, along with an uncomfortable-looking stone kneeling bench—or maybe it was a foot rest since there was a straight-back chair next to it with a leather belt hung across the back.

A hearth in the opposite wall had its fires banked for the night, the embers still sparking bits of red and orange. Oil lamps hung on either side of the hearth, casting the room into shadows, making Elizabeth feel closed in. The only other source of light was from a candle standing on a table next to a massive sofa upholstered in red velvet. Placed as the sofa was in front of the curtain, it practically blended in. Were it not for the black lacquered frame, Elizabeth would have missed it. She looked around. A trunk and a cart holding glass decanters were the only other pieces of furniture. Besides the chair, the sofa was the only place to sit.

"How do you like the décor?" the duke asked, his glacier-blue eyes seeming to glitter like ice from the reflection of the dim light.

She decided not to tell him the room reminded her of an animal's lair. Elizabeth doubted the duke wanted to hear that description. She swallowed. She'd never been a good liar. "It is different."

"Ah, diplomacy." He laughed and then gestured to the sofa. "Come, my dear. Please sit."

Elizabeth would have preferred the straight-back chair, but it was across the room so she sat on the edge of the sofa.

"Would you like a drink? There is sherry, ratafia, cognac—"

"No. I am fine, thank you."

The duke tilted his head to study her. "Are you nervous?"

"No…no. Why should I be?" Elizabeth folded her hands to keep them from fidgeting. She certainly didn't want the duke to think she was scared of him.

He walked over to the cart, poured himself a brandy,

and returned to join her on the sofa. "This room has some of my favorite things."

Elizabeth looked around, wondering what he meant. There were no pictures on the walls nor any *objects d'art* standing around. Maybe he had artwork stored in the trunk and wardrobe, but why hide them if they were his favorite things?

"I only invite certain people here."

She started when she realized he had moved closer. Not close enough that they were touching, but much closer than should be appropriate, given that they were alone. She remembered Bridget's warning. Elizabeth sidled slightly, bumping into the sofa's arm, and chided herself. Why hadn't she sat in the middle?

"There is no reason to be scared."

"I'm not scared." Elizabeth resisted the urge to jump up, since that would just prove his point. She needed to get down to the business of why she was here. She lifted her head and looked straight at the duke. "Did you believe Bridget's story?"

He looked amused. "That she didn't care to bed the earl?"

"The man attacked her."

"Hmmm. From what I was told *you* attacked the earl."

"Only because he was strangling Bridget. Did you not see her bruises?"

The duke shrugged. "Bridget has bruises elsewhere as well."

"What…" Elizabeth let her voice trail off as she remembered earlier conversations about Bridget and Carla sharing the duke's bed. Surely he didn't mean he hurt them. She was letting her imagination run wild because the room made her uncomfortable. "Are you saying your servants get flogged?"

"Flogged?" He seemed to consider the word. "I suppose that might be accurate."

'But that's inhumane. Everyone here works hard. There is no reason to strike them to punish them."

"To punish them? I do not see it that way."

"No one *likes* to be hit, for goodness' sake."

The duke smiled. "You are quite wrong, my dear. Pain can quickly turn to pleasure. It just takes an expert hand."

Elizabeth felt her blood chill, finally realizing what he meant. Her eyes shifted to the wardrobe and then to the trunk. Were those things he treasured so much objects of torture? Was that why he kept them hidden? She didn't want to find out.

"I had better leave." She made a move to get up, but his hand on her arm brought her quickly down. She tugged but he tightened his grip until it felt like a vise.

"Let me go."

"Not quite yet. When I spoke to the earl this afternoon, he wanted me to have you arrested. I told him I would think on it." The duke leaned over her to put his brandy snifter on the table beside the candle, then turned to her, his face inches away from hers. His eyes glittered silver. "I could be persuaded to forget—"

The door to the solar banged open, the frame splintering. Broc stood in the doorway. "Let her go or we will settle this now, once and for all."

The duke released Elizabeth and stood. "I was wondering if you'd come." He smiled. "Well done, brother. You have finally freed me."

****

It wasn't until they were away from the manor and walking toward the woods that Elizabeth stopped on the path suddenly and looked at Broc.

"What did the duke mean, calling you 'brother'?"

Broc sighed. He'd expected the question as soon as Elizabeth's mind had cleared enough to think clearly. He'd managed to keep the secret hidden from nearly everyone. Only Colton had guessed at the relationship, thinking it odd that Broc had arrived shortly after Byron claimed the duchy and that there seemed to be animosity between them.

"Byron is my twin."

Elizabeth's eyes widened. "Your twin? You look nothing alike."

"We're fraternal."

Her brow creased. "If you're the duke's brother, doesn't that make you a marquis? Or at least a lord? What are you doing working as a head groom?"

"I like working with horses," Broc answered. "As for a title, Byron has pronounced me bastard-born."

"How can you be a bastard if you're his twin? You have the same mother."

"The same mother, yes, but not the same father."

"What? I don't understand," Elizabeth said.

"Byron likes to say dogs have litters in which the pups have different sires," Broc replied, "and that mine was a mongrel."

"That is ridiculous," Elizabeth said. "Just because one of you is dark and the other fair, doesn't mean... Well. Surely your mother defended herself."

Broc shook his head. "She only said we were both her sons." He wished he could tell Elizabeth the whole truth. His mother had been a white witch—a healer—and his father had been mortal. Byron's had not.

"But your father claimed you?"

"No. My father was killed before we were born." Broc couldn't very well explain that Byron's father was an incubus who had assaulted their mother in retaliation for saving a villager. Broc's father died trying to protect her. "We were raised by an uncle, Lord Sutton of Willishire near York."

Elizabeth nibbled on her lip, a gesture Broc found particularly alluring. He looked away from her mouth. "You look troubled."

"I'm just trying to understand. If your brother won't acknowledge you, why would you follow him here?"

"It is a long story," Broc said. Far too long—and unbelievable—for her to accept, even if he were allowed to tell her who he really was. "You might say I know my brother's intentions aren't always honorable, particularly when it comes to ladies."

"You knew I was in danger tonight?"

"I wasn't sure until I talked to Bridget and she told me Byron had summoned you to his solar. It is…not a good place for a woman to go."

Elizabeth shuddered. "The room gave me the chills. It felt…almost evil."

If only she knew. "I should have cautioned you. I am sorry."

"You have nothing to apologize for. I am the one who should be thanking you for arriving when you did." She smiled up at him. "So, do you rescue damsels in distress often?"

Elizabeth's smile was his undoing. Broc let his gaze drop to her mouth. Her full lips were curved and parted and inviting. When the tip of her tongue darted out the corner, he groaned and then heard the quick intake of her breath. His gaze traveled to her eyes. They were luminous in the moonlight, the pupils dark and wide with desire. Her scent wafted to him on the light evening breeze and he took a step closer.

Her arms came around his neck as she pressed herself against him, her head tilted upward for his kiss. Somewhere on the edges of his conscience a voice was telling him to stop, but another stronger urge had taken control. Broc knew he couldn't have Elizabeth—not in the full carnal sense, not without facing eternal damnation—but he could have this one moment. His mouth came down on hers, claiming those luscious lips.

And he knew he'd tasted heaven.

****

Elizabeth woke the next morning and stretched on her pallet, not quite sure if she'd been dreaming of Broc's kisses. His lips had been soft, but firm. Gentle, yet demanding. The kiss had deepened, his tongue exploring her mouth fully while she reveled in the taste of him, in the scent of him. She'd wanted so much more when he'd abruptly stopped and they'd returned to the servants' quarters. That was why she thought she had dreamt the whole thing. From what she'd seen around here, no man stopped himself, especially not when someone was as willing as she was.

Then Elizabeth remembered the nightmare in which the evening began. The duke's overtures had been all too real. Broc *had* rescued her, just like Sir Galahad. And, like that virtuous knight, he'd not taken advantage of her, either.

Elizabeth got up, not sure if she liked virtuous knights or not…or, for that matter, why had she started thinking about knights at all? The world around her was a harsh reality, not given to heroes wearing shining armor.

She dressed quickly—the other maids had already gone to the kitchen, which made her late once again. But, after what happened with the duke in his solar last night, she'd rather be cleaning ovens than be available.

"I am sorry I'm late," she said to Alma a few minutes later when she arrived in the kitchens. "I'll ask Ina or Sara to wake me up from now on."

The cook gave her a pitying look. "Ye won't be worrying about that anymore."

Elizabeth furrowed her brow. Had the duke actually decided to help her? Even after what happened last night? Or, perhaps, he thought she'd be compliant if he did? If that was the case, she would have to be firm. There wasn't any way she would go back to that solar.

"What do you mean? Have I been assigned elsewhere?"

Alma shook her head. "Ye will be leaving."

Elizabeth stared at her. The duke was sending her away? She didn't want to leave Broc. "Where am I going?"

"London."

"London?" Maybe when the duke had gone there, he'd secured a governess position for her. That might explain his unwelcome attention last night. He'd expected a thank you of sorts. She'd be glad to thank him—verbally. "Did His Grace secure a position for me?"

Tears welled in Alma's eyes. "Ye are being taken to Newgate for striking the earl."

Elizabeth felt her mouth drop. "To prison?" Dear

Lord in Heaven. The duke was retaliating for her refusal—well, it was a rescue, but the blasted man knew she'd already refused him—and having her arrested.

She had to get to Broc. He'd know what to do. She bolted for the door, only to run headlong into two burly guards who grabbed her arms.

"You are coming with us."

Chapter Ten

Broc struggled to free himself in what felt like pitch blackness, but the more he moved, the tighter the restraints became. He wasn't sure where he was or how he'd gotten here. His arms were wrapped around something behind him. He became aware of the rough bark of a tree against his bare back. Amidst the smell of pine and earth he detected the taint of magic. Demon magic.

He squinted into the unnatural darkness. This was Byron's doing. Broc had unfettered the invisible bonds that had kept his twin's power confined to the manor house when he'd entered and broken the wards. What else had he unleashed? And why was he bound?

The hair at his nape rose. Elizabeth. Elizabeth was in danger and Byron wanted to make sure Broc could not come to her rescue again. He tugged at the ties holding him, clenching his teeth to keep from moaning when he felt whatever was holding him cut into his flesh.

A torch was thrust so close to his face that it singed his hair. The light blinded him as much as the ebony night had. Then, as the torch lowered slightly, he heard Byron's laugh, which turned into a howl.

Broc blinked, willing his eyes to refocus. At first, he didn't recognize where he was, but as his senses returned he realized he'd been taken to the rocky outcrop above the ravine at the edge of the forest. His twin stood not far away, but the Adonis façade was gone. His brother had sprouted horns, his nose and mouth had elongated into a muzzle, and his eyes blazed red.

He'd only seen his brother let the beast out on one other occasion—when he'd ripped out the throat of the real heir to the duchy. Broc fought the unusual sensation of panic he felt rising and forced himself to be still. "What have you done to Elizabeth?"

The beast grinned, its long fangs sharp and deadly, but at least no blood dripped from them.

"Answer me, demon."

Byron snarled and then resumed his human face. "Don't call me that."

"It is what you are."

He growled again and waved the torch menacingly. "Perhaps I will just burn you and put an end to this."

"Then you will deprive yourself of the pleasure of torturing me first," Broc replied and slowly wiggled his fingers. He'd discovered, when he stilled himself, his bonds had loosened somewhat. They could very well be illusionary. Suggestion had a powerful effect on the mind, and he had allowed his thoughts to become chaotic over Elizabeth. He had also momentarily forgotten the most fundamental fact about wizardry.

White magic was stronger than black magic. Broc's magic had been inherited only from his mother, whose power had been as pure as angels.

He needed to put forth a call, but to do that, mental shields needed to be in place so his twin would not discern what he was doing. That meant Broc needed to distract him.

"Since I am not going anywhere soon—"

"You are not going anywhere at all," Byron said

with a smirk.

"In that case, you might as well tell me what you did to Elizabeth." Broc braced himself for the worst and silently put out his call.

His brother's smirk widened into a sinister smile. "Your stupid wench made a bad mistake when she struck a member of the nobility. I decided to have her sent to Newgate, where she will either rot in a cell or be hanged." His eyes glowed red again. "Of course, I imagine a number of guards will have their way with her first."

Broc reined in his temper. He needed to stay calm for the magic to work. He began to weave the invisible threads that would deliver a message to the boars that their territory was being challenged. He knew he had the power to calm animals but he'd never tried to anger one. Would they come?

Broc had no idea how long he'd been ensorcelled. Was Elizabeth already in London? Broc knew she had the inner strength to withstand prison conditions temporarily, but had the charges against her been enhanced enough to merit hanging? He had to get to her.

In the distance, thunder rumbled.

Byron looked up and his eyes narrowed. "You think to bring a storm? I can harness the lightning as well as you, brother."

"Why would I summon lightning when I am bound to a tree?"

Byron considered for a moment and then broke into a feral grin. "Perhaps lightning is not a bad idea at all." He held his hand to the heavens. "It will save me the work of using the torch on you."

Lightning flashed around them, but no bolt

descended. Broc wiggled his fingers again. His bonds were gone. The storm ruse had distracted his twin enough to drop his enchantment. Broc put his own shields in place before his brother could spellbind him again.

The wind picked up suddenly, a strong gust extinguishing the flame from the torch, leaving them in darkness. Byron muttered an incantation and the flame relit, only to die out once more as a squall of rain poured down. He cursed.

Broc smiled. The shrieking wind would cover the sound of what was coming.

Byron bellowed at the forces of nature, which only increased the lightning, rain and wind. He didn't hear the snorting of the beasts nor the pounding of the hooves until it was too late.

The boars broke through the forest line, long tusks gleaming like sharp swords in the midst of the storm. Byron dropped his torch, preparing to hurl a curse to stop them, and stepped back as they charged.

But he was standing too close to the edge of the outcrop. His foot slipped on the slimy, wet shale and he tumbled backward just as the tusks of the first boar caught and lifted him, sending him over the edge.

Byron screamed as he fell, and then there was silence.

The storm ceased as quickly as it had begun. The boars snuffled and pawed the ground and then turned to trot quietly back into the forest.

Broc watched as a dark column rose from the depths of the ravine. For a moment, he saw the hideous face of the incubus in its midst. Lightning flashed once more and the incubus was gone.

Moonlight burst through the clouds, illuminating the path home.

****

Elizabeth huddled on the floor in the corner of a damp, dank cell that had a slit for a window too high up to see out. A wooden bench that served as a bed was bolted to the wall. At the moment, the other female occupant of the cell—a middle-aged woman with graying hair—was occupying it. She might have been pretty once, but her features had hardened and she sported a bloodied, bruised lip.

A foul-smelling chamber pot in the opposite corner made Elizabeth wrinkle her nose. The older woman laughed, her mouth twisting grotesquely because of the swelling.

"Ye'll get used to the smell in time," she said, wiping dirty fingers on her ragged gown and then extending her hand. "I'm Mattie."

Elizabeth was loath to take it, but she knew better than to cause offense. "I am Eliz—Lizzie."

"Well, Lizzie," Mattie said, releasing her hand and leaning back against the wall. "Like I said, ye will get used to the smell. 'Tis better than the stench of rotting flesh in the men's quarters."

"Rotting flesh?"

"Aye. The men are chained to the walls with no clothing or blankets—"

"But it's December and near to freezing in here!" Elizabeth stared at Mattie. "Why does the warden not give them clothes?"

"So the gaolers won't have to do laundry, I suppose." Mattie shrugged. "It's punishment too."

"Have they all been found guilty of crimes?"

168

Mattie started to laugh again, then patted her thickened mouth. "Court is only held eight times a year. Ye have to wait your turn."

"But that's…" Elizabeth paused, more dread filling her stomach like lumps of coal. "When is the next time court will be held?"

"Probably March, when the lords all return for the Season."

March. Three months. Elizabeth looked around the small, barren cell. How was she going to survive that long? "But people are innocent until proven guilty."

"Where did ye get that notion? If ye are accused, ye sit here and wait."

"But March is three months away—"

"It might be longer than that, depending on how many untried are ahead of ye. 'Tis the reason some of the men's flesh rots on the other side of these walls. The air fevers some of them. Then there are the rat bites—"

"Rat bites?" Elizabeth drew her knees up to her chin and tucked her still semi-clean gown under her. "Can't solicitors do something about this?"

"Aye. If ye have coin, ye can have a better cell with a pallet of straw. With enough gold, ye can even have a bath now and then and hot meals. Otherwise, ye eat gruel and moldy bread."

Coin. Money. The lumps of coal in Elizabeth's stomach suddenly felt like lead. She had no money. Suddenly the servants' food at Chadworth didn't seem bad. At least the porridge had been hot and the bread not moldy. The creek had allowed her to keep clean… She closed her eyes, remembering how Broc had shown her how to heat the water over a fire. Broc. He probably didn't even know what happened to her. Elizabeth squeezed her eyes tighter to avoid crying, but a few tears managed to escape.

"Crying will do ye no good in this place," Mattie said.

Elizabeth popped her eyes open and she wiped at her face. "I know that."

"Come." Mattie moved over and patted the bench. "Sit beside me."

"Thank you." Elizabeth moved to the bench gratefully. Already her legs were feeling the effects of a damp, hard floor. "How long have you been here?"

"Thirty two days." Mattie pointed to marks on the floor. "I kept track by how often the sun rises and light comes through the window."

"What did you do? I mean," Elizabeth added quickly, "what are you accused of?"

Mattie was quiet for a minute. "My husband wanted to marry a younger woman."

Elizabeth blinked. "I don't understand. I know divorce is not common, but—"

"I did not want to bring such shame to my family," Mattie said, "so I told him I would not leave."

"What did he say?"

"He laughed and said he could make me leave." Mattie looked around the cell. "He was right."

Elizabeth frowned. "But he can't have you put in prison for that."

"Maybe not, but I'm accused of stealing a pair of candlesticks from a chandler. When the magistrate arrived to question me, he found the pair in the pantry."

"How did they get there?"

"The chandler's shop is next door to my husband's tailor shop. They are friends." Mattie shook her head.

"No one believed me."

"That is awful! It's not right, either. What will happen to you?"

"I will probably be fined." Mattie's expression turned glum. "I doubt I can pay it, so I'll probably go to debtor's prison."

"You don't have a relative or friend who can lend you money?"

"I have a sister in Cornwall, but she's barely managing to scrimp by as it is."

"But debtor's prison is a vicious cycle. If you can't afford to pay the fine and you go to prison, you'll never be able to pay."

"Which will make my husband very happy because then he can live with his mistress." Mattie dabbed at her eyes and then lifted her chin. "Enough about me. What crime are ye accused of?"

"I struck an earl."

Mattie's eyes rounded. "Ye did what?"

Elizabeth explained what had happened. "The earl had it coming."

"Aye, he did," Mattie agreed, "but the nobles don't see it that way. Neither do the courts. Servants have few rights. And a duke's friend…" She let her voice trail off and then sighed. "Ye poor dearie."

Trying to squelch the uneasiness welling up inside her, she asked, "Why do you say that?"

"Ye will be flogged for certain, if not hanged."

Elizabeth felt her blood chill. "It can't be that serious. I didn't kill the man."

"Much will depend on what the duke has to say about the matter. Next to the royals, dukes hold the most power in the land." Mattie frowned in concentration.

"From what I remember of my husband's dealings with the Duke of Chadworth, he does not like to be thwarted."

Elizabeth's body went numb and not from the cold. There was no doubt she had already thwarted the Duke of Chadworth.

****

Broc slowed Warrior to a walk on the uneven cobblestones of London's streets. He'd pushed the animal as hard as he'd dared and the horse was tired. The stallion had more stamina than any horse he'd ever owned, but limits were limits. As it was, they'd only stopped for hour-long rests so the normal two-day carriage trip to London had taken one day of riding hard, with no sleep. Broc had already wasted a day trapped in Byron's enchantment and then another clearing things at the estate after his brother's body had been recovered. That meant Elizabeth had spent three days in Newgate—the "hell above ground" as it was called by many. The formal charges of assault against a lord of the realm had been signed by the duke, which meant Elizabeth would be shown no leniency.

Broc dismounted in front of the granite-arched gate at Old Bailey, looped Warrior's reins over a hitching rail, and tossed a guinea to a waiting street urchin to watch his horse. The lad grinned as he caught it, showing a missing front tooth. Then he lifted his ragged shirt to show a wicked looking dagger stuck in his pants' band. Broc nodded and patted Warrior's neck. "You'll be in good hands while I'm in there." The horse pawed the ground, then extended his neck to nuzzle the boy who'd already taken a wide-legged stance of defense.

The iron portcullis was up and Broc used the iron knocker on the heavy oak doors. A guard slid open a small window in the door. Broc held up a paper with the duke's seal. "From the Duke of Chadworth regarding female prisoner Elizabeth Shelton."

A moment later, he heard the bolt slide and one of the massive doors swung open. The guard grinned at him. "That one is a real looker. Be a shame if the duke changed his mind about the charges before some of us could sample her goods."

Broc fought the temptation to put the man on his arse, preferably missing a few teeth. The comment was exactly what he didn't need to hear. He'd spent the last three days worried to his gills that Elizabeth had already been taken advantage of. A lot of women sold themselves for better treatment—the guards were not above threatening the ones who didn't. The whole prison system reeked of corruption, bribery, and injustice.

"I am the Duke of Chadworth's brother. Keep your comments to yourself."

The guard's face paled. "Yes, your lordship. I meant no disrespect, your lordship. I—"

"I need to see the warden."

"Yes…yes….at…at once," the man stammered and gestured to another guard standing inside the central courtyard. "His lordship needs to see the warden."

The second guard nodded. "This way, my lord."

As Broc followed the man into the dark, dungy hall toward the office, he could hear the wails and groans and occasional scream from the recesses of the prison. He grimaced, wishing he could use magic to change this place, but changing the course of mortal history was forbidden.

Once they reached the warden's office, Broc handed his paper over. "It bears my brother's seal. I think you will find everything in order for Miss Shelton's immediate release." Broc hoped news of the duke's death hadn't reached London—or at least Newgate—yet. That news could come at any minute. Although the seal was legitimate and his own forgery of his brother's handwriting perfect, he'd prefer not to be questioned about the date it was written or why the duke had suddenly changed his mind just before he died. What was important was that he get Elizabeth away from here.

The warden scanned the letter and then nodded to the guard. "Bring the woman here immediately."

"Yes, sir."

It seemed to Broc a half-century passed before he heard the guard's heavy footsteps along with lighter ones in the hall. He assumed a somber pose and stern expression as he faced the door. He hoped Elizabeth wouldn't make a wild dash for him. Broc didn't want the warden to suspect there was anything personal between them. The more formal this whole process appeared, the sooner they would be out. Still, he held his breath as Elizabeth entered. She looked dirty and disheveled, but he didn't see any bruises or injuries. Her eyes widened when she saw him and she started to smile, then frowned as he looked above her head. She took a step toward him, then checked herself.

The warden dismissed the guard, then turned to Elizabeth. "You are free to go."

"The duke and the earl have decided to drop the charges," Broc added, still not meeting her gaze. He'd had to do a bit of mesmerizing to get the earl's "agreement," but that was not important at the moment. Only that Elizabeth played along so he could get her away. "I have come to escort you back to the estate."

She looked a little puzzled. "I am most grateful."

"Let us be on our way, then." Broc walked to the door to open it for her, but she hadn't moved. Did she not understand the importance of leaving before the warden decided to question anything? "Come."

"I…" She looked from him to the warden and back. "There is a woman…Mattie…in my cell. She is accused of stealing candlesticks, which she didn't do."

"Prisoners lie," the warden said.

Broc nodded. "The warden is right. He—"

"No. She didn't take them. Her husband…" Elizabeth sighed. "It is a long story, but I believe her. In any case, the candlesticks were returned, so she shouldn't even be here. Please…help."

Broc heard the sincerity in Elizabeth's voice. He also saw the determination in her eyes. Time was of the essence here and he didn't want to spend a lot of it discussing this matter. Whether the woman was guilty—and there was a good chance she wasn't—bribery usually trumped justice at Newgate. Broc turned back to the warden. "How much would the woman's fine be? Perhaps I could pay it as a charitable contribution from the duke."

The warden cleared his throat and appeared to be considering the matter. Broc smiled pleasantly. "Might I offer a small compensation for yourself as well, for your trouble? Perhaps ten sovereigns?"

The warden's greed won out at the offer of so much gold. "I believe that can be arranged. It is quite kind of you—and the duke—to help the poor woman out."

"Of course. Have the woman brought out front." This time, Broc took hold of Elizabeth's arm to make sure she followed him, but he needn't have bothered. She practically danced her way to the door.

They waited—this time outside the gates—for what seemed another half-century before Elizabeth's cellmate was brought out. The two women hugged while Broc fidgeted, hoping some newsboy wouldn't come running down the street shouting that the Duke of Chadworth had died.

"We need to be on our way," Broc said, laying a hand on Elizabeth's arm. "The sooner the better."

"He is right, dearie. We both need to be gone from London," the older woman said and looked up at him. "I thank ye for your kindness, sir. I'll be heading to Cornwall to my sister's, now that I'm free."

Broc knew prisoners were rarely released with any money, even if they had some when they were brought in. He reached into his pocket and pulled out several five-pound notes. "For your journey."

Mattie clapped a hand to her mouth and tears sprang from her eyes. "'Tis a small fortune, my lord."

"Think nothing of it," Broc answered. He was only too glad to spend the duke's money.

She took the money gratefully, tucking it inside the bodice of her torn dress, and then hugged Elizabeth again. "'Tis enough to help my sister out as well. God bless ye."

"Here." Broc handed her several more bank notes. "Take these too." Without another word, he turned and lifted Elizabeth into the saddle and sprang up behind her. "Safe journey," he said, not sure if he meant himself or the woman.

****

Elizabeth looked around the room at the coaching inn well away from London where Broc had decided to stop for the night. It was sparsely furnished with a scarred wooden dresser that held a chipped china pitcher and basin, a small table with two chairs, and a narrow bed. The wallpaper was faded, but when Elizabeth sat down on a mattress of real feathers, she thought she'd found heaven in this present life. After prison conditions, the inn could well have been a palace and this chamber as fine as any hung with silk banners and velvet curtains.

"Tell me again how you found me so soon," she said to Broc who stood by the window looking out at the road. They hadn't really spoken much on the ride here, save that he'd told her the duke was dead and that the sooner they were out of London the better. She hadn't argued that point. He'd apologized for the conditions of the inn he'd chosen, but he'd thought it better not to draw attention to themselves. Elizabeth had assured him she'd sleep out in the open in a deluge of rain as long as it meant being out of that miserable cell.

Broc turned from the window to smile at her. "When I returned from…from following the trail of a wounded boar, the maids all started chattering at once. I finally made sense of it when Alma managed to get them to let her do the talking. Then they practically shoved me to the stables to go after you. It seems that you've made a lot of friends at the manor."

Yes, she had, Elizabeth realized. When she'd first arrived, the other women had thought her snooty—and maybe she was—but having seen and experienced how hard the servants worked without much reward had given her a sense of compassion. "I hope, with the duke gone, that we servants will be treated better."

Broc gave her a strange look. "I can assure you the servants will definitely have better working conditions."

Elizabeth widened her eyes as a thought struck her—one that she should have thought of sooner. "You will inherit the duchy, won't you?"

"I suppose so. I don't care much for titles."

"But it's the authority you will have," Elizabeth said. "Think of how you can change things at Chadworth. You can make everyone's lives better…" She paused as another piece of reality hit her like one of Warrior's hooves in her stomach. "And some young woman is going to be very lucky to become your duchess."

His brow furrowed. "I'll not marry except for love, regardless of what's expected."

Elizabeth felt her heart skip. "So you don't have someone you already fancy?"

Broc smiled, his eyes deepening in color. "There might be someone."

"Oh." Elizabeth felt suddenly stupid. "I didn't mean to pry. I should have known you had a lady in your life."

"Not a titled one, but yes, quite a lady."

She felt her face warm.. "It's none of my business."

"But it is." In three quick strides Broc was beside her, kneeling on the floor. He picked up her hand and kissed it. "You are the lady."

"Oh," Elizabeth said again and wondered if she could manage something besides a one-syllable word. Her cheeks grew hot, but this time not from embarrassment. "I—"

"Hush." Broc brushed a kiss across her lips and then another.

Elizabeth coiled her arms behind his neck, nearly sliding off the edge of the bed. His arms wrapped around her waist, bringing her off the bed onto her knees as he pressed her against him. He deepened the kiss, not taking her fully when she opened her lips to him, teasing her with his tongue until she began to moan. She was about ready to take charge and thrust her own tongue into his mouth when someone knocked at the door.

They both groaned as they broke apart. Broc set her back on the bed and rose. "That will be your bath."

"My bath?"

He grinned. "I thought you might like one."

Elizabeth tried not to squeal as he opened the door and two young boys carried in a half-bath followed by a half-dozen maids carrying steaming buckets of water. "A hot bath! And real soap," she added as she saw one of the maids put a bar on the dresser.

She thanked the servants and then, as soon as they'd gone, she turned to Broc. "This is absolutely the best thing anyone has ever done for me."

Broc turned to the door. "I'll leave you to enjoy it, then."

Elizabeth smiled. "You could join me."

He hesitated, an odd mixture of expressions crossing his face. Then he reached for the knob. "I need to see about getting you a horse for tomorrow. Have your bath. I will return shortly."

Elizabeth stared after him, listening to the sound of his boots fading down the hall. From the way he'd kissed her, she'd been sure he'd want to stay. Maybe that strange code of honor he had—like Sir Galahad—had made him leave. Elizabeth smiled to herself. Broc had implied she was his lady. She felt her body tingle as she stepped into the tub and then sank down into the soothing hot water.

As soon as she finished her bath, she'd climb into

that wonderful bed and wait for Broc to return.

****

Broc kept a running argument with himself all the way down the stairs and out the door and to the stable. What had he almost done back there? He grimaced. He *knew* what he'd almost done. He'd never gotten emotionally involved with a subject before, and he'd sworn—at least to himself—that he wouldn't with Elizabeth. Somehow, she'd managed to break the shell of protection he kept around his heart. A heart that beat faster at the thought of her waiting for him in a room with a comfortable bed.

He chided himself again. What he was contemplating was sheer madness. It was *forbidden* to take his physical pleasure with the women who were sent to him. That rule had never bothered him before, but he was about to blow it to smithereens soon.

Broc bought a solid bay gelding for Elizabeth, hardly hearing the stable master extolling the sound characteristics of the horse. He probably paid too much, as well, but he hardly cared. The thought of melding his flesh with Elizabeth's made him as giddy as an untried boy.

He didn't want to waste time bathing, but neither did he want to go to Elizabeth's bed with the dust of the road covering him and smelling like a horse, so he stopped at the barber's and took a quick dip in a public tub kept for travelers. Luckily the water was clean and not cold, although Broc didn't think the frigid water of the Chadworth creek would have been able to diminish his desire at the moment.

Dressing, he slicked his wet hair back and returned to the hotel. Broc wished it wasn't winter and flowers had been blooming. He wanted to make tonight very special.

He took the stairs two at a time and paused at the door, wondering if he should knock. Then Broc grinned. He would surprise her. Turning the knob, he stepped inside.

The room was empty.

Chapter Eleven

The soft notes of her alarm penetrated Elizabeth's dream. Somewhat sleepily, she thought maybe Broc had sent a flutist to play outside the door while she enjoyed her bath. As the alarm grew louder in sound and intensity, the fogginess of her mind cleared and she opened her eyes to stare at the ceiling.

The twelve-foot plaster ceiling of her tenth-floor apartment in Manhattan, not the low wood-beamed ceiling of a small room in a coaching inn with faded wallpaper. She was lying in a king-size bed with satin sheets and a silk coverlet, not a narrow feather bed with a worn quilt. The designer outfit hung on a rack, the shoes on the floor where Emma had placed them. Elizabeth squinted at the clothing. It looked neither practical nor comfortable.

She glanced at the clock. Nearly eight o'clock. She'd napped for over an hour. The gala had already begun. Dinner was to be served at nine. She'd have to hurry to get dressed to get to The Cloisters in time.

Outside, the storm howled, its intensity increasing because of the wind tunnel effect between the tall buildings. She got up and padded over to the window. Snow swirled, making the streetlights below look like fluttering candles…just like the candles on the nightstand in the coaching inn.

Elizabeth shook her head as she started to dress.

She'd never had a dream so intense before. She could still recall the scents from the kitchens at Chadworth and the cacophony from the huge dining hall. She also remembered the poor living conditions of the servants and the extravagant excess the duke's guests experienced. Elizabeth had never had a dream about a man like Broc before, either. He still seemed so *real*. Her body still tingled in places she usually didn't even think about. Oddly enough, another emotion still niggled at her... She had been falling in love with Broc. A man in a dream. How could that be?

Elizabeth finished dressing and went downstairs to find Jones waiting in the hallway, keys on the table.

"Are you ready for me to bring the car around, Miss Shelton?"

She frowned slightly, realizing the servants always addressed her as "Miss" while she called them by their first or last names. It sounded uppity and smacked too much of the separation of classes in her dream. "Call me Elizabeth, please."

The butler arched one brow. "Are you certain?

Elizabeth smiled. "Quite certain. And..." She looked toward the living room window, already frosted over. "...why don't you just call me a cab? There's no reason for you to have to wait for hours for this event to end before you can go home. The storm is just going to get worse."

Jones had been in the process of lowering his brow when it arched again and he scrutinized her. "Are you feeling well, Miss...Elizabeth?"

"Yes, of course. Why do you ask?"

"It is just... Never mind." He cleared his throat. "However, I am not about to abandon you to a cabbie in this kind of weather. They drive like March hares on a good day. The roads will be icy by the time you come home. You could get into an accident. The Mercedes will be much safer."

Elizabeth blinked at him. He was concerned about her welfare? She just assumed he did his job because he got paid well. Then she thought about Emma taking a personal interest in what Elizabeth would wear tonight and making sure it was ready before she left, even though it would take her an hour—or more in this weather—to get home. Did the maid really care? And even the cook who knew Elizabeth would be having a late dinner had left something hot and nourishing on the stove. Were they simply doing their duties, or did they actually like her? Before Elizabeth had the dream, she hadn't really thought much about servant's personal feelings and attitudes. She felt her face heat with shame that she hadn't even known Emma had a child…and, with her own picky eating habits, she'd gone through several cooks in a row and hadn't bothered to learn anything about them, either. Ironically, she'd been ripe for a rude awakening to the plight of servants in the dream that still seemed as though it had actually happened.

She looked toward the window again. "On second thought, don't call me a cab. I've decided not to go out tonight."

"But you are already dressed."

Elizabeth glanced down at her clothes. "This is hardly appropriate for the weather, is it? It doesn't matter, though. I won't be missed."

"Your mother will expect your picture in Sunday's paper."

"She will just have to deal with that. I'll send a check

to the chairman of the event for the charity they're sponsoring. That's what really matters anyway." She picked up the car keys and handed them to Jones. "Here. Take the Mercedes home. As you said, it's safer. You can bring it back on Monday."

He looked at her hand holding the keys and knit his brows. "Are you sure?"

"Yes. I'm not planning to go anywhere." Elizabeth put the keys in his hand and folded his fingers over them. "Besides, you should be home. It is Christmas Eve, after all."

****

Broc closed the ledger and shoved it alongside a stack of parchment, then leaned back in the chair behind the big desk. He rubbed his eyes, tired with the tedious task of making sure all of the duchy's money was accounted for.

Almost seventy-two hours had passed since Elizabeth had left. Broc told the servants at the manor that she'd run away the first night they'd stopped at the inn, although he knew full well she had returned to her own time. His mission had been accomplished. Elizabeth had learned the lessons of empathy and compassion and, before Broc could violate eternal law, she had been whisked away from him.

He should be grateful that she was safely back in the twenty-first century and he hadn't been sent to the fires of perdition for almost seducing a woman placed in his care. Instead, he was restless, easily agitated, and increasingly irritable. Three very good reasons he'd retired to the library with orders not to be disturbed.

The knock on the door told him someone had not gotten his directive. "Enter," he said, striving to keep his tone neutral.

Molly opened the door, balancing a tray of food with one hand. "I've brought ye stew and warm bread."

"I am not hungry. You can take that back to the kitchen."

"Well," she said, ignoring his remark and coming in to set the tray down in front of him. "Ye have not eaten in two days, and I'll not have ye starving since ye put me in charge of the household."

Broc eyed her warily, hoping the promotion was one he wouldn't regret. Knowing how stringent the former housekeeper was with rules and how miserly the butler when servants pilfered a bit of meat, Broc had given them both pensions, sent them on their way, and put Colton and Molly in charge of running the manor. They both had enough experience—and obvious determination, if the glare Molly was giving Broc was any indication.

"I'm not leaving until ye eat something," she said and crossed her arms across her chest.

He suspected she wouldn't budge until he did as he was told. So much for him being the next duke. Molly and Colton weren't fazed by the addition of a title. Broc sighed and picked up the spoon. Their lack of awe was precisely why he trusted and liked them. He took a bite and then realized that he was hungry. It didn't take long to finish the bowl. "This is very good."

Molly beamed and sat down uninvited. "Alma put in a bit of extra mutton for ye."

Broc paused. "Are the servants getting mutton tonight as well?"

"Aye. The servants are eating the same as ye, just like ye ordered. Grateful they are, too, being so close to

Yule. 'Tis like a celebration."

"The season has nothing to do with it. I want that order to be permanent. Our stores are plentiful. There is no need to ration food."

Molly nodded. "'Tis not a servant that would not thank ye for that."

"I don't need thanks." Broc broke off a piece of bread. "The day before Christmas I want Alma and the maids to cook up a massive feast…as much as Byron had for the house party."

"Ye are planning for guests?"

"No. I want the servants to divide the food and take it home to their families for Christmas. No one is to work on that day."

"But ye will need—"

"I will need nothing. Besides," Broc said before he popped the bread into his mouth. "I can take care of myself for a day."

Molly stared at him for a moment and then jumped up to bustle around the desk and planted a kiss on his cheek. "Ye are a kind man. Do ye know how glad the servants will be to spend Christmas Day with their loved ones? Ye will make every servant at Chadworth very happy. Ye will."

"It is the least I can do after they survived Byron." Broc pushed the tray back. "Please thank Alma for the supper."

"Aye," Molly said, picking up the tray and heading for the door. "'Tis glad we are ye are making so many good changes."

"Thank you." Broc stared at the door after she left, not really seeing it since he was lost in contemplation. *Spending time with loved ones at Christmas,* Molly had said.

His mother had always striven to make Christmas a happy time, even though Byron had shown resistance to kindness even then. In recent centuries, Broc hadn't given much thought to the season. His mother was gone and he hadn't been close to anyone else.

Now he was. He'd found Elizabeth. Could he join her?

Broc stood up and began to pace, for the first time in three days feeling exhilarated. He'd been allowed to travel to the twenty-first century to learn her ways. Would he be allowed again?

He stopped and looked at the ledger on the desk. The duchy's accounts were in order. His twin had spent money freely, but he'd had the intelligence to keep profits coming in as well. With Colton and Molly in charge, the manor would continue to run efficiently. Besides, the duchy didn't really belong to him any more than it did Byron. Perhaps a distant relative to the duchy existed somewhere.

Broc resumed pacing. If he wrote Queen Victoria, voluntarily giving up the title, she could bestow it to someone worthy. Broc could tell her he'd decided to pursue interests in America. It wouldn't be a lie. He just wouldn't mention which century he was pursuing those interests in.

Would he be allowed to go?

He returned to his desk and sat down to watch the flames in the hearth dance in colors of red and yellow and orange. When he'd been given this mission, the master had appeared amidst fire. When Broc accepted, the flames had responded and turned blue in acquiescence. Would they do so again?

Broc closed his eyes. While he had been in the twenty-first century before, he'd lost his warlock power and was strictly mortal. Could he exist only as a mortal in that world permanently? Elizabeth was there. Did he want to exist in this world without her?

He knew he didn't. He was willing to sacrifice immortality to live with Elizabeth for all her mortal days. The question was, would he be allowed to?

Broc opened his eyes and looked into the fire. It burned bright blue.

He smiled, picked up parchment and pen and began his letter to Queen Victoria.

Caroline: Chapter One

The icy mixture turned to slush on the windows of the train as it sped out of the city toward Long Island. Already the landscape was frosted in white. By morning, everything would be covered in a snowy blanket. It reminded Caroline of winters in the Minnesota farming country where she and her husband Danny had grown up, even though the scene outside didn't include rolling hills or open land.

She leaned back in her seat. Her mom had called asking she come out to join the family for Christmas, but Caroline told her the museum would be packed with holiday visitors and she couldn't get away. It wasn't an untruth, but it was an excuse…and the same one she'd used last year. She wondered how long it would be before her parents figured out the real reason she didn't want to go back to Minnesota.

Not that she had anything against the state. Growing up in Mayberry, RFD, had its benefits. Farms that had been settled in the 1800s were passed down through the generations. Everyone in the town of fifteen hundred knew everyone else. The three churches—as well as high school sporting events—were the social centers of the town. Neighbors were neighborly, always ready to help.

Caroline sighed. Those memories were now bittersweet and she couldn't handle them. She had gone home for Christmas three years ago because Danny was overseas. She had been sitting at the kitchen table at her in-laws' farmhouse, playing with Danny's huge wolfhound, when the doorbell rang. Two soldiers, one with Danny's dogtags, gave her the news her husband had been killed in an ambush outside the compound. Within twenty minutes, the townspeople had gathered round, filling the living room and hall, offering sympathy and bringing tons of food. For the next five days, her parents' house had been filled with neighbors, as well as Caroline's sisters and their husbands, all of them lamenting the perils of war and why did Danny have to go to Afghanistan in the first place. He had been an officer. Why didn't he just have an administrative job somewhere behind a safe desk?

She knew all too well why Danny had gone. They'd both been bitten by wanderlust while in high school—in world history class, to be specific—and they'd wanted to explore the world. While in college, Danny decided he wanted a military career where he might be able to change the course of events in oppressed countries. Caroline preferred to scour the past in books to avoid repeating mistakes that led to war.

When Danny transferred to West Point, she'd gotten the curator job at the museum. At the time, she thought it was the perfect place to continue her own research. Now, the museum had become the perfect haven in which she could hide. As autonomous and busy as the city was, she could lose herself among the crowds and be alone with her thoughts.

If she went to Minnesota, she'd have to contend with her sisters' happy marriages. One had a baby last year and the other was pregnant. She didn't want to be confronted with questions or even inquiring looks as to when she might get married again, either. Her parents—and Danny's as well—had hinted that she was still young, with her life ahead of her, and it would be understandable if she started dating. While Caroline admitted—only to herself—that she missed having a man around, especially on cold winter nights when he could keep her warm, she'd also decided she'd never let herself love again. It hurt too much when it was lost. Better not to get involved.

Besides, the town would also be bustling with holiday festivities, which would only dampen her already dismal mood. Old-fashioned streetlamps were hung with garland and banners were strung across the main street. Christmas carols played in every store, and the churches not only held special services and nativity plays but also hosted potluck suppers. If "Peace on earth, good will to men" was possible, it manifested in the small towns of rural America. Caroline didn't want to be the Scrooge who screwed it up.

The train slowed and then lurched to a stop. Caroline gathered her things and got up, only to be jostled by other passengers retrieving items from overheads. She was practically pushed along the aisle and out onto the blustery platform where people rushed by her to get to waiting cars. No one paid her any attention, and she blinked the sting of snow from her eyes. At least, she thought it was snow.

Her tiny apartment, filled with books, was waiting for her. Sometimes she wished she could just transport herself to another time period—one in which she would be happy—but such thinking was the stuff of faerie tales. She was no longer a child. Even though she'd come to accept what happened to Danny, a part of her felt empty.

192

Caroline gave herself a mental shake. The psychologist she'd seen while learning to cope had suggested that, when the "moods" came on, she should do something enjoyable. Caroline squared her shoulders. She'd put on her fleecy bathrobe, make some hot chocolate, and spend her evening researching mistakes the Scots had made at Culloden in 1746 that cost them their national identity. She wouldn't think about Minnesota.

As Thomas Wolfe said, "You can't go home again."

Chapter Two

Caroline woke from dozing in her recliner and snapped the book shut that was lying open on her lap. What on earth was all that clanging and shouting about outside? And were those shots being fired? The village she lived in on Long Island wasn't prone to drive-by shootings.

Putting the book aside, she padded the few feet from the chair to the door and opened it cautiously. Instead of the short walkway that led to the parking lot, she was looking out at a large courtyard where men dressed in Scottish plaids were running across it, yelling in Gaelic, and swinging huge claymores above their heads. At the nearby garrison, she could hear guns being fired and horses galloping away.

Caroline slammed the door shut and leaned against it, eyes closed. She must be having a recurrence of her anxiety disorder. She hadn't had an episode in over two and a half years, but Christmas upset her. Or maybe it was reading about the battle of Culloden and how many Highlanders had been killed senselessly by the Duke of Cumberland, otherwise known as The Butcher. That must have triggered memories of Danny's murder in Afghanistan.

Slowly, she opened her eyes and then took a sharp breath. She was no longer standing in her living room, either. Gone was her beloved recliner, her leather sofa, and the small, old-fashioned TV on its stand. Instead, the room was filled with several satin-brocaded chairs on spindly legs, a horsehair sofa, and various small tables on which sat pictures and ornaments. Her plain vanilla walls were gone, too, replaced by pale gold wallpaper with scrolling green vines. Heavy velvet draperies and large valances covered the two front windows where blinds had been. The room reminded her of a Georgian-era parlor.

Caroline took a deep breath. This was an hallucination. The psychologist had told her this could happen when she was least expecting it. The first time, the day after the funeral, she had transported herself to the mountains of Colorado where she and Danny liked to hike. The second time had been to the Caribbean where they'd lazed on a sailboat and snorkeled. Each episode felt like it lasted several days, although usually only a few hours had gone by. After that, there'd been two or three more, but they were brief flashes, rather than full-blown scenarios. Caroline had quit taking the anti-anxiety meds two years ago, but she wished she had some now.

Breathe in. Count. Breathe out. Again. Caroline repeated the exercise several more times. The room didn't change back nor did the shouting outside stop. *Okay, then.*

The doctor had taught her rather than to fight the illusion just to flow with it. She always retained her sense of reality, just in an alternative setting. She could handle this.

Tentatively, she made her way over to one of the brocaded chairs and then nearly jumped out of it as the door blew open with a heavy gust of icy wind. Caroline started to get up to shut it when a wolfhound bounded in and then stilled, looking at her with eyes the same color as his shaggy gray-brown coat. She gave a startled cry, not because the beast was so massive, but because it looked identical to the one Danny had…the one who had died only months afterward. This was a whammy of an hallucination.

Caroline extended her hand toward the dog, feeling somewhat silly since he probably didn't exist, and then gasped as he moved toward her, pushing his large head under her hand to have his ears rubbed. He felt so real.

"Aren't you beautiful," she crooned.

The animal wagged its tail, then turned suddenly, tail stiff, and emitted a low growl toward the door.

Caroline looked up to see two large men wearing plaids and holding daggers in their hands. The dog growled again.

"Get on with ye," one of the men said.

When the animal didn't move, the other took a brass vase off a table and threw it at him. The dog sidestepped and Caroline jumped up. "Stop it! Don't hurt him."

"Will ye listen to that? An *English* woman who acts like she cares," the first one said.

"Aye," the second one replied. "What's yer name, lass?"

"Caroline Campbell. Why?"

The two men exchanged looks and then broke into grins. "Looks like we got luckier than we thought," the first one said.

Caroline felt the dog's nose nudge her arm. She put a hand on its head. "What do you mean by that?"

"We're MacLeans," the first one said, "and we don't like Campbells."

"Aye, she'll make a fine hostage to exchange for the Earl of Loudoun," the second one added.

The Earl of Loudoun. The earl was John Campbell, a Scot who sided with the English. He also fought under the Duke of Cumberland at Culloden.

Caroline felt her blood chill, as they led her out with the dog following behind them.

****

From the safety of the forest not far from the MacLean campsite, the wolfhound shook himself and waited for his body to assume its human form. His charge had arrived and he'd barely gotten to Caroline Campbell before his soldiers did.

Gavin MacLean wanted to will his transformation to hurry, but he knew it always took a few minutes before his animal form would surrender to his human one. Shifters who rushed things often ended up dazed and confused for days, and Gavin couldn't take a chance on that happening—not with the lass being a Campbell.

Damnation. Why did she have to have that accursed last name? The MacLeans weren't the only clan who hated the Campbells. The MacDonalds—who would be arriving soon—still thirsted for blood after the massacre at Glen Coe decades ago. At least half the highland clans who had joined Bonnie Prince Charlie's cause had no use for Campbells either since they'd allied with the English.

His men had raided the Inverness garrison—or rather, the castle-like house next to it, where dignitaries were housed—this evening in hopes of catching John Campbell before he set off for Moy Hall where Prince Charles was staying. The wily bastard had slipped past them. As disappointed as he was that Campbell had eluded them, Moy Hall had already been alerted the earl was on his way. They'd be ready. Unlike his men, who'd cursed long and loud at not capturing the man, Gavin knew there had been another reason for the raid. Caroline Campbell.

Gavin watched his men through the trees as his body slowly elongated and became upright. Sinew and muscles rippled as his chest expanded and his biceps thickened. His shaggy hair darkened and curled to collar length while his eyes returned to their normal gray color. He squinted, having lost the dog's sharp sight.

Caroline had been placed close to the fire, her wrists and ankles bound. She looked terrified. Gavin frowned. He didn't like seeing women tied, and his men should have known better. He reached for the extra tunic and tartan he always kept hidden when there was a chance he might need to shift. He certainly did not need to scare Miss Campbell further by emerging naked from the woods.

As he strode across the small glade, Gavin saw Caroline look up and her eyes widened in shock when she saw him. He hoped he didn't have any dog fur clinging to his face. He motioned to one of his men. "Untie her."

"But she's a Campbell."

Gavin looked at the man who'd spoken. Shamus was one of the best fighters Gavin had, but he fell short on civility and generally had no use—save one—for women. Gavin looked around to the rest of the group. "Do ye think the ten of ye canna keep an eye on the lass without binding her?"

Some of them got sheepish looks on their faces while Jamie, the youngest in the group, went forward to untie her hands and feet. A look of relief crossed

Caroline's face, and for the first time, Gavin realized how delicate her features were. Red curls framed a face with high cheekbones. Her small nose was straight and her lips wide and full and pink, perfect for kissing. Gavin blinked. Where had that thought come from? By the saints! He didn't need to be attracted to her. He moved his gaze to hers and sucked in a breath as she gave him a trusting look with eyes as green as pine.

"Thank you," she said, still rubbing her wrists.

"I am Gavin MacLean. Are ye hurt?"

She shook her head. "No. I just don't know why I'm here."

Shamus snorted. "Ye're a Campbell."

"Yes. Caroline Campbell. I haven't done anything wrong."

"Doesna matter. Ye're a hostage."

She threw Gavin a questioning look and, for the life of him, he wanted to comfort her. "Ye will come to nae harm with us."

Shamus spit. "But—"

"Enough. Until my brother recovers from his wounds, I am the acting laird. The lass will come to nae harm." Gavin turned to her. "Ye may feel free to walk about if ye wish."

"Thank you," she said again, but before she could get up, the thundering of horses' hooves was heard along the road through the forest and, a moment later, a dozen MacDonalds burst into the glade. Caroline stared at them.

Shamus grinned at Gavin as the men dismounted, pulling their whisky flasks from their saddles as they approached the campfire. "The woman may be safe from us, but do ye think she'll be safe from MacDonalds once the night wears on? 'Tis only one woman in camp—"

"The lass will be safe." Gavin set his jaw when Shamus looked skeptical. "Miss Campbell will be sleeping with me."

She made a strange sound—something between a gasp and a choke—and when Gavin turned to her, he saw the terrified look was back in her eyes.

By the saints, he didn't mean *that*. He meant he would protect her, but he would have to reassure her later. Right now, Calum MacDonald was striding toward him.

****

Caroline huddled deeper into her fleece wrap, wishing she could make herself invisible. The lecherous glances from a couple of the MacDonald men—not to mention all of them taking healthy swigs from their flasks—made her realize the danger she was in. Gavin had said she'd come to no harm. She looked at him now, exchanging back-poundings with the MacDonald leader. Gavin wore only a short tunic with a tartan wrapped around his waist, the end of which was slung over one shoulder like a sash. That left a lot of him exposed, and from what she could see he was all brawn and muscle. Everywhere. She'd heard him tell Shamus he was the acting laird, but even if she hadn't heard that, she'd know he was in charge from the strong set of his jaw and the penetrating look of those stormy-gray eyes…eyes that had felt as though they were seeing right through her clothes a few minutes ago. She wondered if she'd be any safer with him.

The MacDonald chief glanced her way and then back to Gavin with a grin. "Ye brought your mistress with ye?"

"She is—" Shamus began and then stopped at a look from Gavin. He grabbed the flask one of the MacDonalds was offering and took a mouthful.

Gavin turned back to the other chief. "Aye, Calum. The lass did not want my bed to grow cold, no matter where it was."

Angus's grin widened. "'Tis obvious when she's already dressed for your bed."

"Aye. I'm looking forward to saying good night to ye shortly," Gavin replied, "and having the lass keep me warm."

Caroline looked down and covered her face with her hands. Her cheeks felt on fire. Dear lord. Gavin didn't mean that, did he? He couldn't. No one was that arrogant. Besides, this was her hallucination and she'd never put herself in danger before. What was happening to her?

"A shy one," Calum replied with a laugh. "Ye doona often see that "

"Does that mean she willna be sharing her goods with us?" one of his men asked.

Caroline scrunched her eyes closed. Maybe if she took some deep breaths she could get her mind under control…

"Ye are right in that," Gavin said, his tone leaving no room for doubt. "The lass belongs to me."

Caroline nearly choked on an inhalation. Wait a minute. She *belonged* to him? What kind of a decree was that? No one *owned* her. She raised her head to look at him. He had the audacity to wink at her. Before she could reply, though, he'd turned away.

"Make yourselves comfortable," he said to MacDonald's men and gestured toward where the

MacLeans were already sitting across from Caroline near the fire. Gavin walked to one of the horses and pulled a tartan out of a pack to bring back to her. He draped the tartan around Caroline and then sank down beside her and put an arm around her shoulders, before looking back at Calum. "Tell me how it went at Moy Hall."

"We sent the mongrel running with his tail between his legs," Calum said when they'd all gotten settled. "Campbell was in full retreat."

"Dirty dog. Coward not to stay and fight," one of his men added.

"Aye," another one said and pulled out a wicked-looking dagger. "I woulda liked to see Campbell blood on me knife."

"Me too. Pity they all ran."

Caroline felt Gavin's hand tighten on her shoulder and instinctively leaned closer to him. His rock-hard body felt comforting suddenly. What would these men do if they knew her last name? She didn't have anything to do with what was happening in this time period, but this episode she was having was spinning completely out of her control.

She saw Shamus eyeing her speculatively. Was he going to tell the MacDonalds who she was in spite of Gavin's warning look? Shamus finally looked away and Caroline realized how much authority Gavin had. She also understood why he'd told the MacDonalds she was his mistress…for her protection. Or, at least, she hoped it was.

"I suspect Colonel Anne might have had a bit to do with it?" Gavin asked.

Calum grinned. "Aye. The lady managed to scare off well over a thousand of Loudoun's men with her household staff banging pots and pans while hiding in the bushes. 'Tis a good thing too that the prince's retinue includes so many clans. The servants yelled their war cries while firing muskets from different directions."

"So the damn earl thought he was outnumbered?" Shamus asked.

"Aye. By the time we got there, the English were already retreating. We just made them run faster." Calum took a swig of whisky. "If Campbell had known Colonel Anne had only a few men—"

"Campbells are cowards," Shamus said.

Caroline kept her face impassive. Now was not the time to argue the point. Instead, she tried to remember her history on Culloden, but could only recall that there was a Jacobite lady who was a fighter.

"That's one fine woman," one of Calum's men said.

"Pity she's married," another added.

Someone in the group snickered. "Course, her husband is nae there."

"The woman might be in need of a good swiving, then," Shamus said. "Too bad I wasna there to accommodate her."

Gavin gave him a disapproving look. "Anne would probably accommodate ye with the handle of one of her pistols to the side of your head."

Caroline almost smiled. She had only seen a brief mention in an obscure book regarding Anne Mackintosh, but she had a feeling she would like her. In this time period it was rare for a woman to even be listened to, let alone have authority.

In this time period. Caroline turned her thoughts inward as the conversation around her drifted to boasts of past victories and battles to come. This hallucination felt different from the others. In those, she had drifted lazily along with no effort, much like someone just prior to waking having disjointed dreams that seem very real. She'd also had a vague sense of well-being, as though nothing could hurt her. Nor had all of her senses been engaged like they were now. The men around her looked three-dimensional, as did the surroundings. Caroline could actually smell the peat on her clothes and taste the acridness of the smoke on her tongue. Her ears even distinguished the slight difference in the burr of the MacDonalds and that of the MacLeans. For certain, she could feel the warmth and solidness of the man she was leaning against.

She'd never before put herself into a situation like this. Caroline tried to organize her thoughts. She knew who she was. She recollected riding the train home, determined not to think about Christmas in Minnesota. She remembered she'd been reading about the Jacobite Rising in which Scotland was planning to return a Stuart king to the throne. She also recalled thinking how she wished she could warn the Scots that their efforts would be in vain and they would lose everything they held dear. Then she'd dozed off in her chair and awoken here.

Here. With a start that made her blood feel like ice in her veins, she realized she wasn't having an episode. This was *real*. She was living and breathing in the year 1746, and she was surrounded by Highland warriors.

Somehow, she had managed to travel back in time. Was it possible that she could change the tide of history and prevent the massacre at Culloden from happening? If these men listened to Colonel Anne, might they listen to Caroline as well? She couldn't tell them she was from the future lest they thought her a lunatic, and she wasn't quite sure what they did with lunatics in this century, but maybe she could help unobtrusively.

"Well, lass?"

With a start, she realized Gavin was speaking to her. She also noted the men had stopped talking and were finding spots to lie down for the night. "Yes?"

Gavin smiled and rose, wrapping strong, warm fingers around her hand as he brought her along up with him. "'Tis time we go to bed."

Caroline started. She'd almost forgotten his prior claim that she was his mistress. Sweet saints. What was she going to do? He towered over her. Her head barely came up to his broad shoulders, and she didn't need to see the bulge of biceps in his arms to know his strength. She could feel it in his hand holding hers. Even if she managed to break away, where would she run? She had no idea where she was other than in Scotland. Besides, running would be futile with more than twenty men in camp. She'd be brought down like a fox being chased by baying hounds. She felt herself begin to hyperventilate and then the air whooshed out of her as she felt herself suddenly being picked up.

"Relax, lass," Gavin said.

But all she could hear were the sounds of the men laughing behind them as he carried her away.

Chapter Three

Gavin knew picking up the lass and carrying her away from the campfire was a big mistake the minute he lifted her. Holding her body so intimately close to his, feeling the soft, satiny texture of her skin, and inhaling the scent of roses wafting from her hair ignited a fire in him…and not the kind of fiery passion that usually burned in him after a victorious rout such as tonight had been.

He really had no choice, he told himself, but to be holding her. Caroline had turned white as fresh snow and looked ready to bolt at the suggestion of going to his bed. In its own way, that intrigued him, since lasses were usually more than willing, but tupping Caroline was not his intention. He couldn't take the chance she would refuse. If any of the men thought she was not his mistress—that he had no claim on her—she would be as vulnerable as a camp follower. If the MacDonalds found out she was a Campbell, she might not survive the night on her own.

Gavin set her down by the small tent out of range of the campfire. Away from the light of the flames, its dark canvas blended in with the night. Usually a second man kept watch from this angle where he would be hidden in case intruders raided the camp, but tonight Caroline would use the tent.

He held the flap open for her. "Ye will have some

privacy in here."

She peered in and then up at him. "I will be alone?"

"Nae, lass. I will sleep with ye."

She frowned. "I know you're probably used to having your way with women, but should I not have a choice?"

"Nae." He saw the flare of fear—or maybe anger—in her eyes, quickly squelched. "I mean, aye."

"Which is it?"

Her voice sounded steady, but Gavin noted the slight tremble to the hand she put to her throat, instinctively covering her breasts as she did. He felt like a dimwitted lout. "What I meant was that ye have nothing to fear from me, lass. I have never forced a woman and I willna do so now." She looked slightly appeased and he went on, "For your protection, 'tis better the men think ye are my mistress. They willna believe it if I sleep outside."

Caroline worried her bottom lip and Gavin found himself watching in fascination as her even, white teeth sucked the plump, soft lip inside her mouth and then released it, moisture glistening in the dim light. May Saint Andrew—better yet, make that an archangel—help him. Being confined with Caroline in such a small, private space was going to require a tremendous reserve of willpower on his part. Animal lust from his shifting had not completely left his body yet, but she had been sent to him for healing. He could not take advantage of her. He needed to remember that. "Ye may rest easy, lass. Now, please enter before the men get suspicious."

She hesitated only a minute and then did as he asked. He dipped down to follow her inside, then took one of the two folded tartans lying inside and spread it across the small area. "This will be more comfortable than grass."

Caroline sat down and looked around. "I'd probably rest easier if that big wolfhound who followed us here would make an appearance. He'd be protection."

Gavin almost choked at the irony of his alter shape protecting Caroline from himself. Of course he couldn't tell her they were one and the same. He normally shifted to a much smaller dog—one that could easily slink unnoticed into enemy camps and listen to plans being made—but the background information he had been given said her husband had owned a wolfhound and Gavin thought appearing to her in that form would create a bond. He smiled when he remembered how protective Caroline had been when the vase had been thrown at him.

"I'm sure the beast is close by," he said as he sat down beside her.

"Is he yours?"

"In a manner of speaking. He belongs to the clan. The men call him Cathal."

"That's a strange name."

Gavin smiled again. "It means 'strong in battle' in Gaelic."

Caroline gave him a tentative smile back. "That makes sense, I suppose. The dogs were trained to hunt and bring down wolves, so why not enemies in battle?"

"Ye seem to understand the breed."

"My husband had one."

Gavin eyed her, wondering how much she remembered about her past. He could hardly come out and ask. "Ye are married?"

"I…I'm a widow."

"I am sorry. How did he die?"

"I...he was killed in battle."

Gavin wanted to ask which battle to determine how much she could recall, but Caroline appeared uneasy, like she wanted to bolt again. The last thing he needed was to have her run from the tent. "I am sorry," he said again and then lay back to stretch out on the ground. "Ye had better get some rest. We will be riding at dawn."

She gave him a speculative look as if to assess the amount of danger he posed. For the first time in his life, he wished he didn't look so intimidating. His size and strength served him well in battle, but not with a lass as skittish as a filly with her first halter. He stayed as quiet as he could. Finally, Caroline must have decided he was the lesser of two evils and lay down as well, careful not to touch him.

Gavin sighed. It was going to be a long, long night.

****

Men moving about woke Caroline from the partial dozing she'd finally fallen into after listening to Gavin's steady, deep breathing for what seemed like hours. It was still dark, but she remembered Gavin saying they would be riding at dawn. Caroline turned over, half-expecting to see him in the dim light, but the tent was empty. She wondered why she wasn't cold because she could distinctly remember Gavin's body heat warming her last night, even though they hadn't touched—he had kept his word on that. Then she noticed he'd covered her with the second tartan. All that wool made it seem warm as midsummer inside the tiny tent.

Caroline sat up and ran her fingers through her hair, trying to dislodge the tangles amongst the curls. She didn't have a comb, so it was the best she could do. She was still wearing her nightgown and fleecy robe, too.

The attire might have served to support the idea she was Gavin's eager mistress last night—her cheeks warmed as she recalled that conversation—but how could she go traipsing through Scotland without proper clothes?

She still wasn't sure how she'd managed to travel over two hundred and fifty years into the past, either. Trying to come to terms with that had kept her awake most of the night. Caroline shook her head. She shouldn't try to delude herself. Gavin—his closeness—had kept her awake most of the night, but trying to make sense of being in the 1700s also kept her mind spinning. If she were conjuring up this whole thing, it was a far cry from the other episodes she'd had. For now, though, she would remember what her doctor had said and stop trying to understand something that should be impossible.

As she started to crawl out of the tent, she noticed a linen tunic and a plaid, neatly folded, just inside the tent flap. Gavin must have put them there for her. Saying a silent prayer of thanks, Caroline quickly changed. His tunic came to her knees and she had to fold the sleeves back several times, but it was much better than going about in nightclothes. Caroline unwrapped the long strip of plaid, trying to figure out how the men wore theirs. She hadn't realized it was near to an art form to arrange the kilt. When she finished, she was sure the whole thing was lopsided, but at least she was covered. The black satin ballet slippers she'd worn with her night robe would have to do. At least, they weren't big and fuzzy.

Once she left the tent, the first thing Caroline noticed was that there were more men in the camp. Lots more. Perhaps another twenty. When had they arrived? How could she not have heard them approach with all those horses? She looked more closely. The new arrivals were drinking from flasks as they sat around the fire. Surely they weren't drinking whisky at this hour of the morning? Dawn was just beginning to break. She looked around for Gavin and spotted him talking to Calum and a blond newcomer, dressed rather elaborately in contrast to the rest of the men. They stood several feet away from the others.

As if he felt her attention, Gavin turned his head and looked directly at her. His eyebrows lifted and a corner of his mouth quirked up. His companions stopped talking and followed his gaze.

In fact, most of the conversation had stopped as eyes turned toward her. Caroline resisted the urge to crawl back into the tent, but she suddenly felt as vulnerable as a snared rabbit facing a pack of hungry wolves.

Gavin said something to the men and quickly made his way to her, giving her an encouraging smile as he put an arm around her shoulder. Caroline wasn't sure if the gesture was protective or territorial, but at the moment she didn't care. He felt good.

"When did all these other men get here?" she asked.

"About an hour ago. Doona fash. Ye will be safe. They are nae staying long."

"Why are they here?" Caoline asked, still feeling wary. "I know you said we would be riding at dawn—"

"That plan has changed, at least for me. There was a rout last night at Moy Hall and the English were turned back." Gavin replied and pointed toward the new arrivals. "Those are MacGillivrays. They're advancing on Inverness castle this morning along with the prince. They just stopped to gather more men."

"The prince? You mean Charles Edward Stuart?"

"Aye." Gavin gestured toward the light-haired man. "That's him over there."

Caroline stared and then tried not to. She was actually in the presence of Bonnie Prince Charlie. The grandson of James II, who'd been exiled because of his religion and belief in the divine right of kings. Caroline could recall the history as though she had an open book in front of her. The English might call him the Young Pretender, but this was the Stuart that Scotland wanted to reclaim the throne from the Hanoverians. The only claim the House of Hanover had to the British throne was the slim thread of the first King George being the son of a granddaughter of James I.

She stole another glimpse at the prince, who was already walking away, followed by nearly every man in the camp. He was slender, even with the armored breastplate he wore. The bright blue sash nearly covered one shoulder. He was of average height, but surrounded by Highlanders the prince looked more like a boy than an adult. Although, if she remembered correctly, Prince Charles would be in his mid-twenties.

"Should you not be going with them?" she asked Gavin.

"I cannot leave you unprotected."

Caroline gave him a tentative smile. "I won't run away. I know I'm your hostage."

He grimaced. "Consider yourself more of a guest, lass."

"Albeit it one who can't leave?" Not that she had any idea of where to go, but perhaps it was best not to let Gavin know that.

"A Campbell—let alone a female one—this far north would not fare well if caught."

Caroline tilted her head at him. "But you—well, your men—captured me."

"Better us than a clan who has cause to hate Campbells."

"Like the MacDonalds? They can't possibly think I had anything to do with what happened at Glen Coe."

"If ye did, ye'd be an old crone by now." Gavin's mouth turned up at one corner. "I can assure ye that ye are quite a bonny lass."

Caroline felt her cheeks warm. She hadn't been fishing for a compliment, although she was pleased he thought her pretty. "What I meant was that my family didn't have anything to do with the orders given."

Gavin gave her a curious look. "Loudoun is an indirect descendant of Robert Campbell, who was in command at Glen Coe. Ye were a guest of Loudoun's."

She couldn't very well tell Gavin she had no idea of how she had gotten there, so she pounced on one word he'd spoken. "*Indirect* descendant. I'm an even more distant relative." Like over three hundred years, but she couldn't tell Gavin that either. "After more than half a century, can't the MacDonalds forgive and forget?"

Gavin shook his head. "Scots have long memories. We still think about revenge against the Livingstons for the Earl of Douglas's Black Supper, and that happened in 1440."

"It's a wonder any of the clans get along at all," Caroline said wryly.

"Aye. There is truth in that," Gavin answered, "but one thing we all agree on, and that is we want the English out of Scotland."

She sensed the tenseness in Gavin, even though his words were not harsh. He wanted to join the fight.

Shamus had called him laird. "I promise I won't leave camp if you need to lead your men."

He gave a lingering look after his disappearing clansmen and then shook his head. "My men will follow Calum until I can join them. My duty is to get ye to Moy Hall. Prince Charles has reinforcements waiting on the main road. With Lord Loudoun on the run, it shouldn't be hard to take Inverness."

Caroline knew they would win that victory without bloodshed. It was future battles she worried about. There would not be another Stuart on the throne. Once Gavin had taken her to Moy Hall, would she be able to dissuade any of the Scots from fighting?

Was there any way she could prevent Culloden from happening and save thousands of lives? Was that why she was here?

Chapter Four

Gavin tried to think of which battle strategies would be used to capture the garrison at Inverness as he rode with Caroline toward Moy Hall, but his mind focused only on the woman who sat across his thighs. She molded to him perfectly as he braced her back with one arm while the other brushed her lap as he tended the reins. He had difficulty keeping his eyes off the amount of exposed leg dangling from beneath the tunic and tartan as well.

He bit back a smile as he remembered seeing Caroline emerge from the tent earlier, his shirt hanging to her knees and the tartan lumpy and lopsided as though she'd slept in it. With her long coppery hair tangled and mussed, she gave the appearance of having spent a rather active night inside the tent. He'd been tempted to straighten the tartan's pleats for her, but decided it might be better to let the other men draw their own conclusions. For her own protection of course.

"What are you smiling about?" Caroline asked as she gazed up at him.

He looked into her eyes, which was a mistake. This morning, their color was the clear green-blue of the sea on a sunny day. Gavin had the feeling he could very well drown in their depths if he lingered too long.

"I was just thinking the MacLean colors suit ye."

"Better than the Campbells'?"

Gavin grinned. "Aye. For sure."

She didn't return the smile. "This place you are taking me…Moy Hall. Do they hate Campbells too?"

"Ye will be tolerated there."

One of Caroline's eyebrows rose. "Tolerated?"

"Aye." Gavin maneuvered the horse around a tree branch that lay in the road. "The MacKintosh household is a wee bit mixed."

"Like how?"

"Ye heard us speak of Colonel Anne last eve, nae?" When she nodded, he continued. "She is a Jacobite. On her own, she recruited nearly eight hundred men to fight for Prince Charles."

"How did she manage to do that?"

Gavin smiled. "She is a very bonny and very persuasive lady."

Caroline frowned. "You called her colonel."

"Aye. 'Tis an honorary title. Women are nae allowed to command regiments, so Alexander MacGillivray leads them. 'Tis his men ye saw earlier at the camp."

"The MacGillivrays don't hate Campbells, then?"

"Och, aye they do."

"You are not making any sense. If this Anne person—and the soldiers she recruited—fight for the prince and hate the Campbells, how will I be tolerated at her home?" Caroline tilted her head back to look at him more fully. "Or do you have some kind of personal influence with Colonel Anne?"

Gavin wondered if there was a slight edge to Caroline's voice or if he had just imagined it. She sounded piqued. For some odd reason, that made him want to smile again, although he managed not to. "She is a friend."

"And that's why she will tolerate me?"

Gavin shook his head. "First of all, she will tolerate ye because ye will be Caroline Chisholm, nae Campbell, and ye will have been a servant at the house where we found ye, nae a guest."

"So I am assuming a false identity? Your men know who I am. What happens if Anne finds out the truth?"

"I will handle my men. 'Tis nae Anne I am concerned about but the others who willna be so tolerant."

"That is the second time you used the word 'tolerant.' Why would Anne be such?"

"Because her husband is a captain in the Black Watch."

Caroline stared at him. "The Black Watch is part of the *English* army."

"Aye. Ye have the right of it. Angus MacKintosh is stationed at the garrison under the command of John Campbell, Lord Loudoun."

Caroline's mouth dropped open and then a look of confusion crossed her face. "But aren't your men—*her* men—on their way to capture the fort?"

"Aye."

"I don't understand. Does she hate her husband?"

"I doona think so."

"Then why would she send men to fight him?"

Gavin shrugged. 'He is on the wrong side.'

Caroline knit her brows. "But how can they live together if they are on opposite sides?"

"'Tis a wee bit awkward, I'll admit, but Angus MacKintosh is the laird of his clan and Anne is the daughter of the Farquharson chief. 'Tis better for them to tolerate each other's differences in regard to England than to have war between the clans." Gavin pointed down the road. "Ye can see Moy Hall now. We will be there soon." He gave Caroline a smile. "Doona fash. Anne will take ye in."

"I think I know how Daniel felt when he was about to be thrown into the lion's den," Caroline said.

"Did an angel nae protect Daniel?" Gavin asked.

"According to the story." Caroline tried to return his smile. "Are you saying Anne is an angel?"

Gavin laughed. "Nae. I doona think anyone has ever called her that."

Caroline squared her shoulders. "I hope she believes I am a Chisholm."

Gavin stroked her back, almost unaware that he did so. "I will explain things before I leave."

"Thank you." Caroline looked toward the trees along one side of the road. "I'd feel better if that wolfhound were about to show himself right now. I felt like I had a friend, even if he was a four-legged one."

Gavin cleared his throat. "I'm sure he will be along soon."

****

Caroline still felt apprehensive when they rode through the gates and into the courtyard at the front of a large, rectangular stone-and-wood house. It wasn't a castle, but the high walls surrounding it certainly would protect it from raids or, as in last night's case, from the English army as well. Caroline was curious as to what kind of woman Colonel Anne was. *Very bonny,* Gavin had said. He hadn't answered Caroline's question about whether he had influence over the lady. With her husband stationed at Inverness, how did she entertain men when she was alone? How did she manage not to get herself arrested for treason? *Very persuasive*, Gavin had also said.

They had just dismounted when the heavy oaken door to the house swung open and a petite, auburn-haired young woman came rushing out.

"Gavin! Did something go wrong?" she asked and then stopped when she saw Caroline, giving her a curious look.

Caroline tried not to stare, but she didn't have much more luck than she'd had with the prince in that regard. The lady was wearing men's pants with a white linen shirt tucked neatly inside and a tartan sash flung over one shoulder. Gavin had been right. Anne was very pretty. Her hair was a deeper shade of red than Caroline's and her eyes a bit more blue, but they shared the same coloring. Was it Anne Gavin had been thinking of when he'd told Caroline she was bonny?

"Nothing is wrong, Anne," Gavin replied. "Prince Charles picked up my men on his way to Inverness. I will be right behind them." He gestured to Caroline. "I wanted to drop my mistress off here to be sure she was safe."

Caroline had been so intent in scrutinizing Anne MacKintosh that what Gavin said almost didn't register. Then her face warmed as she remembered she was supposed to be his adoring mistress.

One of Anne's eyebrows rose. "You've never brought a mistress here before."

Gavin put an arm around Caroline's shoulders and drew her close. "Well, this one is verra special. Her name is Caroline Chisholm."

A part of her wanted to resist. She didn't much like

being touted as his mistress, although she understood Gavin's reasoning. To his credit, at least he said she was special. But that still made her feel like a second-class citizen. It probably didn't matter since women had no rights in the seventeenth century anyhow. She was thinking in twenty-first century terms. In a very ironical way that any modern feminist would have found appalling, mistresses and lemans did have a social standing of sorts, depending on the status of the man who claimed them.

But this wasn't London society. Caroline was looking at a woman whom men called "Colonel." A woman who had recruited hundreds of men to fight for the prince. How would Anne judge her?

"Caroline was a servant at the garrison's guesthouse and a good informant," Gavin went on, apparently deciding to enhance his story. "But when we raided last night, hoping to catch Loudoun before he set off for here, I realized the lass would be in danger since she was the one who left the door unlocked for us. I couldna take the chance she had been seen."

"I suppose not," Anne said, but she sounded skeptical.

Caroline couldn't blame her for that. The story sounded a little fantastical even to her ears, but it was clever of him to have a reason for bringing her along—besides being his mistress.

"What happened last night?" Gavin asked Anne. "I knew the prince would be safe because your mother-in-law sent young Lauchlan to warn ye, but how did ye manage to turn back fifteen hundred English soldiers with just a handful of men?"

Anne laughed. "It wasn't even a handful. There

were only five…and they were servants, nae soldiers."

"What?" He gave her an incredulous look. "How—
"

"By being resourceful. I gave my smith, Fraser, and four others pistols and told them to hide in the bushes, each firing at a different time and then to move around and fire from different positions."

Gavin smiled. "So the English would think there was a large army prepared to do battle?"

"Aye." Anne shrugged. "It helped that my people were calling loudly for MacDonalds and Camerons to advance as well as the prince's lords Lochiel and Keppoch to flank Loudoun's men."

"So Campbell thought he was facing the Highland army." Gavin's smile broke into a wide grin. "Ye accomplished the rout with just five men. If Campbell ever finds out, he'll be so mortified he might voluntarily exile himself to France."

"I doubt it." Anne shrugged again. "I dinna ken if my husband rode with Loudoun last night or not, and I dinna want Angus killed."

Angus was the MacKintosh chief, Caroline remembered. Anne must truly care for her husband if she went to such measures to protect him. Caroline tried to remember this particular part of history. For some reason, Colonel Anne's story was not one she'd read about. But then, much of history was written by men who weren't particularly willing to admit women played strong, even pivotal, roles.

"Well, I'd best be going if I want to catch up with my men before all the fun is over," Gavin said as he drew Caroline closer and bent down to nuzzle her neck. "Keep the bed warm for me, will ye, lass?" He winked and without waiting for her answer, vaulted onto his horse.

Caroline opened her mouth, but no words came out. She was stunned by how his warm breath had tickled her ear and by how soft and gentle his lips had been as he pressed a kiss to her nape. Saints alive, a tingle had shot straight to her belly.

"Ye look a wee bit bewildered," Anne said as Gavin galloped off. "Does the mon nae kiss ye often enough?"

Caroline blinked and refocused. She'd been standing there like some smitten preteen who'd just seen a boy-band rock star. She was supposed to be an accomplished lover, for heaven's sake. Anne's look was openly curious. Caroline would have to be careful since she suspected not much escaped Anne's notice. "Gavin is always surprising me."

"A fine trait…" Anne started to say, but was interrupted when a buxom, blonde maid came hurrying toward them.

"Has he gone already?" the girl asked, looking disappointed.

"Aye, Elsa. Laird MacLean had to join his men."

"But he kens…" She let her voice trail off as she looked at Caroline. "Who are ye?"

"This is Miss Chisholm," Anne replied. "She is a…an acquaintance of Laird MacLean."

Elsa scowled. "Why are ye here?"

"She is my guest," Anne answered firmly. "Please go back inside and see that the blue room is made up for her."

"Aye, my lady," Elsa said, although she still glowered as she turned away.

Caroline had a sinking feeling in her stomach. "Elsa seems to be somewhat enthralled with Gavin."

"Aye, she feels he favors her with conversation when he is here." Anne smiled. "But then, Gavin favors all of the maids with words."

She wondered what else he favored them with. Did Elsa have some reason for thinking what she did? Caroline surprised herself at feeling a nip of jealousy. Why would she care whom Gavin favored? Just because he had protected her from his own men as well as the MacDoanlds didn't mean anything other than concern for her welfare. He hadn't touched her, even by accident, in the tent last night. The snuggle just now had been for Anne's benefit. Caroline needed to remember their role-playing was just that and nothing more. "Thank you for not explaining the circumstances."

"Aye. 'Tis better to use a wee bit of discretion, at least for now," Anne said. "'Tis up to Gavin how much he wants the household to ken."

"I agree."

"Gavin said your last name was Chisholm?" Anne said as they turned to walk toward the house. "Ye sound English."

Drat. Now what was she supposed to say? She wished Gavin had shared more of the background she was supposed to have. "I...I grew up in Berwick. The town has changed hands between the Scots and English many times, so I suppose I do sound more English than Scots."

Anne gave her a sideways look. "Clan Chisholm doesna live around Berwick."

Drat again. Caroline was horrible at lying, or even ad-libbing. "I...I was fostered with other kin."

Anne opened the door and gestured for Caroline to precede her. "Ye sound educated as well."

Caroline felt like she was becoming entangled in a very sticky web not of her making. She was reminded of Sir Walter Scott's *What a tangled web we weave, when first we practice to deceive* except that he wouldn't be writing those words for another sixty-plus years. Which, of course, was neither here nor there, but her thoughts were running helter-skelter. "My mother insisted I learn to read and write." That much was true at least.

"Aye, such skills would serve ye well as an informant," Anne said and paused at the foot of the stairs. "You probably would like to rest. Your bedchamber will be the second door on the right, next to the room Gavin uses when he's here."

"Yes, thank you, I would," Caroline answered and started up the steps. She wasn't sure which rattled her nerves more…that she'd be next door to Gavin or that she could feel Anne's eyes trained on her back.

Caroline suspected the woman knew she was lying, but what would Anne do about it?

Chapter Five

As Gavin and his men returned to Moy Hall later that evening, he felt apprehensive about seeing Caroline again. What in the world had possessed him to so intimately caress her neck with his mouth that morning? She hadn't resisted, but he'd felt her stiffen and he hadn't missed the look of shock on her face. Even though he'd wanted to impress upon anyone watching from the windows that Caroline was under his protection, he probably shouldn't have taken that approach. But by all that was sacred, he wanted to do it again.

Part of the problem was that his inner beast was only half-civilized. Even though Gavin chose to shift to domesticated animals instead of feral ones, the beast's spirit lived within him and it wanted to act on instinct. On the ride back, the wolfhound had gnawed at the edges of his mind, whining to materialize so it could be petted by Caroline again. That longing had grown stronger the closer they came to Moy Hall. As they rode through the gate, Gavin gave a firm mental nudge to the dog and forced himself to think rationally.

How would Caroline react to him this evening?

After seeing to his horse, Gavin pulled a fresh tunic from his saddle bag and took the time to strip his shirt and wash in the horse trough outside the barn to rid himself of the dust of the road. In clean clothes, wet hair slicked back, he made his way to the back door and through the kitchen. Caroline and Anne were probably already seated for dinner.

"Are ye nae going to stop and say hello?" Elsa asked him as he walked toward the hall and dining room.

She tugged at her bodice as she made her way to him, throwing her shoulders back to accentuate her breasts and giving him a full view of them half-exposed. Normally, he would have indulged in a bit of flirtation, but tonight he could only think about who awaited him. "Hello," he said, smiling briefly, but not pausing. He also ignored Elsa's pout. A lot of women were attracted to him because they sensed his inner beast, only half-tamed. While there were times he valued that benefit, at other times it felt more like a curse.

As he entered the dining room, Anne looked up from her chair at the head of the table. Alexander MacGillivray was already seated to her right and Caroline to her left, which placed her back to Gavin. He paused a minute to take in the beauty of her long coppery hair flowing loose and unbraided. He wished he could see her face so he could capture her emotions.

"Come in," Anne said. "We were just about to get started."

"I hope I'm nae late," Gavin replied and took the chair next to Caroline's. She gave him a sideways glance and he was tempted to repeat his performance from this morning, if only for the sake of MacGillivray watching, but Gavin didn't want to embarrass Caroline. He contented himself with lifting her hand and turning it over to place a kiss on her palm. Her eyes widened, but she didn't pull away. Reluctantly, he released her hand.

"I was just telling Anne how successful we were today," Alexander said. "With Campbell retreating to the

Black Isle, the soldiers left at the garrison didna have much taste for blood."

"Aye. 'Twas a coup without bloodshed," Gavin agreed and then glanced at Anne. She wore a pinched expression and he said, as gently as he could, "As far as we could tell, Angus went with Campbell."

She nodded. "I am glad he was nae hurt."

"I'm glad also that your husband is safe," Caroline said. "There's always a horrible chance they won't come home."

"That is always the fear," Anne replied.

Caroline looked pensive. "Sometimes I wonder if it's worth the risk."

Gavin glanced at her. When he'd been given this assignment, he'd been told her husband had been killed in battle. He knew she'd grieved long.

"'Tis the way of it. War is war," Alexander said. "If we doona fight for what we believe in, we are cowards."

"I don't mean to imply that," Caroline answered, "but look what happened at Dunbar. King Edward massacred the entire town, women and children too."

Alexander's jaw set. "Which is one more reminder why we Scots fight."

"But for the women whose men don't come home…" Caroline stopped and then sighed. "It is hard."

"Those who are left behind have their own battles," Gavin said. "They may not be on the battlefield and there may be no blood let, but the fight to live again is just as hard."

Caroline looked at him and frowned. "I hadn't thought of it that way."

"I suspect each of us has our own battles," Anne said. "Some are just not as visible as others."

"Well, then," Alexander said, lifting his wine glass as Elsa brought in bowls of soup. "A toast to today's coup where no one was killed."

"Aye," Gavin replied and lifted his glass and touched the rim to Caroline's. He looked deeply into her eyes, willing himself not to sink into the depths of them. "A toast to survivors everywhere."

****

Survivor. Yes, she was that, Caroline thought as she took a sip of wine in response to the toast. Her psychiatrist had helped her through the stages of grief, and she had moved into the final phase of acceptance some time ago. That still didn't make it easier to trust life. There were no guarantees. Even though she had grown more and more lonely over the past year, she didn't know if she could bear her heart breaking again should she allow someone past her emotional shields.

What she *could* do, though, was try to prevent other lives from being senselessly taken. No one here knew how disastrous the final battle of Culloden would be.

Caroline was about to take a second sip of wine when Elsa placed a soup bowl in front of her, nearly knocking the wine glass out of Caroline's hand. Wine splashed on the table and soup sloshed over the bowl's rim, but luckily none of it landed on Caroline.

"Do be careful, Elsa," Anne said.

"Yes, my lady," Elsa replied and then grudgingly added, "It was clumsy of me."

"It is all right," Caroline said, using her napkin to soak up the liquid. "I should have been more aware."

Elsa ignored her and moved on. She leaned so close over Gavin's shoulder that Caroline was pretty sure the girl's breast brushed against him. She remembered Anne saying Elsa thought Gavin favored her. Did he?

Caroline glanced sideways, but his expression had not changed nor had he said anything more than a perfunctory thank you to the maid. Still, it was probably just as well Elsa had not been in the room when Gavin kissed Caroline's palm. Sikes, but the feel of his warm, firm lips had turned her tummy to mush and caused her thighs to quiver. She'd no idea how sensitive her palm could be. Even now, the feel of that kiss still lingered in her memory, but maybe that was because she also had another recent memory of Gavin at the horse trough. Just before coming down to dinner, Caroline had looked out her bedroom window in time to see Gavin strip his shirt and plunge his head and shoulders into the water. Muscles had rippled across his broad back and when he'd straightened and reached for his tunic, water dribbled along the hard planes of his chest and dribbled down the ridges of his belly. The man could have been sculpted out of marble. Saints alive, but she'd almost forgotten how beautiful a male body could be.

"Are ye gathering wool?" Gavin asked.

Caroline turned to him. "What?"

"'Tis a saying. Ye looked as though ye had your mind elsewhere."

She could feel the heat of a blush spread over her cheeks. The angels have mercy! She couldn't tell him where her mind had been or what it had been focusing on. Gavin's intense look wasn't helping any, and Caroline was sure her face must look afire. "I…I was just thinking over the events of the day."

"I imagine it has been quite trying for you," Anne said as Elsa and several other maids brought in a platter of meat and various side bowls. "You can rest easy now.

You are safe here, and I doubt anyone will come looking for you now that Lord Loudoun has gone."

Alexander looked perplexed. "Why would anyone from the garrison come looking for the lass?"

"She was a servant there who served as an informant for the Jacobites," Anne answered. "Such a position is risky."

Alexander frowned. "Shamus said she was MacLean's mis—"

"*Miss* Chisholm is under my protection," Gavin said firmly.

Elsa gave her a dark look. Caroline wondered if it was because Elsa didn't like the idea of Gavin's protection, or if the girl had actually understood the inference that Alexander almost made about being Gavin's mistress. She had been given the room next to him, after all.

Luckily, another maid served Caroline's food. Given Elsa's glowering expression, Caroline wasn't too sure Elsa wouldn't have had another accident which would have successfully landed in Caroline's lap.

"Well, then," Alexander said, still looking somewhat puzzled but apparently taking his clue from Gavin, "Miss Chisholm is indeed fortunate to have found a…benefactor, given the circumstances."

"Yes," Caroline replied. At least Shamus had not told Alexander MacGillivray that she was a Campbell. "I am quite thankful." The words were no sooner out of her mouth when she realized how being quite thankful could be interpreted.

She glanced quickly at Gavin. He watched her with darkening eyes and a slow, easy smile played on his lips. "I am glad that is how you feel."

She looked away just as quickly, feeling her cheeks warm again. She wasn't exactly sure how he meant that. She certainly was not going to ask, but she doubted she'd be getting much sleep tonight, even tired as she was.

His bedchamber had a connecting door to hers. She didn't recall if it had a lock on it or not, but she suspected if he chose to enter, a lock wouldn't stop him. Given her own strong physical reactions to him—sensations she hadn't felt in three years—not to mention the image of him half-naked by the horse trough earlier, made her wonder if she'd really mind if he did open the door.

Was that what she wanted?

Thousands of Scots were doomed to die at Culloden, unless she could somehow persuade them to stop this campaign. Gavin MacLean would more than likely command one of the charges that would lead to his death. She did not want to—*could not*—allow herself to feel anything for him.

But her body was rebelling against her tightly reined-in thoughts. Caroline felt Gavin watching her and looked up. She gasped at the hungry look in his eyes that had no need for the food on the table. She felt her eyes widen as a pleasant warmth spread to her belly.. She had quite forgotten how strong physical desire could be. Until now.

****

Gavin nearly spilled his wine when Caroline told MacGillivray she was very thankful to have a benefactor. He knew very well she didn't mean an innuendo with the remark, but his wayward body was thinking along a different line. He watched a soft pink blush spread over Caroline's cheeks as mesmerized as if a snake charmer held a cobra out in front of him.

231

Handling a cobra might be safer than where his thoughts were headed. While he had been gone for the day, a transformation of sorts had taken place with Caroline. Under the light of the dining room chandelier, her hair glowed coppery and gold. His oversize tunic and tartan were gone, replaced with a watered silk gown that shimmered in shades of blue and green, matching the changing color of her eyes. No doubt it was one of Anne's dresses since she didn't wear breeches all of the time, but it fit Caroline perfectly, the soft fabric clinging to her curves. The neckline was cut modestly—another trait that Anne liked—and showed just a hint of cleavage. Oddly enough, Gavin thought it more intriguing when such lovely assets were mostly hidden than when they were half-exposed. And lovely assets they were, soft and plump and perfect for the size of his hand. Recalling how her derrière had fit so firmly against his thighs while in the saddle didn't help in refocusing his mind on what he should be concentrating on—healing her soul, not ravaging her body.

Never had he had such a strong desire to mate with a mortal. His mission was to ease her wounded heart into opening again, allowing her to love again. Passion was part of that, but he had been given no directive to kindle that flame.

But then, he'd had no directive not to do so. After all, to truly love was to give all of oneself to another. Wasn't it? Gavin had never been in such a situation before, but his observations of humans led him to believe that was true. Would he be allowed…?

Outside, thunder rumbled.

"Oh, dear. I wonder if we're in for a storm tonight," Anne said.

Only if he didn't stop his base thoughts. Gavin knew a warning when he heard one. "The sky to the west was clear when we rode in."

"But it doesn't take long for the weather to change," Anne replied, "especially this time of year."

Alexander nodded. "Doona fash. The storms move in fast, but they move out quickly."

Unless Gavin kept up the fanciful drivel in his mind. The heavens might do far more than toss a passing storm their way if he violated his mission. He tried to concentrate on the victory they'd had this day.

But to the victor go the spoils. No doubt his men and MacGillivray's were already enjoying the attention of willing wenches plying them with smooth whisky in the soldiers' quarters. He let his gaze return to Caroline. She caught his look and he felt himself stop breathing just as her breasts lifted with a sharp intake of air on her part. Did her eyes just widen and darken? Did she want him as much as he wanted her? He knew there was no lock on the connecting door between them.

A lightning bolt flashed brilliant white outside the window.

Gavin sighed. The door would be staying closed for tonight, but it was going to be another long, sleepless night.

He would need to get used to those now that Caroline had come into his life.

Chapter Six

Caroline had lain awake most of the night, first listening to the sounds of Gavin going into his bedchamber, then wondering if the door between them would open. She wasn't sure if she waited in apprehension or anticipation.

Either way, nothing happened. The chamber next door had grown quiet and stayed that way. The thunder and lightning had stopped as well, leaving only a whisper of wind through the trees. Caroline had finally drifted into a fitful sleep punctuated with dreams of battlefields, men being hewn down, and Gavin leading a charge.

She slept late, and by the time she went downstairs for breakfast, the small, informal room used for family dining was empty, save for Elsa removing plates. She wasn't exactly the first person Caroline wanted to encounter. From the sour expression on the maid's face, the feeling was probably mutual.

Caroline went to the sideboard where chafing dishes had kept the morning food warm. The candles were extinguished. leaving cold porridge, a strip of ham, and some scraps of coddled eggs in various dishes. She thought she saw a smirk on Elsa's face, but she wasn't sure. The maid did not offer to replenish anything. Caroline helped herself to a scone from a plate and chided herself for sleeping in.

"Do you know where I might find Mrs.

MacKintosh?" Caroline asked. She really wanted to know where to find Gavin, but it wasn't a question she was about to pose to Elsa.

"Her ladyship is usually in the garden house picking vegetables for the midday meal this time of day."

Caroline thought the maid's emphasis on midday was a reference to how late she'd slept, but she figured it would be better if she didn't remark on that either. "Thank you. Where is the garden house?"

Elsa gave her a look that said any dimwit should know. "Behind the kitchen."

"Thank you," she said again and walked down the hall toward the kitchen. The cook turned when she entered and gave her a friendly smile which Caroline returned. The smell of roasting meat over the large hearth in the kitchen made her mouth water and her stomach growl. She quickly stuffed part of the scone in her mouth and went out the back door.

Once she got outside, she could see why Elsa had given her the dunce look. The vegetable garden lay to the left and was huge, probably covering an acre as it sloped down a hill to what Caroline thought might be an apple orchard, the branches still barren. This time of year the neatly tilled garden rows were still furrowed, waiting for the last frost. She could imagine the bounty once summer arrived.

But that would be after Culloden, and many of the Scots would not be alive to see the harvest.

The garden house, which would be called a greenhouse in modern days, was located only a few yards from the kitchen's door. As Caroline entered, warm, moist air struck her face along with the earthy scents of potted plants and the pungent smell of herbs growing in small containers. The room appeared empty until Caroline spotted a door at the far end and walked toward it. When she opened it, a cold blast of air hit her this time and she realized this room had two small open windows, serving as a modern refrigerator would to keep harvested vegetables fresh Anne stood near one wall along with a maid, choosing potatoes from one of the large baskets. She turned as she heard Caroline approach.

"Ah, there ye are. I told the maids nae to disturb ye. Did ye sleep well?"

Caroline didn't think Anne would want to hear that she'd not slept well, nor the reason. "The bed felt wonderful."

Anne looked at the scone in her hand. "Was there nae food left?"

"I…" Caroline didn't want to tell her hostess Elsa hadn't offered to get her anything. "I just wanted a nibble this morning." She prayed her stomach wouldn't rumble and betray her. "Can I help with something?"

"Thanks, but we are finished here and about to go back inside."

"If you have a minute, I'd like to ask you a question first," Caroline said.

Anne raised an eyebrow and then handed the basket to the maid. "Mora, would ye take this inside, please?"

The girl bobbed a small curtsy and took the basket. Caroline waited until she'd closed the door and then turned back to Anne. "I know this is going to sound strange and that it isn't any of my business, but how much influence does your husband have with Mr. Campbell, Lord Loudoun?"

Anne looked surprised. "He is a captain in the Watch, so Lord Loudoun values his opinion. Why?"

"From the conversation at dinner last night, the earl and his men have retreated to the Black Isle. Will they stay there?"

"Doubtful." Anne gave her a small smile. "Campbell would nae have retreated unless he thought he had the whole of the Highland army waiting for him here. When his scouts find out otherwise, he will return, angry for being duped."

Male egos. If only Caroline could persuade Anne to get word to her husband to stay where they were, perhaps they would not meet up with the Duke of Cumberland to join forces. "Lord Loudoun would have to recapture both Inverness and Fort Augustus to regain his power bases."

Anne gave her a curious look. "Fort Augustus? Prince Charles has nae taken it."

Yet. Caroline could have bitten her tongue. She could hardly tell Anne that the prince's army would advance and capture the fort without trouble in the next few days. "I would imagine that would be his next move since it's nearby."

"Aye, it would be the smart thing to do," Anne agreed. "And maybe Fort William as well. 'Tis closer to the west Highlands. The English may not resist if they hear the other two forts have been taken."

"Yes, they will."

Anne raised an eyebrow. "They will?"

This time Caroline did bite her tongue. She couldn't keep making these comments like she knew the outcome. Well, she *did* know the outcome, but who in their right mind would believe she was from the twenty-first century? They'd think her insane at the very least, or worse, think she was a witch. She didn't think anyone had been burned at the stake in the 1700s, but people got suspicious easily. "I… While I was at the garrison guest house, I heard talk that Fort William could withstand a siege due to getting supplies through Loch Linnhe."

Anne frowned. "Aye. My husband knows Captain John Scott, the commander there. 'Tis nae likely the man will surrender."

He wouldn't. The Highlanders would waste valuable time that could have been spent training to meet Cumberland's men, but Caroline couldn't say that either. "Do you suppose you could persuade the prince to keep his men here?"

Anne shook her head. "Prince Charles wants to retake all of Scotland, and the sooner, the better. He has eyed England also. Even General Murray hasn't been able to contain the prince's ambitions."

And that was where the disaster lay. From her knowledge of history, Caroline knew Bonnie Prince Charlie was not a strategist and that many of the Highlanders were only interested in reclaiming Scotland, not invading England. The clans, under different chieftains, were not highly organized or well disciplined like the English forces. The prince, if he had listened to battle-hardened leaders, would have been better to stay put and train. If he would not listen to his generals, or men like Gavin and Calum MacDonald, there wasn't a prayer Anne would be able to change his mind.

A slim thread of hope lay in keeping Lord Loudoun's men where they were. "Do you think you could get a message to your husband?"

"A letter would have gone through while he was at the garrison in Inverness, but now at the Black Isle, it would be difficult." Anne gave Caroline another curious look. "What would you have me say?"

"That a lot of bloodshed could be avoided if Lord Loudoun would let this rout take its course and winter where he is."

"That message would fall on deaf ears," Anne said and started toward the door that led to the warm part of the garden house. "Angus and I have had this discussion many times. Neither of us will change our minds."

She shouldn't be surprised, Caroline thought as she followed Anne. Pride was strong, no matter which side of a war someone was on. She doubted she'd have any more luck with Gavin, but she would try talking to him as well.

Anne opened the door between the rooms, nearly knocking Mora and Elsa over as she did. "What are ye doing here?" she asked.

"I…we…were…" Mora let her gaze drift to Elsa who lifted her chin.

"I came to clip some chives to go with the potatoes," she said.

Anne looked at the basket Mora was still holding. "Ye had best get started on those if we're going to have them for the midday meal."

"Aye, my lady," Mora answered and scampered away, followed by a slower walking Elsa.

Caroline watched them leave. Why had they been standing so close to the door when the herbs were against the other wall? How much had they heard?

****

Caroline spent the rest of the morning, what was left of it, helping Anne and the cook prepare the food. She found it both surprising and interesting that Anne, the daughter of one Highland laird and the wife of another, actually helped with the work, but then, this was the

Scottish countryside, not London society.

The MacDonalds, along with Gavin and his men, had ridden to Inverness at dawn to confer with the prince, so Caroline didn't have an opportunity to talk with Gavin until late afternoon when they returned. Even then, she had to wait while the maids served the meal that had been kept warm for them and she had to watch Elsa hovering around Gavin with her ample breasts brushing his shoulders at every opportunity.

Caroline wasn't sure why that bothered her since she'd observed plenty of women in the twenty-first century being just as obvious, but watching Elsa rankled.

Finally, Gavin left the table, saying he'd forgotten something in his saddle pack. Carolne slipped out the kitchen's back door and followed him to the stable. Maybe if she could speak to him alone, without any other men around, he might listen to what she had to say.

Gavin turned around as she entered the tack room. He took a rolled parchment out of his pack as a corner of his mouth lifted in a crooked smile. "Do ye wish to be alone with me, lass, or did ye decide it wise to play the part of my mistress and follow me out here?"

Caroline felt her face flush. It was probably the same color as her hair. Did Gavin really think she'd followed him for a…a romp in the hay? Literally, she thought, since there was a big stack of the stuff just outside this room. "No."

"No?" An eyebrow rose. "Ye *are* alone with me."

"Well, yes, I did want to catch ye alone."

His smile widened. "What would ye like to do?"

"Do?" Caroline nibbled her lip, feeling her face grow hotter. "Nothing. I want to do nothing."

His gray eyes turned darker and he set the parchment

aside. "Let me reword the question. What would ye like for me to do?"

This was just getting worse. More heat infused her face. Could humans spontaneously combust? She felt like she might. "I don't want ye—you—to do anything either."

Gavin tilted his head. "Shall we just stand here and look at each other, then?"

"No. I mean, yes." Good grief. It wasn't like her to sound so addled. She was practically gibbering. She gathered her wits. "I need to talk to you."

"What is it ye wish to say?"

Given her conversation with Anne this morning, Caroline knew John Campbell wouldn't be abandoning the fight, which meant the Highlanders wouldn't either, so she decided to try a different tactic. "How long do you think it will be before Lord Loudoun decides to return?"

Gavin looked surprised at her question. "I suppose as soon as he learns the entire Scottish army isn't awaiting him. Our swords are ready."

"I don't doubt it," Caroline said, "but the English have muskets that can stop you long before you can reach them."

Gavin shook his head. "Muskets misfire and the aim isn't that good. Besides, they have only one shot and it takes time to reload the powder."

"You're still going to be outnumbered."

He shrugged. "We've always been outnumbered, lass. Our lads have been taught to fight two or three to one since they were old enough to hold a small sword. Our claymores can inflict a lot of damage with one swipe. Campbell has less than a thousand men left."

"The Duke of Cumberland has nine thousand more."

Gavin frowned. "Who told ye that?"

A little white lie wouldn't hurt if she were to be believed. "I overheard it while I was a guest at the garrison house. He is marching to Aberdeen and a flotilla of English ships will sail up the coast to aid him."

Gavin gave her a sharp look. "Ye ken this for certain?"

"Yes." She wished she could tell him how she knew, but she couldn't. "According to what I heard, the duke will spend a month training before he advances toward Inverness." Caroline took a deep breath since her next sentence would be the most important and might prevent the massacre at Culloden. "The prince has time to go west into the hills and prepare to defend from there."

"The prince will see it as retreating."

"From what I heard, Prince Charles is not trained for warfare." Caroline decided to add a bit more ammunition to her argument. "Didn't Robert the Bruce use guerilla tactics to win at Bannockburn?"

"Aye."

Gavin looked as though he were about to say more, but stopped suddenly and lifted his head like a hunting dog scenting prey. "What is it?"

"I thought I heard something."

Gavin took two steps closer. Caroline could feel his body heat and picked up the pleasant scent of soap and leather that clung to him. Her own senses sharpened and she heard shuffling of straw and a footstep. Before she could turn to see who was there, Gavin's hands encircled her waist. He drew her close and brought his mouth down on hers.

****

Her lips were incredibly soft and pliant, and molded

perfectly to his. Gavin knew he was lost when she opened for him, inviting his tongue inside. The spicy scent that clung to her along with the sweet taste of her mouth made him wrap his arms tighter, bringing her soft curves against his hard ridges. She mewled softly deep in her throat, making him hungry for more, much more. He wanted to taste every inch of her. Instead, he angled his head and deepened the kiss, shockwaves rippling through him when she thrust back, meeting his demands as though they had done this many times before.

Shakily he broke the grasp of desire and leaned back. A part of him expected thunder to rumble, but none came. Except for the sound of their raspy breathing, all was quiet. Whoever had been outside the door was gone.

Caroline had a dazed expression on her face and Gavin wondered if he was wearing one too. Never in his long, long life had he ever reacted so quickly and so intensely to a kiss. His beast wanted desperately to shift and let primal urges run the gauntlet. Inside his head, the wolfhound howled.

"I should apologize," he said. "Someone was outside—"

"I heard it too." Caroline smiled and traced his mouth with a fingertip. "Don't apologize. I found I very much wanted that."

"You did?"

"Yes, even though I know you did it because whoever was there needed to think we are lovers." Caroline sighed slightly and stepped away from him. "It has been a long time since I've let myself feel anything."

Gavin knew, although he couldn't tell her. He smiled. "To be honest, I enjoyed kissing ye as well." When Caroline looked at him, her blue-green eyes still dark with desire, he knew he shouldn't have said that. The saints have mercy. He wanted to take her right here. Right now. He strove for control. "We probably should be getting back before someone comes looking for us."

Caroline nodded. "Thank you for keeping my identity a secret," she said as they walked back toward the house.

"'Tis the least I can do. No sense in having ye be hated for something ye didn't have a part of."

"Thank you for believing me too."

Before he could answer, Anne came into the yard. "There ye are," she said, giving Gavin a curious look before turning her attention to Caroline. "I was wondering if ye would care to join me in a game of chess? Or do ye nae play?"

"I do," Caroline said, "but it's been awhile."

"I am nae that good myself."

Anne linked arms with her and Gavin watched them walk away. He thought about what Caroline had said earlier. Could she possibly know that General Murray and the other Highland chiefs had already tried to persuade the prince to fight from the hills where they were familiar with the terrain and the English were not? He wondered too how she knew about Cumberland and his numbers and the English flotilla. She had not been a guest at the garrison, so she could not have overheard any plans. Her knowledge came from the future.

Usually, the mortals sent to him did not recall their real lives until whatever lesson they were sent to learn had been accomplished. Caroline was unique in that she seemed to remember her past quite well.

Gavin wondered if she also knew what the outcome of this war with England would be. Would Scotland lose?

Chapter Seven

By the time Caroline took her seat at the evening meal, she had managed to compose herself, at least somewhat. What had happened in the barn earlier had unnerved her, yet it had set her body on fire as well. Emotions, deeply buried, had stirred and risen to the surface at the touch of Gavin's lips to hers and then erupted like a volcano when his tongue had ravished her mouth. Even now, every nerve ending felt scorched.

She glanced at Gavin, seated at the far end of the table this evening. Since Calum MacDonald and his men had not returned, Anne had invited Gavin's men to dine with them and she'd given him the honorary position of host. Caroline missed his presence beside her like it had been last evening. Instead, young Jamie sat beside her, more intent on his food than conversation. Across from her, Shamus glared whenever she looked his way. Was he the one they'd heard in the stable?

Even if the man had not already said he hated Campbells, there would be no doubt in Caroline's mind, given his hostile looks. If he had seen Gavin kissing her, it had probably just added fuel to his animosity. Yet Caroline was beginning to see the wisdom in Gavin's story. She didn't think Shamus would go against orders to keep quiet, but being the laird's leman insured the other men would stay quiet as well. It also gave her a certain amount of protection, even if she really wasn't

Gavin's mistress. Like dry tinder, something ignited deep in her belly at that thought. Did she *want* to be his lover?

Her musings were interrupted as the maids brought in the first course. At least, Elsa was serving the other side of the table, and Caroline wondered if Anne had arranged it so. Then Caroline realized that working on the other side meant serving the host while Mora, the maid on her side, served Anne, the hostess. Caroline tried not to let her agitation show. Elsa was a clever girl.

They were finishing dessert when they heard horses thundering through the gate. "The MacDonalds must be back," Anne said and motioned to Mora. "Make sure some food is kept warm. They'll be hungry."

"Shall we meet them in the grand hall?" Anne asked as she put her napkin down and stood.

Caroline followed the others and looked around as they entered the grand hall. The room was large enough to have been a ballroom had this been London, but not quite as big as a castle's Great Hall. Like the more medieval room, this one had sconces attached to the walls for lighting and large hearths at either side with trestle tables set up in rows to feed soldiers. Unlike a castle, it had no raised dais at one end nor anything that looked like a throne chair. Since the walls were paneled in wood, it lacked the traditional tapestries, as well.

Boots could be heard making their way down the hall. A minute later, Calum MacDonald strode through with four of his men, two of whom were holding up and half-dragging a man between them. A prisoner, judging from the bruises on his face. Caroline tried not to wince.

Anne frowned as they came to a stop in front of her. "Lieutenant Howard? Why are ye nae with my husband?" She put a hand to her mouth. "Has Angus been killed?"

"As far as we ken, MacKintosh lives," Calum replied before the English soldier could. "This one was caught trying to escape disguised as a Scot."

"I had a duty to get—"

"Silence!" Calum said, his voice not loud but deadly. He turned to Anne. "The mon was wearing a MacDonald tartan when he was found."

"Filthy English wearing our colors," one of the other MacDonalds said.

Calum nodded. "The only reason the lieutenant is alive is because he was MacKintosh's aide."

Shamus spit. "He's still English."

"And MacKintosh is still Scot, even if he is confused on which side he should fight," Gavin said.

"Thank you, Calum, for bringing him here," Anne said. "We doona need another senseless killing."

"He is *English*." Shamus spit again.

"Keep a civil tongue," Gavin warned.

Elsa and Mora brought in jugs of ale for the MacDonald men and busied themselves serving tankards while giving the prisoner curious looks.

"I'm sure accommodations can be found where Lieutenant Howard can be watched and pose no danger," Anne said and looked at Gavin. "Would ye go and check the lock on the door to the cellar? That will do for tonight."

"Aye," Gavin said and nodded to one of Calum's men. "Come with me to make sure it meets your requirements as well."

He had no sooner left when another dozen or so men appeared in the doorway. Caroline had not seen them before and they were wearing tartans she didn't recognize, either, but then, Prince Charles had recruited many different clans. She noticed Elsa giving the younger men in the group appreciative looks.

Their leader, a big man with reddish hair and a hardened expression, approached Calum. "Where is the lass?"

Calum pointed toward Caroline. "Over there."

The group of strangers turned to her. The force of their sharpened gazes made her feel pinned to the wall like a butterfly under glass.

Their leader shook his head and looked back to Calum. "She is nae one of ours."

One of theirs? Who were they?

The question answered itself when Anne spoke. "Laird Chisholm. I had no idea ye were coming. I'll have the maids set the table for your men."

"I doona wish to intrude," the man said in his graveled voice. "Calum said MacLean rescued an informant from the garrison who was a Chisholm. We came to take her home." He glanced at Caroline again. "But this lass is nae a Chisholm."

Chisholms. Lord have mercy. Her alibi had been exposed and Gavin had left the room. Her basic instinct was to bolt for the door, but her feet were rooted to the floor as though her shoes had been cobbled to it. She opened her mouth to speak, but no words came out. Transfixed, Caroline stared at the men while in her periphery vision she saw that Elsa and Mora had stopped serving and were blatantly watching what would transpire. What should she do?

The two MacDonald men who had been holding Lieutenant Howard up unceremoniously dumped him on a bench as they looked at the Chisholm laird and then at Gavin's men. "Who is she, then?" one of them asked.

Caroline didn't dare look at Shamus. She could tell Gavin's men were uncomfortable since they were shuffling their feet and looking away. So far, their silence held. Would Shamus be the one to break it? She could feel him studying her even though she kept her gaze averted.

"Ye will have to ask our laird," Shamus finally said.

Caroline let out a breath she didn't know she'd been holding. Shamus was respecting Gavin's orders.

The relief was short-lived, however, because Lieutenant Howard raised his head and looked across the room. His eyes widened suddenly and he turned to Anne. "I was wondering what happened to our guest," he said, pointing toward Caroline. "She just disappeared after the raid."

"Your guest?" Anne asked. "I thought she was a servant."

"A servant?" The man tried to smile, but his split lip stopped him. "Oh, no. She was a guest of the captain's. She'd just arrived that afternoon." He looked back toward Caroline. "I am glad to see you are well, Miss Campbell."

Caroline felt as though a bucket of ice water had been thrown over her. All motion froze in the room. Men stopped with tankards lifted halfway. Elsa's and Mora's mouths hung open. Anne's face was pale, her hands clenched together.

Slowly, one person came to life. Calum MacDonald advanced slowly, not taking his dark eyes off her. "Miss *Campbell*?" he asked.

His tone sounded more lethal than a cannon fired.

Caroline looked wildly around. Gavin was gone. She was alone. She wanted to run, to flee, but there was nowhere to go. Would anyone believe her if she tried to explain? Not that she could explain she was from the future. Judging from the hostile looks, no one would even listen to her. Could she deny her name? Maybe claim her maiden one? She'd always been proud of Danny's name and family. She looked around. These men would not deny belonging to their clans. Neither would she. If they wanted to kill her, they would, but she couldn't be a coward. Danny hadn't been a coward.

Caroline squared her shoulders and lifted her chin. "Yes. I am Caroline Campbell."

****

Gavin heard the roar that rolled down the hallway and echoed off the walls before he even got to the cellar door. He wheeled, wondering if the English lieutenant had been foolish enough to try to escape. Gavin didn't expect to see Caroline surrounded by men angry enough for a lynching when he got back to the grand hall. His beast roared silently as he charged forward.

"Stand aside!" he commanded as he elbowed his way through the horde. "Touch her and ye will answer to me. I care nae who goes down first."

Several men cursed as he jostled them, and he saw more than one create a fist, but he didn't care. If they wanted to fight, he'd take them all on.

Later. First, he had to get to Caroline.

The pack had her cornered. Her face looked white as washed linen, but her eyes glittered like sun reflecting off water and her chin was up. Gavin pushed past two MacDonalds, causing more swearing, and gathered Caroline to him, putting a protective arm around her shoulders.

"What is the meaning of this?" he demanded.

Calum cocked a thumb. "Ask him."

Gavin swung his head around, for the first time noticing the Chisholm men. He bit back a few choice words of his own. What damnable luck. They must have been at the garrison earlier, although he hadn't seen them. Before Alistair Chisholm could answer, Caroline did.

"They know I am a Campbell."

Gavin's beast growled and he quickly turned it into a cough as the men around them began to mutter. "And how…" He stopped, his eyes riveting on the English soldier. More damnable luck. The man must have seen her at the garrison house.

Gavin looked at the two other lairds, standing to his side. "She has no part in this war."

"She's a Campbell," Calum said.

"And she dared to usurp our good name," Alistair added.

"Aye! Aye!" The rumbling grew louder as some of the MacDonald and Chisholm men pressed forward, only to be blocked by Gavin's men quickly forming a circle around their laird. The other men began to throw punches.

Silence fell as Anne fired one of her pistols into the ceiling.

"There will be no fighting in my house."

If the situation hadn't been so tense, Gavin would have grinned. There wasn't a Scotsman within miles who didn't know how accurate Anne was with a pistol. She stood back from them, calmly holding the second pistol she always kept loaded.

"Gentlemen. I suggest ye all be seated."

Both Calum and Alistair nodded and their men, still grumbling beneath their breaths, retreated to the trestle tables. Gavin's men took positions near the door. Anne motioned for Elsa and Mora to bring in the platters that had been warming. For the moment, tension had been diverted.

Beside him, Caroline drew a shaky breath. "I think it would be best if I went to my room."

"Aye," Gavin agreed. "I will have Jamie escort ye and have him posted outside your door." If out-and-out conflict with the two other clans was to be avoided, Gavin would have to conference with Calum and Alistair, but he wanted to make sure Caroline was safe. He motioned to Jamie and gave the young man his orders. "Stay vigilant. Do not allow anyone into her chambers."

"Aye," Jamie said solemnly and escorted Caroline toward the stairs.

As Gavin watched them leave, he wished he could be the one assuming that duty. Only he had a feeling he wouldn't be standing outside the door.

****

Caroline closed the door to her bedchamber and leaned against it, finally allowing her body to tremble. Her knees weakened and she sank to the floor. She had never been so fearful in her life. She knew what mobs could do—twenty-first century newspapers' headlines screamed with incidences—but she'd never encountered such behavior face-to-face nor had she ever been the target of mob mentality.

She buried her face in her hands. What if Gavin hadn't appeared when he did? If he hadn't come back?

But he *had* come back. He hadn't hesitated to push his way through the angry men even if it meant a fight. Gavin had protected her and defended her against men who were normally his friends. It was what an honorable soldier would do, what an honorable man would do.

Caroline raised her head and stared at the single candle emitting a halo of light from the night table. Like that single source of light, Gavin had stood alone. Caroline knew his own men didn't like her any more than Calum's or Alistair's, but Gavin had been willing to stand against them all to keep her safe. His friends and his men. Did that mean he cared for her on a personal level? Oh, Lord. What if one of the MacDonalds or Chisholms had run him through with a knife or sword because of her?

She started to cry and it was like a dam breaking, releasing the pressure of water it had held back for too long. The tears were not of fear or loss. She'd shed enough of those over the past three years. These were tears of joy. The breaking dam had also released her emotions and she was able to feel again.

And that feeling felt suspiciously like the beginning of love.

****

Gavin trudged up the stairs to his bedchamber close to dawn. He felt as though he'd spent hours on the battlefield and perhaps he had, only this battle was fought in Anne's library instead of on a moor.

Calum and Alistair had demanded answers and Gavin had tried to be as truthful as he could, short of telling them Caroline had been sent from the twenty-first century. He told them she had been married to a Campbell who'd been killed in battle and that she'd come north to understand if any war was worth a man losing his life. MacDonald and Chisholm had looked at him as though he'd gone daft, and he knew how it sounded to men who were used to battles and accepted dying as part of that. But it was the truth for Caroline, even if she didn't realize it herself.

Luckily, Anne told them she'd harbored the same concerns. Every time the Scots engaged in battle with the English, she was afraid Angus would die. Calum and Alistair had eyed her only slightly less dubiously, but in the end, they agreed there would be no retaliation.

It had taken hours and a great deal of whisky for them to come to that decision.

Gavin yawned as he reached the second floor. He would relieve Jamie of his post, then slip inside Caroline's bedchamber. Much as Gavin desired to crawl into bed with Caroline and hold her close, that would have to wait until they could have a good discussion about where their feelings were leading. Instead, at least for tonight, he would shift to the wolfhound, so Caroline would feel safe when she woke.

"Has anyone been by?" he asked Jamie.

"Just a stable lad. He said he had a message from you for Miss Chisholm. I mean, Miss Campbell. I told him she wasn't to be disturbed."

The hair rose on Gavin's nape. "Do ye have the note?"

"Aye." Jamie dug into his sporran and produced a dirty piece of paper. "I thought ye might be testing my mettle since ye told me nae to let anyone pass."

Gavin unfolded it. *We have to talk. Meet me at the loch's shore at midnight.*

All of his hair bristled. "Have ye checked on her?"

Jamie looked startled. "Nae. I doona poke my head into a woman's chambers unless I am invited to."

On any other occasion, Gavin would have applauded him for that. But not tonight. Who had written that note? He pushed open the door to reveal a bed not slept in. Gavin rushed in.

"She is not here."

"What?" Jamie stepped inside, his eyes wide. "I swear, laird, I dinna leave the door for a single minute. She could not have left."

Gavin's gaze swept the room. The gown she'd been wearing last night lay in a crumpled heap by the door. The tartan he'd given her that first night was folded over a chair. Other than that, there were no signs of her. He looked toward the open window. This afternoon had been a rare almost warm day, somewhat like early spring. Had she opened the window to air out the winter mustiness?

Jamie noticed it too. "Mayhap the lass decided to escape?"

Gavin frowned. The wolfhound remained silent. If there was to be a hunt, the dog would be trying to shift. He wasn't.

Gavin's own hair began to crackle. He walked to the window and looked out. It wasn't much of a jump to the top of the rear cupola that shielded the back door. From there, it would be easy to slip to the ground. Better to let Jamie think Caroline had done that. He turned around. "We will search for her when light breaks."

But Gavin knew they wouldn't find Caroline.

She had gone home.

Chapter Eight

Caroline opened her eyes to stare at a white ceiling, then moved her gaze to take in the cream-colored walls. Not pale gold with green vines. There were no heavy velvet drapes on her windows either, only blinds. She looked around the room, knowing what she would find. Leather sofa. TV. Outside, a car door slammed and an engine roared to life. Caroline sat up in the recliner, looking at the closed book in her lap. She was back in the twenty-first century.

Had she actually left? Or had her time in the eighteenth century been only a dream? Caroline laid the book aside and got up to go to the door. She unbolted the locks and cracked it open. Although it was still snowing outside, the light of a new day greeted her. At least the newspaper had arrived. She bent down to retrieve it, then closed the door and looked at the date. Christmas Day.

She must have slept straight through the night in the chair. How odd, since she much preferred to stretch out on her comfortable bed. She hadn't even touched her cocoa, now sitting cold in the cup on the side table.

Caroline flopped down in the recliner once more. The events in her dream—or hallucination, if that was what it was—had seemed so real. She could recall the sights and sounds vividly, which usually didn't happen with one of her episodes. Those were always fuzzy, as though she were peering through fog, and they faded rapidly. But the more she thought about the MacDonalds, the MacLeans, Anne and Gavin, the clearer they became.

Gavin in particular. Not only had she let her guard down with him, but she'd allowed herself to feel emotion. Had even welcomed it as much as she did his kiss. Even now, she could feel his arms wrapped around her, holding her close as though he never wanted to let go. She hadn't wanted to let go either. That surprised her most of all. Even if it was only a dream, she'd opened her heart to a man again, wanting to feel love.

That was the gist of it. Caroline picked up the book on Scottish history and opened it to where the bookmark was. Culloden happened. Nearly two thousand Scots lost their lives on that moor. Not only did Bonnie Prince Charlie flee to exile, King George dissolved the clans and banned the skirling of pipes and the wearing of tartans. In her dream, she had tried to prevent all of that, but of course, a person couldn't change history.

But perhaps she could change herself. Caroline looked up at the picture of Danny hanging on the wall. He wore his dress uniform and, strangely, it reminded Caroline of Gavin and Calum and Alexander wearing their kilts, in command of their men. Danny would have approved of them because they wouldn't stand down, wouldn't retreat in the face of the English army. All of them had courage.

If we doona fight for what we believe in, we are cowards.

Was she a coward? Or did she have the courage to try and love again?

She looked at the picture on the wall. Although the pose was stern, as befitted an officer, Danny's eyes seemed to be smiling at her as if encouraging her to go ahead.

Before going ahead, she would have to go back. She had to face all those wonderful memories of the happy times she and Danny had in Minnesota, live through them once more, and then let them go.

Caroline picked up her cell and dialed her parents' number. "Merry Christmas," she said when her mother answered.

"Merry Christmas, darling," her mother replied. "How nice to hear from you. We wish you could be here."

"I was thinking about that," Caroline said. "The planes are not usually full on Christmas Day. I can catch a flight out this afternoon. Will you save some dessert for me?"

For a minute there was only silence and then her father came to the phone. "Your mother is trying to decide whether to become hysterical."

"I didn't mean to upset her."

"Upset me?" It was her mother again. "Sweetheart, you've given me the best Christmas present ever."

"So you'll save me some pie?"

"Honey, we'll keep the whole dinner warm and waiting. Hurry home."

Caroline thought of the old cliché, *Home is where the heart is*, as she hung up. Home might not be Minnesota any longer, but going there allowed her to finally say goodbye. Now she could start to build her life again.

****

"How could the lass just have vanished?" Jamie asked glumly the next morning after a score of men had searched the roads and forests for several hours and come back to Moy Hall empty-handed.

"Campbells are a stealthy lot," Shamus said.

"But a lass? On her own?" Calum asked. "'Tis strange."

"Maybe she had some help getting away," Shamus answered. "The window was open. A Campbell might have been slithering around out there waitin' for her. They're snakes in the grass, I say."

Gavin gave him a sharp look, wishing he could tell the warrior he wouldn't have to worry about Caroline anymore. But he couldn't, any more than he could tell young Jamie it wasn't his fault Caroline had gone. He could see Jamie felt wretched.

"With the recent thaw, we would have found tracks," Alistair replied.

"Aye. All of our horses are accounted for," Anne said and glanced at Gavin before turning back to the rest of the men. "We can send out search parties again in the morning, but she's probably in Inverness by now."

"Doubtful we will find her there unless she's foolish enough to go to the garrison," Calum said, "and the lass dinna strike me as stupid."

Gavin nodded his agreement. Caroline wasn't stupid, nor would they find her in Inverness, but not for the reason they thought.

****

Long after the men had gone to the barracks and Calum and Alistair to their guest chambers, Gavin sat broodingly looking into the fire in the library's hearth. The wolfhound inside him was restless and even half a dozen drams of whisky couldn't calm the beast.

Gavin startled at a knock on the library door. Who in the world was still up at this hour? "Yes?"

Anne poked her head in. "May I come in?"

"It is your library," Gavin said and attempted to stand, but Anne waved him down. She took the chair opposite his and studied him for several minutes.

"What?" he finally asked.

"Ye know where she is, don't ye?"

Gavin tried not to squirm under Anne's level-eyed gaze. "Why do ye say that?"

"I think ye felt she was in danger here."

"Do ye think she was?"

Anne smiled. "Ye are being evasive, much like Angus when he doesna want to answer a question. My answer is yes, she may have been. Elsa didna like her."

"Elsa?" He hadn't given any thought to the maid since he was more concerned with calming the MacDonalds and Chisholms. "Do ye think she would have harmed Caroline?"

"The girl fancied herself in love with ye," Anne replied. "I wondered why she was loitering in the garden house the morning Caroline and I chatted. I saw Elsa follow Caroline out to the barn as well. The girl was jealous, no doubt."

"She has no claim on me."

"When has that ever made a difference?" Anne handed him a folded piece of paper. "I think this might confirm it."

Gavin took it. The printing was irregular and many of the words were misspelled as though it had been written by someone barely literate, but the message was clear.

Cozun. I tell my laird abut yer visitr. Martin

"I doona understand. Who is Martin?"

"Elsa's cousin who is a groom for Alistair

Chisholm. Mora told me the note fell out of Elsa's apron pocket. When I confronted her, she admitted she'd written her cousin."

"But why?' Gavin held up a hand to answer his own question. "She wanted Chisholm to come get Caroline?"

Anne nodded. "Elsa wanted Caroline gone. She'd heard the men's conversations that the clans would meet with the prince at Inverness, so she sent the note telling her cousin to let Alistair know a kinswoman was here. She wouldn't admit it, but I think she might have hinted that Caroline was being held against her will."

"Elsa is a sly one," Gavin said.

Anne nodded again. "There is more."

"More?"

"Aye. Once we found out Caroline was a Campbell, Elsa told Mora she was going to lure Caroline down to the loch by sending her a note from you saying to meet her there. Mora came to me because she was scared." Anne hesitated. "I think Elsa intended to drown Caroline."

The note. Thank God Jamie had followed orders and not delivered it. By all that was holy, Caroline might have been killed tonight.

The thought stunned Gavin. Having Caroline returned to her own time already weighed heavy on him, even though he knew it was inevitable. Having her killed—murdered in the wrong century under his watch—was something he couldn't accept. Wouldn't accept. Then another thought stunned him. He didn't want to live in this century if she wasn't in it. He'd known he was losing his heart to Caroline when he let his emotions loose. Love transcended time. He would go to her.

The wolfhound yelped once in approval and then was silent.

"I think you did the right thing," Anne said.

Gavin frowned, having a bit of trouble understanding, lost in his thoughts as he was. "Right thing?"

Anne studied him. "Ye sent her somewhere safe, didna ye?"

Yes, Caroline had been sent somewhere safe, at least from Elsa. Gavin intended to make sure Caroline stayed safe in the twenty-first century as well. "Aye, Caroline is safe. I will be going to check on her, so ye may not see me in a while."

Anne gave him another thoughtful look and then stood. "May your guardian angel protect ye, then."

Gavin smiled. Angels indeed.

Caroline had been sent to him for a purpose, only he hadn't realized he needed to learn a lesson as well. He couldn't wait to see her again—in her own time.

Epilogue

Caroline stomped snow off her boots before she entered the coffee shop on Monday afternoon. She was tired, since she'd taken an overnight flight back from Minnesota, but the trip had definitely been worth it. She felt better than she had in three years.

Maggie and Elizabeth were already seated at their favorite table. Not wanting to wait for coffee, Caroline made her way through the crowds standing in line and headed straight for her friends.

"I had the most amazing dream on Christmas Eve," she said as she tossed her coat and cap on the extra chair. "Wait until you hear."

Maggie and Elizabeth exchanged glances. "We had strange dreams too," Maggie said. "This is so weird. I kind of feel like I've been gone for months."

"But we haven't," Elizabeth said and gestured toward the bar not far away. "Those same guys that were here Friday don't look like they've moved."

Caroline glanced over. The guys all had their backs to them, probably playing on laptops, but Elizabeth was right. They were dressed the same as Friday. She turned back to her friends. "Tell me about your dreams, then I'll tell you mine."

"You go first," Elizabeth said to Maggie.

"Okay. Like I said, it was so weird. I woke up in a meadow in Ireland. There was this really good-looking man sitting in the grass nearby. He had coppery hair sort of like the middle guy at the bar over there. But get this. The year was 1815."

"And, in my dream, I woke up in the courtyard of a manor house in England," Elizabeth said, "in 1838."

The hair at Caroline's nape rose. "You both dreamed you went back in history?" When they nodded, she swallowed hard. "So did I. Scotland. 1746. And…there was a really good-looking man in my dream, too."

Elizabeth raised an eyebrow. "I met one too. Only he had a twin that was evil."

"I didn't have any good twin-evil twin thing going on," Caroline said, "but I was captured by Scots who hated the Campbells."

"Were you harmed? In the dream, I mean," Maggie asked.

Caroline shook her head. "No. The man—Gavin MacLean—protected me. I was treated more like a guest than a hostage."

"I was living with my aunt and uncle," Maggie said, "only this time they were wealthy and associated with Irish aristocrats. They even had maids."

"And I was a servant," Elizabeth said.

"*What*?" Maggie and Caroline asked in unison.

Elizabeth nodded. "It's true. I was a serving girl in the hall of a duke. I honestly didn't think I was going to survive. If it hadn't been for Broc—he was the good twin—I don't think I would have made it. It all felt so horribly real."

"I know what you mean," Maggie replied. "Finn— that was the good-looking neighbor—befriended me. He took me to the village where small children were working right alongside their parents to earn enough to have food. None of them could read or write because education was forbidden when the English imposed the Penal Laws. I felt like I was really there too." Maggie paused. "I know this is probably going to sound silly since it was a dream, but I thought about it a lot yesterday. I want to make a difference. Education is a cause I can believe in. I'm going to get my certification to be a teacher."

"I did a lot of thinking yesterday too," Elizabeth said. "The dream really made me realize not only how unappreciated servants are, but also how they are stuck at levels from which they cannot advance." She hesitated as well, an odd expression that Caroline had never seen flitting across her face. "I've decided I'm going to start a charitable foundation that will give minimum-wage workers an opportunity to advance. I talked to our firm's attorney about it this morning."

"Wow," Caroline said. "You two have made some big decisions."

"Did your dream inspire you in any way?" Maggie wondered.

"Actually, it did." Caroline wished now that she had some coffee…or maybe something stronger. "I think I received courage."

"Courage?" Elizabeth looked puzzled. "I always thought you were really strong, given what happened with Danny."

"Not really," Caroline answered. "What I did was withdraw from the world. Oh, I held a job and I didn't drop my friends, but I didn't want to let myself feel anything. I created a nice, safe cocoon for myself where I wouldn't get hurt again."

"Ah," Maggie said. "And being a hostage—in your

dream—made you think differently?"

"In a way. You see, I knew what was going to happen at Culloden. So many of them would die. I tried to tell Gavin and the others not to fight, but no one listened."

"They didn't believe you?"

Caroline shook her head. "Even if they had doubts, it wouldn't have mattered. One of the men said if he didn't fight for something he believed in, he was a coward. Those clans believed that Scotland needed to be free...and they were willing to die for that freedom, much like Danny did." She thought a minute while her friends remained silent. "I realized then that I hadn't been free either, although I wasn't being physically oppressed. I've been hiding from life these past three years, tucked away in history where I know what the outcome will be." She took a deep breath. "I know there are no guarantees, but I want to reconnect with people—on an emotional level—again."

"Does that mean you're going to be willing to start dating?" Maggie asked.

Caroline smiled, feeling more at peace with herself than she had in years. "Yes." She looked at the three men still working on the laptops. "I might just start with the dark-haired one over there."

"Did ye hear that?" the dark-haired man at the bar asked his companions.

"I think ye accomplished your mission, Gavin," the one in the middle answered.

"And ye, too, Finn. It sounds like Maggie found a cause she can believe in."

"Don't forget Elizabeth." Finn cocked his thumb toward their companion. "Broc did a fine job in helping her develop empathy."

"I think the women taught us lessons as well," Broc answered. "I finally stopped hating my brother and that released his spirit."

"Aye," Gavin said. "Caroline taught the MacDonalds—and myself—there might be worth to some Campbells."

Finn nodded. "As a prince, it surprised me that when someone has the luxury of being treated as an aristocrat—and the power and wealth as well—not everyone wants it. Maggie didn't."

"I think we all learned another lesson." Gavin looked at his friends. "We each learned to love a mortal."

"Yes, it's why we are here, without our magic," Broc said.

"'Tis a strange feeling," Finn said. "I've never given up my powers before."

"Well, we have nae given up our souls," Gavin replied. "Even human souls are immortal."

"'Tis true. We were given a choice." Finn agreed. "And we chose to follow our hearts this time."

"Rafael knew what he was doing when he sent us those lasses," Gavin said.

Broc smiled. "Archangels always do."

"Besides, it's still Christmas." Finn looked at Broc and then at Gavin. "Are we ready?"

"The question is, are they?" Broc responded.

"We'll find out," Gavin answered as all three men clicked the laptops shut.

Then they turned, slipped off the barstools and walked toward the women they loved…now and forever.

And, as Charles Dickens' Tiny Tim would say, "God bless us every one!"

Afterword

If you enjoyed Caroline Campbell's story, you might want to join three other young women who travel back in Time to try and prevent the massacre at Culloden from happening. You'll find their stories in Cynthia Breeding's "Ghosts of Culloden" trilogy: *Highlander Unleashed*, *Highlander Untamed*, and *Highlander Unconquered*.

A word about the author...

Cynthia Breeding lives on the Gulf Coast of Texas with a very non-spoiled poodle-mix and enjoys walking and horseback riding on the beach, as well as sailing.
www.cynthiabreeding.com

Thank you for purchasing
this publication of The Wild Rose Press, Inc.

For questions or more information
contact us at
info@thewildrosepress.com.

The Wild Rose Press, Inc.